Up in Smoke

With a roaring of jeers and catcalls exploding behind the barricades, Chandler emerged from the rear of the car and turned to face the crowd. Grinning, he thrust up his arms in a V as though he were a hero acknowledging a reception by admirers.

"What nerve," Peg said with a half laugh. "Who the devil does this guy think he is, President Eisenhower?"

"It's not from Ike that he's borrowed that gesture," replied Woolley as the noise of the crowd increased with each taunting wave of Chandler's upthrust arms. "He's a product of a later generation. This is in-your-face Sixties sock-it-to-'em-baby Richard Milhous Nixon."

"You ought to know, Professor," Nick gibed.

Woolley stroked his beard. "As a matter of fact, I do feel a twinge of nostalgia."

As he spoke, the jeering crowd chanted, "S.O.S., S.O.S., S.O.S., Snuff Out Smoking, Snuff Out Smoking, burn the books, burn the books."

Someone shouted, "Let's get the author!"

Another screamed, "Death to Chandler!"

Surging forward, the crowd broke through the barriers and shoved aside the handful of vainly resisting police. In an instant the protesters flooded across the street. With waving signs and fists, they rushed the limousine.

Other Nicholas Chase Cigar Mysteries by
Harry Paul Lonsdale
from Avon Books

SMOKING OUT A KILLER
WHERE THERE'S SMOKE, THERE'S MURDER

UP IN SMOKE

A Nicholas Chase Cigar Mystery

HARRY PAUL LONSDALE

AVON BOOKS
An Imprint of HarperCollins*Publishers*

This is a work of fiction. Names, characters, places, and incidents are products of the author's imagination or are used fictitiously and are not to be construed as real. Any resemblance to actual events, locales, organizations, or persons, living or dead, is entirely coincidental.

AVON BOOKS
An Imprint of Harper Collins*Publishers*
10 East 53rd Street
New York, New York 10022-5299

ISBN: 0-380-80300-3
www.avonbooks.com

First Avon Books paperback printing: April 2001

Printed in the U.S.A.

10 9 8 7 6 5 4 3 2 1

For my nephew, Tom Detwiler

PART I

Smoke Dreamer

Let stocks go up or downward,
and let politicians wrangle,
Let the parsons and philosophers
grope in wordy tangle,
Let those who want them scramble
for their dignities or dollars,
Be millionaires or magnates, or senators or scholars.
I will puff my mild Havana, and I quietly will query
Whether, when the strife is over,
and the combatants are weary,
Their gains will be more brilliant
than my cigar's expiring flashes,
Or more solid than its dead and sober ashes.

ARTHUR W. GUNDRY, *MY CIGAR*

One

WHEN THE ELEVATOR stopped on the ninety-eighth floor of No. One World Trade Center, Madeline Lewis stepped into a lobby of dark wood-paneled walls and huge leather arm chairs and sofas. The decor was what she had expected to find in the offices of the savvy man whose magazine had sounded a clarion call to males to assert their gender unabashedly in the form of a symbol of masculinity, the cigar. While providing articles on men's fashions, cars, sports, fine liquors, wines, travel, manly jewelry, and entertainment, *Cigar Smoker*'s primary purpose was to exhort readers to rebel against feminism and anti-smoking zealots by lighting up stogies, not sheepishly in the privacy of homes, offices, men-only clubs, and other male enclaves, but proudly and defiantly in public.

Festooning the walls of the lobby were portraits of famous cigarists: 1930s' New York's pudgy and pugnacious Mayor Fiorello LaGuardia with a long stogie in his mouth as he dashed to fires and smashed slot machines and kegs of prohibited beer; leering Groucho Marx with a cigar at a rakish angle as he demonstrated his funny low-slung stride; W. C. Fields brandishing a half-smoked Corona as if it were a sword unsheathed against the enemy, whether it be a sheriff come to run him out of town, a nagging wife, or a nettlesome child; John F. Kennedy puffing away on an elegant cigarillo while sailing off Hyannisport; President Bill Clinton with an unlit cigar as he wheeled a golf cart on the way to the first tee; Milton Berle; George Burns; he-man superstars Arnold Schwarzenegger and Bruce Willis lounging in one of their Planet Hollywood restaurants; and TV's gap-toothed late-night talk show host David Letterman.

At the center of these icons was a large oil portrait of Melvin Chandler. Middle-aged with squared jaw, cobalt eyes, and brown hair becomingly streaked at the temples with strands of gray, he had on a dark blue suit. The left hand grasped a copy of his magazine. In a pincer-like grip of thumb and tips of the first two fingers of the right was a long, lighted cigar. Beside the portrait in gold letters was the name of the magazine. Below it in smaller script was a sentiment of the poet John Galsworthy: *By the cigars they smoke, ye shall know the texture of men's souls.*

"You can also tell a lot about a man's soul by where he works," Madeline thought as she entered a spacious, elegantly furnished office with walls adorned by oil paintings. At a massive antique desk and looking like a model in an ad in his magazine, Melvin Chandler wore a brown-and-white houndstooth-checked jacket, red-and-blue striped tie, and yellow shirt with cuff links in the shape of cigars.

On a credenza behind the desk stood a computer flanked by framed photos of himself and four former presidents, the current occupant of the White House, two ex-mayors of New York, the present one, and the governor of the state. Standing apart from these were a smaller framed photo of a boy of about six years of age and a picture of a young man whom the gossip columns invariably identified as print mogul Melvin Chandler's playboy son, Richard.

With his back to a panoramic view of New York harbor and the Statue of Liberty, Chandler smiled at her benignly from across his desk. She knew she was attractive in her very becoming navy blue outfit that underscored her short blond hair and flawless suntan. "Please sit and enlighten me about the business of peddling books, Miss Lewis," he said. "Or may I call you Madeline?"

She sat in a black leather chair. "I've been Maddy as long as I can remember."

"Maddy it is," he said from a tall, red leather wingback. "Please call me Mel."

"What is it about peddling books on which you need enlightening?"

"How much money will it take to assure that *Smoke Dreamer* hits the best-seller list?"

"Which list do you want your book to hit?"

"The *Times,* of course."

"The one in New York or the one in Los Angeles?"

He smiled. "Make it both. I read somewhere that President Nixon once gave one of his henchmen a half-million dollars to get a book Nixon liked onto the *New York Times* list."

"You can't buy your way onto a list for the simple reason that the means by which newspapers compile them is a trade secret that, as far as I know, no one has ever ferreted out. It's a complicated system involving designated book stores, quantities sold, and at what rate they're sold. Nixon was wasting his money."

"Having known Tricky Dick, I'm sure it wasn't his dough. So what you're telling me is that no matter what I might spend on trying to put my book over, there's no guarantee *Smoke Dreamer* will become a best-seller?"

"Books get on lists because people want to read them. A book sells itself."

"Maddy, no product in this world has ever sold itself. That's why specialists like you are in the publicity business."

"On that point," she said, getting out of her chair and striding to the window to look at the view, "may I ask you a question?"

Chandler turned to face her. "Fire away."

"Your magazine has a large publicity staff—"

"Fifteen people at last count."

"So why hire an outsider to publicize your book?"

"They've got their hands full with the magazine. I don't believe in dividing responsibilities. I need someone who'll do nothing but push *Smoke Dreamer.* If you want a job to be done right, you should get the best hired gun in town. Ben Salter, my assistant, says that's you."

"I've earned that reputation by carefully choosing clients. I'm here because I never take on a job for an individual without first looking him in the eye. My policy as a publicist is to work only on behalf of a client I can trust. I could never have been a publicist for Nixon."

"You've read my manuscript," he said, smiling. "You know all about me."

"If that's true," she said, returning to her chair, "you've written the first autobiography in history that isn't full of lies."

"Maybe I did omit or skip over a couple of things in my life that are nobody's business," Chandler said, smilingly. "That doesn't mean my book isn't any good. Even though I wrote it by myself, and I did, every word of it, I think it's a terrific read."

"It is indeed. The Melvin Chandler on its pages has had quite a life. It's a classic in the American success story genre. Poor boy lifts himself by his bootstraps and publishes a magazine that dictates masculine style. And in keeping with the great tradition of business tycoons, the Melvin Chandler in the book is an unscrupulous and ruthless martinet. You crushed Lawrence Gordon and his competing magazine. You fired a man who'd been your managing editor from the get-go. In private life you are a cad who dumped a long-suffering wife after twenty years and then made a career of chasing bimbos. Names of the people whose friendship you abused in one way or another make up half the book's index, from Charles Appleton to Steve Yedenok."

Chandler grunted. "Charlie and Steve were weaklings. The divorce was as much my wife's doing as mine. I canned Dave Selden because he'd lost his initiative. *The Smoking Life* failed because of Larry's incompetence. He was a copy cat, and an inept one to boot. Selling out to me was the smartest thing he ever did in his life. But I fail to see what the devil my business practices and my personal life can possibly have to do with the question before us. Is Madeline Lewis going to take on the job of publicizing my autobiography?"

"It's precisely because I know how you operate professionally and personally that I must insist on your guarantee that how I handle your book will be entirely up to me. The moment you or anyone else tries to interfere, I'll resign and keep the fifty-thousand-dollar fee for my services, which is to be paid up front. I'll bill you for expenses."

"When I hire an expert, I never interfere."

"What is the proposed publication date?"

"My editor says that it's slated for November. She thinks women will want to give it to their men for Christmas."

"I noted in your book that you were expelled from Harvard University. Have you any ill feelings toward the school?"

"Getting booted was the sweetest break I ever had. Why do you ask?"

"I can think of no better way to draw attention to your book than staging a ceremony at which you give the college a lot of money. It could be either an outright grant with no strings, or an endowment of some kind in your name. Or in honor of someone you admire or to whom you're grateful. Somebody you love or loved. If there is such a person."

Chandler grinned. "What a stunt! I love it. How much do you think I should fork over?"

"As I recall, you paid a hundred grand at auction for the monogrammed gold pocket cigar case that once belonged to Winston Churchill, which you wrote off your taxes as a business expense. I can't see you giving your alma mater less than a million."

"A million it shall be, deductible as a charitable contribution, of course," he said with a grin as he lifted the lid of a large mahogany desktop cigar humidor. "As long as we're going to kick off the book on my old stomping grounds, I think I should throw a huge cigar night party at a place where I was a busboy in the lean old days. It's called Farley's. And how about me signing books at a cigar store run by an ex–New York cop that I once picked as tobacconist of the year? I forget his name. Ben Salter can tell you. By the way, you're to keep Ben informed of your plans."

"I propose that you put him to use now by sending him to your bank for my fifty-thousand dollars. In cash. I'll be waiting in my office. Ben knows where it is."

Chandler withdrew two long cigars with gold and black bands from the humidor. "Shall we celebrate closing our deal with a couple of genuine Cuban Cohibas?"

"I've always found a cigar is much more becoming to a man's profile than a woman's. Did you get them before or after the embargo on their importation?"

"They're a gift from Fidel Castro himself in appreciation for an editorial in my magazine. I called for the lifting of the embargo," said Chandler as he carefully returned one cigar to the humidor. "He sent them by way of our office in London. Then it was a simple matter of putting them in another box to get them through customs at J F K airport." Mouthing the unlit second cigar, he smiled slyly. "How can I be sure that you won't take my fifty-grand in cash and then not hold up your end of the deal?"

"I've read your autobiography, Mel. I'm not a fool."

When she was gone, he took the Cohiba from his mouth, slipped off the band, clipped the end of the cigar with a desktop cutter in the shape of a guillotine, and put a match to it.

"WHAT A REMARKABLE WOMAN."

Slight of build with lank sand-colored hair and brilliant blue eyes set deeply in the kind of androgynous face which could never be seen illustrating articles on the masculine pastimes and manly styles in *Cigar Smoker*, Benjamin Salter looked up from a paper-strewn desk. "I was sure you'd approve of her."

Looming in front of the desk, Chandler plucked the Cohiba from his lips. "She's a really classy dame, but a ballbuster. She's the kind that when you're done screwing her, you've got fingernail scratches down your back. I'd love to find out if I'm right. That dame is a hot ticket. Where did you find her?"

"We met at a birthday party for a friend of mine a couple of years ago. We kept in touch, and when you finished your book, I thought she'd be great at publicizing it. I'm glad you agree."

"She wants her fee in cash. Fifty-grand. Take it out of the Sutton Place safe and deliver it to her office right away."

"She works from her home. She's got the top half of a townhouse on East Eightieth."

"Well, get your ass in gear. I don't want you keeping that extraordinary dame waiting."

Fifteen minutes later, Salter found Maddy Lewis sipping

coffee at a table in the rear of a café on the mezzanine level of the Borders book store at the World Financial Center.

"Your meeting with the old man didn't last very long," he said as he pulled up a chair. "What did you think of him?"

"Melvin Chandler was exactly what I'd expected in a man of his generation, position, and reputation who publishes men's magazines—conceited, rich, and randy."

"He thinks you're a classy, ball-busting dame," Salter said, grinning as he sat opposite her. "He says that any man who gets you in bed will have his back raked by tiger-like claws."

Maddy set down her cup and studied her fingernails.

"Not that he'll ever find out for himself," Salter continued. "He's got such bad circulation because of a heart condition that he hasn't been able to, uh, function in that way since Donny was born. Ironic, isn't it, that a man who's made a fortune with a magazine that advises men how to romance the ladies is no longer able to follow through?"

"What about the money?" she asked. "Are you on your way to the bank?"

"It's in the safe in the Sutton Place house."

Her eyes widened. "I've always wanted to see that place. And his art collection."

"I'm sorry to disappoint you, Maddy, but all those Picassos, Renoirs, and practically every painter Mel ever read about in museum catalogs are fakes. To quote the man you're now going to work for, 'Why should I pay through the nose for the real McCoy when I can get fakes that are just as good and no one will ever know?' The only oil painting in the house that's an original is the one of Richard."

"There's none of the second son?"

"Before Mel could get one done of little Donny, he and the second Mrs. Chandler were killed, as you know, in a hit and run when they were at Mel's place on Cape Cod. I should say Anita's place, since she got it and the house in Boston in the divorce settlement."

"I still want to see the Sutton Place house. Or are you worried that Richard will be there?"

"He won't. He had another row with Mel and fled with his

latest girl friend to the house on the Cape, where I imagine they are screwing like champions surrounded by images of Mel's late hero, John Fitzgerald Kennedy. The guy's been dead for forty years, but every issue of the magazine contains a photo of him puffing away on a cheroot. I thought Anita would redecorate, but she didn't. That's probably because she never uses the place. When Anita wants to be in the sun, she goes to Miami Beach."

Maddy said forcefully, "I want to see the Sutton Place digs, Ben."

He thought a moment, then shrugged. "Oh, why the hell not? Then we'll go to '21' and celebrate your new job with a superb lunch."

"Oh, by the way," she said as she slid from the booth, "Mel is giving a million dollars to Harvard University."

Salter's eyes went wide open. "When did he come up with that idea?"

"I suggested it. He loved it!"

Salter smiled. "When Richard hears about this, he'll go ballistic."

Three

AMONG SEVERAL LARGE and sturdy shipping cartons containing boxes of cigars which had been delivered on what Nick Chase expected to be a traditionally slow Monday was a large, thick padded envelope. Opening it, he found a book. Wrapped around it was a letter on the stationery of *Cigar Smoker* magazine which read:

Dear Mr. Chase:

With the compliments of Melvin Chandler I enclose an advance copy of his autobiography, Smoke Dreamer. *It is scheduled to be published in November. The book will be launched in the Boston area when Mr. Chandler hosts one of his famous "cigar nights," to be held at Farley's restaurant. It is his hope that you will permit him the honor of also appearing at your store to meet your customers and sign copies of* Smoke Dreamer.

I believe you'll find Mr. Chandler's story entertaining and informative. In the hope that after reading it you would like to welcome him to the Happy Smoking Ground, I will contact you during a forthcoming visit to Cambridge to arrange a convenient date for the signing.

Very truly yours,
Madeline Lewis, Special Assistant to Mr. Chandler

The jacket of the book featured a full-length color portrait of Chandler holding a cigar and wearing a red velvet smoking jacket, matching fez with tassel, open-necked shirt with a dangling undone bow tie, tuxedo pants, and red slippers. He was standing in a humidor room that appeared to be twice the size of Nick's store.

The flap copy said, "A confirmed cigar smoker since college days, Melvin Chandler at the age of fifty and at the pinnacle of a successful career in business and publishing almost single-handedly resurrected cigar-smoking as the ultimate symbol of the good life for men."

Nick opened the book to the introduction and read, "Have a cigar! Those words are surely among the happiest phrases in the language."

"I'll say," Nick muttered as he stopped reading to light an H. Upmann Corona, his first cigar of the day.

"Chances are, your father celebrated your birth by handing out cigars to friends," said the author of *Smoke Dreamer* as Nick resumed reading. "As a remembrance of meeting Ava Gardner in a bar in Spain, Ernest Hemingway presented the movie queen with the band of his cigar. When astronaut John Glenn returned to earth after piloting America's first spaceship, he was given the equivalent of his weight in Havana cigars. Great Britain's wartime Prime Minister, Winston S. Churchill, held Dunhill cigars in the crook of fingers raised in a V as a symbol of British defiance and an expression of confidence that he would soon smoke another while celebrating the triumph of freedom over tyranny. With the possible exception of a glass of champagne uplifted in a toast, nothing man-made has been employed more frequently to celebrate something, whether personal, social, political, or economic. There is no way of knowing how many such happy moments have been marked by smoking a cigar."

Lifting his eyes from the page, Nick recalled a day in the 1940s. He and three pals in the fifth grade at P.S. 57 in Brooklyn had swiped a pack of cigarettes and a five-for-half-a-buck box of Primadoras from a corner store and raced to a playground to smoke them. By the time he was in recruit training at the police academy, he was up to smoking a six-pack of Grenadiers a day. For twenty years as a homicide detective he had been able to afford cigars bought in boxes of twenty-five at a dollar each from Nat Sherman's on Fifth Avenue. He had handed out two-buck Montecristo No. 3's to mark the births of his son Kevin and daughter Jean, who every day more and more resembled her mom of blessed memory. Now, more than thirty years after Maggie's death, their father was a retired ex-cop and owner of a tobacco shop whose green-and-gold sign alerted passersby on Brattle Street that within The Happy Smoking Ground they would find "The Finest in Cigars, Tobacco, Pipes."

An authentic wooden Indian stood on the sidewalk. To the left of the store's white door a brass plaque was engraved with:

No less true, and set aside all joke,
From oldest time he ever dealt in smoke;
His capital all smoke, smoke all his store,
'Twas nothing else; but lovers ask no more—
And thousands enter daily at his door.

During Nick's two decades of purveying tobacco in all its forms, thousands had indeed passed the Indian and the plaque to explore the delights awaiting them in display cases and in the walk-in humidor. Most were students and faculty from nearby Harvard University.

As he leafed through the book lying before him on the sales counter, he came to a section of photographs of its author in various pictures: Melvin Chandler posing as a child in short pants; as a dashing and rakish-looking youth; with a college friend and with him again as the friend served as best man at his wedding; the bride and groom kissing; proudly holding his young son on his lap; and as the distinguished-looking middle-aged publisher of slick magazines for men which instructed them on the playthings of the self-indulgent life. Three pages of candid photographs showed Chandler enjoying the company of beautiful women on his yacht, with men of commerce, politics, and show business in ballrooms and banquet halls the world over, and amid workers in vineyards of the Cognac region of France; the lush tobacco plantations of the *Vueltabajo* region of Cuba; and the tobacco fields of the Dominican Republic.

Filling two pages were several photos of Melvin Chandler as host of celebrity-studded parties given in the 1990s in the interest of promoting the monthly editions of his magazine. Called "Cigar Nights" and held in grand ballrooms of deluxe hotels in New York, Los Angeles, San Francisco, Chicago, and Atlanta, they afforded the privileged guests tastings of the world's finest premium cigars, superb cognac and brandy, great whiskies, and varieties of single-malt scotch.

The caption below a picture of Chandler surrounded by movie stars at the first of these affairs, held in Beverly Hills, asserted, "Not since Hugh Hefner's *Playboy* in the 1950s has a magazine so gloriously celebrated and encouraged the indulging of one's masculinity. In *Cigar Smoker* Melvin Chandler exhorted men to celebrate their achievements with the trappings of success—fine clothing, sublime cuisine, superb beverages, and the ultimate symbol of the good life, the premium cigar."

As Nick continued to leaf through the book, the door opened and in walked an elderly man who'd spent most of his life lecturing in Harvard classrooms before his retirement. Wearing a gray tweed jacket with brown elbow patches and appearing every inch the professor of history he'd been, Roger Woolley was slender as a sapling. Jutting from a gray Van Dyke beard, a black bent briar pipe was clenched in the left side of his mouth. His right hand held an ebony walking stick with a silver top in the shape of the head of Sherlock Holmes. Tucked under his left arm was a bulky package wrapped in heavy brown paper and tied with white string.

"You're up and about early, Professor," Nick said, closing the book.

"I'm on my way to the post office and then to a university committee meeting."

"Am I correct in my deduction that the bundle you're toting contains the latest mystery solved by your private eye, the intrepid Jake Elwell?"

"I completed the damned thing last night," Woolley declared, nudging the door closed with the walking stick. "I'm dropping it off to be duplicated. What a godsend photocopying has been for those of us who labor as authors. No more carbon paper. Gone forever are the dirty fingertips and smudged pages."

"The next step, Professor," said Nick through a puff of smoke as Woolley crossed the store to the counter, "is finally to retire that old Underwood upright and get a computer."

"If the typewriting in the flat above yours well into the small hours of this morning disturbed you, it couldn't be helped. Jake had a brainstorm around eleven o'clock."

"The sound of your typing is like soothing rain on a tin roof."

"Liar. What is that you are reading?"

"It's an advance copy of a book titled *Smoke Dreamer*. It came in this morning's mail."

Woolley gently placed his stick on the glass counter top, but held on to the package. "Are you being solicited by the publisher to provide a gushy blurb for another how-to guide seeking to cash in on the craze in cigar smoking? It seems to me there have been enough of those tomes in the past decade."

"This is the memoir of the man who started the stogie revival."

Woolley's eyes went to the author's name.

"Good lord! *Melvin Chandler* has had the effrontery to pen his life story?"

"I doubt that he used a pen," Nick said, laying the Upmann in an ashtray. "Mr. Chandler's assistant sent me this copy. Chandler hopes to have a book signing in my store."

Woolley smiled slyly. "Of course he does. One hand is being asked to wash the other. It is obvious that you are expected to return a favor to the man whose publication once named you tobacconist of the year."

As Woolley lifted his stick and pointed toward the wall behind the counter, Nick turned and gazed at a framed cover of *Cigar Smoker.* Beneath a photo of a younger and slenderer Nick Chase in the blue uniform of the New York Police Department was the headline:

CUFFS TO CORONAS
Cigar Smoker's Latest Hall of Famer
Went from Top Cop to Premier Cigarist

Thanks to numerous pages of lavish advertisements for cigars and cigar-smoking accoutrements, copies of the current edition of the magazine stacked next to the cash register were much thicker than the one in which an article had explained why and how a homicide detective gave up police work in New York City to open a tobacco shop.

"That article was published over ten years ago," Nick said. "If I'm being asked to return a favor, it's taken Chandler a long time to request it. But even if that is the case, where's a better place for the author of a book on the subject of cigars to sell them than a cigar store?"

"When are you expected to play host for this dubious event?"

"The book is being published in November. The plan is to have it coincide with one of Chandler's cigar nights to be held at Farley's. There'll be free premium smokes and snifters of superb cognacs. I'm sure I can wangle you an invitation."

"No thanks."

Nick's eyes went wide. "Since when has Professor Roger Woolley stopped accepting invitations to parties?"

"In the unlikely event of my receiving one," Woolley replied as he adjusted the bulky package under his arm, "I would want no part in boosting further the ego of Melvin Chandler, and I'm sure he's not interested in seeing me again."

Nick picked up his cigar. "Again? I had no idea you knew him."

Woolley set down the package. "Some twenty-five years ago I was a member of the disciplinary committee which expelled him from Harvard."

"What did he do to merit ejection from the groves of academe? Cheat on a final exam? Plagiarize some material for a paper? Cut too many classes? Vote Republican?"

Although no customers were present, he whispered, "Chandler was charged with a small case of grand larceny."

"There's no such thing as *small* grand larceny. How much did he steal, and from whom?"

"It was a thousand dollars," Woolley continued *sotto voce*, "embezzled from the account of Chandler's club, of which he was treasurer."

Nick studied the ash of the H. Upmann. "What did he swipe the money for?"

Woolley struck a wooden match and lit his pipe. "Chandler pleaded *nolo contendere*, so we never found out the motive. I was convinced the club's president and vice-president knew why, but Charlie Appleton and Kevin Rattigan refused to cooperate with the investigations."

Nick shook his head ruefully. "I hate an unsolved mystery."

"My impression," Woolley continued, "was that Chandler had lost some kind of wager. The man was a notorious gambler. Others felt his extravagant lifestyle had caught up with him in the form of a bill collector, probably sent by one of the tony Boylston Street haberdashers. Even as a college student Chandler had fancied himself a fashion plate. He was always more interested in dazzling women sartorially than in pursuing his studies."

"I had the impression in the Sixties that if a college guy wanted to score with a girl he wore bell bottom jeans, tie-dye shirts, and love beads and joined the anti-war movement."

"Chandler was all for the war, which in his case represented no personal threat because he had a medical deferment for a heart defect. Had he been subject to being conscripted, I might not have voted to expel him. As to women, if a girl in whom Chandler was interested had exhibited any interest in politics in 1968, she would have been a 'Co-ed for Nixon' or for some other such right-wing group."

"You were a Hubert Humphrey man, of course."

"Heavens, no! I worked for Eugene McCarthy. He would have succeeded had it not been for Bobby Kennedy jumping in after Gene proved that Lyndon Johnson could be beaten."

Nick puffed the cigar. "Chandler's lack of a Harvard sheepskin doesn't appear to have hurt him. He's got to be worth several million bucks."

"Accumulation of wealth," said Woolley, picking up his bundle and stick and turning to leave, "is never a criterion in defining success."

"Good golly, all these years I've been cruelly misled."

"Neither," added Woolley, "is having one's name on a book jacket."

Four

AFTER A MORNING which saw only three customers, Nick busied himself in straightening boxes of cigars on the shelves of the walk-in humidor when he heard the front door close hard. Stepping from the glass-walled room to see who had come in and again finding Woolley, who was looking red-faced, he said, "All right, Professor, what happened at your meeting that's gotten your dander up?"

Angrily tapping the floor with his walking stick as he stood by the door with a glowering look, Woolley demanded, "What makes you think my dander's up?"

"Whenever you bang something, whether it's the floor with a walking stick or my door, you're on the warpath. Ergo something at the meeting raised your hackles."

"You and your detective's mind," said Woolley, striding across the store. "Until I sold you this building and you moved into the flat below mine, I had no concept of what Dr. John H. Watson had to endure while sharing quarters with Sherlock Holmes."

"Whatever mental distress and physical discomfiture Holmes inflicted on the good doctor was amply compensated in the fees Watson collected from the *Strand* magazine for writing his stories about them. Just as you've profited twice by writing books about my involvement in two murder cases."

"And masterly involvements they were!"

"You still haven't told me what happened at the meeting."

"That sanctimonious old fart Andrew Reynolds happened," said Woolley. "He actually demanded that we turn down a one-million-dollar gift on grounds that it has been proffered by someone who accumulated his wealth through tobacco. Once upon a time, Reynolds was a three-pack-a-day man—unfiltered—and now the doddering old fool has appointed himself the avowed archenemy of smoking of all kinds."

"The ex–cigarette smoker usually becomes the most rabid anti-tobacco zealot," Nick said, returning to the humidor to stack boxes of Partagas Robustos. "Cigar and pipe smokers who give them up—and very few do—are too gentlemanly to try to tell someone else how to live his life. Who's the million-buck benefactor?"

Woolley followed him into the room. "None other than Melvin Chandler."

Nick barked a laugh. "He's giving a million dollars to the school that kicked him out?"

"So said his executive assistant. Benjamin Salter flew up from New York to present the proposal to the gifts committee and to request that we arrange some kind of ceremony to coincide with Chandler's coming to your store for the book signing. It's another brazen attempt to gain his tome even more publicity."

"He's going to have to sell a bunch of books to get back a million dollars."

Woolley grunted contemptuously. "What's a million to an egomaniac?"

"Given your animosity for the man," Nick said, leaving the humidor and closing the glass door, "I'm surprised that *you* didn't kick Salter out of the meeting."

"I would never allow personal feelings about someone to cloud my judgment," Woolley said in a wounded tone, "especially in a matter of benefit to the university."

"I assume that you persuaded the other members of the gifts committee to vote aye."

"Certainly. However, that pig-headed Reynolds vows to

voice his dissent publicly by way of letters to the editors of the Boston newspapers, the *New York Times*, and, of course, the *Crimson.* He hopes to urge like-minded individuals to rally against smoking of all kinds by staging protests when Chandler is here. I warned him that in so doing he will only provide Chandler more of what he seeks, which is publicity for himself."

"Isn't it possible," Nick said, going behind the sales counter, "that Chandler's gift is a sincere expression of repentance for the misdeed that got him kicked out of Harvard? For that kind of dough the guy deserves an honorary degree."

"If you think giving a million dollars can buy a Harvard degree, you've got another think coming," said Woolley indignantly as he followed Nick. "I also have a seat on that committee. Although I'm an *ex officio* member with no vote, my opinions are listened to. And respected."

"For a man who retired from the academic world twenty years ago," said Nick, "you do manage to keep your hand in things. I'm amazed that you find time to grind out your charming Jake Elwell thrillers so regularly."

"Now, *there's* a pot calling a kettle black. Where would the police have been if a retired detective named Nick Chase hadn't been on hand to get involved in investigations of the Rupert and Hardin murders? In both cases the culprits would have gotten away with it."

"My involvements in them were happenstance. Your memberships on committees, six of them at last count, are willful."

"You somehow make it sound criminal."

"Andrew Reynolds can write as many letters to the editor as he wishes; he's not going to keep Melvin Chandler from promoting his book. And history proves that no matter how many voices are raised against them, people who choose to smoke are going to go on smoking. This is a continuation of the battle over smoking that began the moment Sir Walter Raleigh first stuffed a pipe with tobacco from Virginia and lit it. Four centuries later, tobacco is still legal."

"Yes, but for how long?"

"I don't think this country will make that mistake. We all know what we got when people who wanted to ban drinking liquor had their way. Prohibition! With what result? The country went on a thirteen-year binge and gave rise to the Mafia."

"That's a lovely speech, Nick," said Woolley, turning to leave, "but it's not likely to get you anywhere come December when Reynolds and his anti-smoking allies in S.O.S learn that Chandler is coming to your store to sign copies of his book."

"What the hell is S.O.S.?"

"It's Reynolds' action group, Snuff Out Smoking. It's run on a day-to-day basis by one of Reynolds' protégés, name of Rob Devonshire."

"Well, the book signing is three months away. To quote that famous cigarette-smoker Humphrey Bogart in the movie *Casablanca,* I never worry about anything that far in advance."

PART II

Smoke Signals

As I puff this mild Havana,
and its ashes slowly lengthen,
I feel my courage gather
and my resolution strengthen:
I will smoke, and I will praise you,
my cigar, and I will light you
With tobacco-phobic pamphlets
by the learned prigs who fight you.

MY CIGAR

Five

NICK AWOKE AT seven in the morning on Friday, the fifteenth of November, to the sound of a window rattling. The weatherman on last night's midnight newscast on WHDH radio, he recalled, had warned of a very cold and gusty day.

Lying on his back and hearing the stirring of the delightful old man who lived upstairs, he became aware of the dark brown taste of yesterday's final cigar lingering in the far recesses of his mouth. He'd leisurely smoked the full-bodied Partagas Almirante from the Dominican Republic in the living room of his apartment in a commodious and slightly dilapidated greenish leather couch on which he did his pre-bedtime reading. The six-inch cigar had come from a box of forty, an early birthday gift from Peg Baron. Because she would be away on the eighteenth, playing her cello with the Boston Symphony in the orchestra's annual visit to New York City, she had presented them ten days early after dinner at Farley's restaurant.

The book which had kept Nick up well beyond his usual bedtime was Roger Woolley's latest Jake Elwell mystery, not counting the one he'd shipped to his publisher in September. At the very moment Nick had thought he'd spotted the killer, Woolley had pulled the rug out from under him with a devilish twist that in the real world of murder could never hold up during a trial. Any defense lawyer worth his retainer would have made a hash of such a flimsy case of circumstantial evidence and hearsay. Fortunately for Woolley's fictional district attorney, the affable but bumbling Horace Harker, the cornered killer had foolishly blurted a confession to both Jake and homicide detective Anthony Purvis. In six Jake Elwell novels Woolley had blatantly patterned Purvis on Lieutenant Jack Lerch of the Cambridge Police Department's murder squad.

According to a midnight radio newscast, Lerch had cracked the strangulation murder of prostitute Lilly Foster in two days and had done so without the help of a private eye. He and his men had solved it with legwork and time-tested investigative procedures.

Nick made a mental note to phone Lerch to congratulate him and got out of bed. Going from the warmth of carpeting against his bare feet to the cold tiles of the bathroom floor, he ran through his day's schedule.

After retrieving the *Boston Globe* from his doorstep, he would have his usual breakfast of black coffee, orange juice, and toast and scan the paper for items reported by his son, Kevin, and any stories of other crimes which might mention daughter Jean, a criminologist with the Boston police. Following a shower and shave, he would dress appropriately for changing the display in the front window of his store to a Christmas-is-coming-and-it's-not-far-away motif.

In the purveying of cigars, pipes, and other smoking-related items, he'd quickly learned as a tobacconist that only Father's Day surpassed Christmas in an upturn in patronage and a change in the nature of customers. With the approach of the two holidays, he could count on an influx of women. Most came looking for advice on what to give the men in their lives. In many instances he counseled that because choices in cigars and pipes were so intensely personal, unless the gift-giver knew what the recipient wanted, his advice was for the customer to select a gift certificate.

When he'd described this policy to Peg Baron and noted that hardly any women followed his advice, but went ahead and purchased cigars or a pipe, Peg had shaken her head in dismay.

"Suggesting that a woman present the man in her life with a gift certificate," she said, "is the dumbest thing I've ever heard. Don't you understand, Nick, that it's never the gift that is important to a woman? It's seeing the expression on the man's face when he opens it. So what if she's picked out the wrong kind of cigar? The man can do what a woman does when she's been given the wrong present. He can take it back and exchange it. Besides, according to you, there's no such thing as a bad cigar."

After ten years of observing Nick Chase smoking cigars, Nick thought as he looked at his reflection in the bathroom mirror, Peg had learned that in giving him a box of Almirantes she'd run no risk. Because every box of cigars sold in his store bore its name, rubber-stamped on the bottom of the box, her only challenge had been buying the cigars from his store without his knowing it. Assuming she'd had an accomplice, he suspected the co-conspirator had been the man he'd heard moving around in the apartment above.

Looking at the bare-chested reverse image of himself in the mirror, he daubed shaving soap from a small tub onto his cheeks, jaw, and neck with a brush from a shaving kit that had been last year's birthday gift from a grandson. This triggered an affectionate memory of Peg's birthday gift and a cake ablaze with thirteen candles, each representing five years. She had connived with the head waiter at Farley's to present it, accompanied by the raucous singing of "Happy Birthday to You" by everyone in the cigar room.

Confronting the lathered face in the mirror, he demanded, "How the hell did you get to be sixty-five years old without me noticing?"

Shaved and dressed, he finished breakfast not having found either of his children's names in the newspaper. But on a page of the lifestyle section he discovered a brief article concerning Melvin Chandler, the forthcoming publication of his autobiography, and the fact that the author would be soon visiting the Boston area to promote the book in a series of events.

"According to Mr. Chandler's business associate, Madeline Lewis," the article said, "the plan includes a cigar night reception at Farley's restaurant, the author signing copies of the book titled *Smoke Dreamer* at the Happy Smoking Ground, a popular tobacco shop on Brattle Street in Cambridge, and a speech to be delivered at a meeting with present members of a student club to which Mr. Chandler belonged when he was an undergraduate at Harvard in the 1960s."

Ripping out the article, Nick muttered, "A popular tobacco shop! Let's hope that brings in a few more customers today!"

Turning to the editorial and op-ed pages, he found a letter over the name of Woolley's nemesis on the gifts committee. Professor Andrew Reynolds had written:

Citizens of the greater Boston region concerned with the proven hazards of tobacco smoking are soon to be confronted with the presence of Melvin Chandler, publisher of an especially offensive magazine devoted to promoting smoking. He plans to promote the publication of his autobiography by appearing at the Happy Smoking Ground cigar store on Brattle Street in Cambridge and during a "cigar night" at Farley's restaurant. All those sharing my outrage over these appearances are urged to join me and others in protesting Mr. Chandler's appearances at those locations. Further information may be obtained by contacting Rob Devonshire at "Snuff Out Smoking." The number is listed in the Cambridge phone book.

Six

THE WEATHER FORECAST of cold and wind notwithstanding, and because he only had to take a few steps to reach the store from the vestibule at the foot of the stairs to his apartment above it, Nick left an overcoat in the closet and put on a brown tweed sports jacket. Looking left as he stepped outside, he saw a hatless reddish-haired stocky young man hanging something around the neck of the cigar store Indian. "Hey boy," he shouted, "what are you doing there?"

As the startled youth bolted and ran eastward, Nick saw something white flapping in the strong, chilly wind blowing down Brattle Street from the square where the fleeing figure mingled with people bundled against the cold. Heads down, they strode toward Harvard, a block north.

As he neared the Indian, he found a sign printed in black letters with a wide felt-tip pen:

CIGARS
STINK.

"One man's stench," Nick grumbled as he removed the placard, "is another's perfume."

Standing on a wooden pedestal shaped and painted to look like a boulder, the six-feet-tall fanciful representation of a native American had a lone white feather stuck into the back of a red headband. Bare-chested, he wore fringed buckskin leggings. A sheathed knife dangled from a beaded belt. The right arm rose in a graceful arc and the hand formed a kind of salute to shield squinting black eyes. Cupped, the left hand cradled a bundle of wooden cigars. Hewn into the base was the name William Demuth & Company.

Research by Professor Woolley had determined that in the 1880s and 1890s the New York City tobacconist had enjoyed a brisk and profitable sideline selling such figures to what one of the firm's advertisements called "segar stores, wine & liquors, druggists, Yankee notions, umbrellas, tea stores, clothiers, theaters, gardens, banks, insurance companies &c." The figures had ranged in dimensions from life-sized for display at the fronts of stores to small figurines for sales counters and window displays. They had been the earliest form of outdoor advertising and were now considered folk art and exhibited in museums of Americana.

Nick's example had been acquired for ten-thousand dollars through a Massachusetts Avenue antiquarian, Stanley Rupert, whose murder two years earlier had drawn Nick reluctantly into the investigation of the case. The Indian had been standing adjacent to the front door of the Happy Smoking Ground since the store's opening, except for varying lengths of time during the spring when the effigy's whereabouts were known only to groups of Harvard law students. They celebrated completion of the school's legendary rigorous first year by kidnapping the statue. This was not an easy task, as the object weighed a thousand pounds. Yet once a year, Nick found in its place a demand that he ransom it with a postal money order for the price of a box of his best premium cigars.

These framed, crudely written extortion notes hung behind the sales counter next to a display containing Nick's gold New York Police Department detective shield and the framed *Cigar Smoker* cover and article naming Nick the magazine's tobacconist of the year.

The only other molestation of the Indian by Harvard students occurred on the weekends of the annual football games with Yale. Left in place, it was adorned on those occasions with placards or banners exhorting victory for the Crimson eleven. This year's contest had occurred in October, with a Yalie triumph.

Grateful that the young man who'd fled after having expressed his disdain for the objects of Nick's livelihood had not chosen to vent it on the wall with a can of spray paint, he entered a store that was rich with a scent that had proved alluring since tobacco was discovered by natives of the two continents which European explorers had called the New World. Spanish sailors had found tobacco being smoked on islands as cigars and had carried them around the world. Englishmen learned to smoke the dried leaves in wood and stone pipes, then took the discovery home to be enjoyed in clay at first and ultimately in finely crafted woods, primarily briar.

Folding the cardboard placard and placing it in a wastebasket, Nick looked around at the shelves and display cases filled with all manner of cigars with names both descriptive and poetic: bonitas, fabuloso, immensa, petit, claro, oscuro, maduro, pyramid, belicoso, torpedo. And those named for illustrious and accomplished men: Churchill, Hemingway, Valentino, Rothschild, Balboa, Columbus, Clemenceau, and even Al Capone.

Three walls of the store were festooned with racks displaying scores of the descendants of the first pipes in a variety of sizes and shapes: apple, billiard, bulldog, pot, prince, straight, half-bent, full-bent, and even the yellow huge-bowled Calabash of the Sherlock Holmeses of stage and film, but not of the Holmes found in the stories by Sir Arthur Conan Doyle. The Sherlock on the printed page chose from what Dr. Watson called "a litter of pipes" on the mantelpiece, and if not a pipe, a cigar from those he kept in a coal scuttle.

Tucked among the displayed pipes of the Happy Smoking Ground was a framed photo of the best known of the Holmes personifiers, Basil Rathbone, clutching a half-bent Peterson pipe, and a color portrait of the actor who had defined Holmes on television, Jeremy Brett. Wearing a long dressing gown and seated in profile with hands clasped around upraised knees, he appeared deeply pensive as he smoked a lengthy straight briar.

Pictures of three cigar smokers had been chosen to adorn the walls: a glowering Churchill holding one of his favored Dunhills as though it were a weapon, W. C. Fields with a half-smoked stogie in the corner of a sullen mouth, and television's Peter Falk as Lieutenant Columbo looking deceptively puzzled in rumpled trench coat. He puffed a stubby cigar whose aroma just might have justified the sentiment expressed on the sign Nick had found hanging on the Indian.

With the Happy Smoking Ground open for business, Nick took an H. Upmann Lonsdale from the box he kept on the counter beside a giant antique brass cash register. He clipped the tip of the cigar, lighted it, and puffed a plume of very pleasant-to-the-nostrils bluish smoke toward the middle of the store. As he smoked and waited for the day's first customer, the phone rang.

He answered cheerily, "Good morning. Happy Smoking Ground."

A gruff male voice demanded, "Are you the owner?"

"This is Nick Chase."

"Did you see the sign on your Indian?"

"It was hard to miss."

"Consider it a warning."

"About what?"

The answer was a click and dial tone.

Minutes later, the phone rang again.

"Now look, fella," Nick answered angrily, "I don't have time for jokes."

A woman asked in a puzzled tone, "May I please speak with Mr. Chase?"

"Sorry! I thought it was somebody else calling. I'm Nick Chase."

"Oh good. This is Madeline Lewis, special assistant to Melvin Chandler."

Surprised, Nick blurted, "You're in the newspaper this morning."

"Yes, and a very nice article it is. I'm calling to ask if it would be convenient for us to get together sometime today. I'd like to talk with you about the arrangements for Mr. Chandler's book signing at your store. I'm staying at the Mayflower Hotel, but just for the day. Do you have an hour or so to have lunch with me?"

"Dinner would be better. I run the store by myself on Fridays. I close at seven."

"That's fine. I'll take a later plane. Shall we meet at seven-thirty at Farley's?"

"It happens to be my favorite spot."

"That's why I suggested it."

"Really? How did you know that?"

"Thanks to the article about you a few years ago in *Cigar Smoker,* I know a great deal about you, Mr. Chase. I've also read about your recent adventures in crime-solving in a couple of fascinating books written by your friend Roger Woolley. I'll see you at Farley's."

Seven

AS NICK NEARED the top of the steps and the opened double-doors of the entrance to the upstairs cigar room of Farley's, he inhaled the rich aroma of the smoke of fine cigars and heard a muted chorus of baritone voices. Within, he found a usual Friday evening crowd of businessmen and academics in a smoky room of dark wood-paneled walls and maroon leather banquettes lit by amber sconces and flickering candles. Tables were draped in red-and-white checkered coverings. He was greeted by the head waiter.

"Good evening, Mr. Chase," he said, bowing slightly. "Right on time, as always."

"Hello, Freddy. I'm expecting a guest, name of Madeline Lewis."

"The lady's already seated at your table."

The only woman in the room, she added a dash of vivid color in the form of a red dress as she sipped a glass of white wine.

Freddy asked Nick, "Shall I bring your usual Bushmills neat?"

"Yes, thanks. And another of whatever she's drinking."

When Nick arrived at the table, she said, "You look just like your picture."

Sitting, Nick asked, "What picture?"

"The one in *Cigar Smoker* when you were named tobacconist of the year."

Nick winced and patted his belly. "That was a long time and a lot fewer pounds ago."

"According to Roger Woolley's book, it was here at Farley's that Natalie Goodman launched her scheme to get you involved in a plan to murder Harry Hardin and make it seem that she was actually the intended victim."

"It was at this very table. It's my regular spot."

"Out of habit or design?"

"From here I can observe the entire room."

"Is it in a rule book that a detective must never sit with his back to a door?"

"You can't learn anything if you're looking at a wall."

"I read in an article in *Cigar Smoker* that Wild Bill Hickok, the lawman of the Old West, always sat back to the wall to guard against being shot from behind. The only time he didn't, that's exactly what happened."

"You appear to be quite an expert on the contents of a magazine for men."

"Only since I went to work for Melvin Chandler. I decided that if I was to take on the job of publicizing his book, I should familiarize myself with the magazine that made him famous."

"And very rich."

She winked. "That too."

Freddy delivered the drinks and asked, "Would you like to order dinner now?"

"I'm afraid I haven't given it a thought," said Madeline.

"I recommend the lamb chops and Farley's famous home-fried potatoes," Nick said.

She smiled up at Freddy. "Lamb chops and Farley's famous home fries, please."

"For two," said Nick.

As Freddy withdrew, she asked Nick, "What can you learn by observing people eating and drinking?"

Nick sipped the Irish whiskey. "Everything. Social status. Their finances. Ethnicity. Education and breeding. How they see themselves and what they want others to believe about them. Who's a snob and who isn't, and why. Who's in love or would like to be. The easy-going and the uptight. The self-centered and the busybodies. Skinflints and the big-hearted."

"You see all that by watching someone having dinner?"

"Once upon a time you could discern a great deal by whether someone smoked. From what they smoked. And the way they smoked, of course. Except in rooms such as this, nowadays all I can tell about someone's smoking is observing whether they linger after a meal. Smokers get up and leave almost immediately. Non-smokers dally."

"Are you able to tell from someone's manner of eating, drinking, and smoking whether he or she is capable of committing a crime?"

"We're all capable of that. The only thing that prevents most people from doing so is the fear of being caught. As to a link between smoking and criminality, to whether a smoker is more likely to break the law, I would not be at all surprised if somewhere research was being done by some anti-smoking zealot to come up with data to show a connection. As for me, I would much rather be invited out to dinner with a cigar-smoking crook than with the Surgeon General."

"Have you ever known of a criminal who didn't smoke?"

"Adolf Hitler springs to mind."

"What about detectives who didn't smoke?"

"What about them?"

"Have you known any?"

Nick sipped the Bushmills again, thought for a moment, then smiled. "None who was as good as me."

"Why did you give up policework?"

"I finally met the bullet with my name on it."

"Oh yes, I remember now. The article in *Cigar Smoker* said you'd been shot and that you got bored being restricted to a desk job, so you retired from the police department. But not, evidently, from solving murders. I know Roger Woolley has written about those cases, but have you ever given thought to writing your own book? With the right publisher and a good publicist, I'm sure it would do very, very well."

"I'm perfectly content running a tobacco store, although there's at least one person who's unhappy with that situation. When I opened for business this morning I found a placard hanging around the neck of the wooden Indian in front of my store. It said, 'Cigars stink.' A few minutes later, I got a phone call telling me that I should consider the sign as a warning."

"Have you told the police about this threat?"

"Making threats is not illegal. Besides, there's nothing the police could do."

"They could find the person who put up that sign. He must have left fingerprints."

"Hanging a 'Cigar Stinks' sign on a wooden Indian falls within the definition of freedom of expression."

"But you got a threatening phone call!"

"I figure whoever put it up and made the call were members of an anti-smoking group. Its leader had a letter to the editor in the *Globe* today."

"Yes, I read it."

"I expect Melvin Chandler has had to put up with lots worse things. Because of the letter and the general fervor of the anti-smoking movement, he's probably going to find himself facing protesters while he's in Cambridge."

"I've found that Mel is not the sort of man to duck controversy. However, in view of the sign on your Indian and the phone call, I'm worried about the wisdom of going ahead with the book signing at the Happy Smoking Ground."

"I have no intention of backing out of my commitment. All I'm waiting to find out is the date and time you have in mind."

"I've scheduled the cigar night here at Farley's for December fourth, a Monday. Would that date be convenient for you? I'd like to arrange the signing for at least an hour. I thought we would begin at noon."

"That's fine with me. Mondays are always slow."

"Good. When I return to New York, I'll have some posters made that you can place in the window of the store, and anywhere else you feel they might be helpful in advertising the event. I'll also place ads in the Boston newspapers."

Peering across the room, Nick saw two familiar figures enter. "Speaking of the police," he said, nodding in the direction of the entrance, "they have arrived."

Madeline turned to look at a short, pudgy middle-aged man in a gray suit and a younger, trimmer one wearing a dark brown sports coat and tan slacks. "The chubby one has to be Jack Lerch," she exclaimed. "Woolley's first book about your adventures in sleuthing described him to a T. The other I don't recognize."

"That's Lerch's new partner, Detective Sid Goldstein," said Nick as the pair made their way toward them across the smoky room. "The sergeant on the case in the book you read was Gary Evert. He left Cambridge to take a job as chief of police in a small town in Vermont."

"Don't they all?"

Reaching the table, Lerch declared, "Well, Nick Chase! Fancy meeting you here."

"I heard on the radio of your latest success, Jack. Congratulations," Nick replied. "And to you, too, Detective Goldstein. It's your first murder since joining the force, I believe?"

"I've worked plenty before this one."

"Fellas, allow me to introduce Madeline Lewis."

She asked, "Was the murder Nick mentioned tough to solve, Lieutenant Lerch?"

He smiled. "Let's put it this way, it's not likely to result in Nick's pal, Professor Woolley, rushing to his typewriter to turn it into another of the best-sellers he grinds out so regularly."

"Will you join us for dinner?" she asked.

Lerch glanced at Nick. "Thanks much, but Detective Goldstein and I have a few things to go over about the case. Odds and ends, loose ends. The kind of things that are never left hanging in one of Woolley's novels."

"I'm sorry you can't join us," she said. "I was hoping to persuade Nick to tell you about a threatening phone call he received."

"Is that so?"

"Nothing for you to worry about, Jack," said Nick. "It was somebody who disapproves of the way I make a living."

Lerch frowned. "What did he say exactly?"

" 'Consider it a warning.' He was referring to a sign that I caught some kid hanging on the neck of my wooden Indian. The caller was probably the same guy. I caught him in the act, but he got away."

"What did the sign say?"

" 'Cigars stink.' It's a prank, I'm sure. When I was a kid I used to call up the tobacco shop on the corner and ask if they had Prince Albert in a can, then yell, 'Well, let him out.' "

Lerch smiled. "I did that, too. But 'Consider it a warning' is not something you should take lightly, Nick. There are a lot of kooks out there. And who knows how many low lifes and killers you sent up the river when you were a cop might be out and looking to settle up accounts with you?"

"The guy who put up the sign was a kid, around twenty, red hair, athletic."

"You saw him actually doing it?"

"If I was ten years younger I could have collared him."

"I want your word that if something else like this happens, you'll let me know."

"I appreciate your concern, Jack, but as you know, I've got two very reliable friends I can turn to if there's trouble, Mr. Smith and Mr. Wesson."

"A pistol in the drawer in back of a counter will do you no good when you're out on the street or walking home after dinner and cigars at Farley's."

"What are you going to do, assign me a bodyguard?"

"If I must, yes."

"I'm sure the idea of spending taxpayers' money to assign a policeman to keep my Indian company by standing guard in front of a cigar store will go over very well with the bean counters at City Hall." A waiter appeared with two orders of lamb chops and home fries. Nick scowled. "After all this worrying about my safety, I'm not sure if I should eat this. It might be poisoned."

A little while later, when the waiter appeared to inquire

whether Nick and Madeline cared to have dessert and coffee, Madeline replied, "Neither for me, thanks."

"If I have coffee," Nick said to her, "I'll have to light up a cigar. If my smoking would bother you, I can skip it."

"I have no problem with the smoke," she answered, "but I do have a plane to catch soon, and I would rather spend the time seeing the layout of the Happy Smoking Ground, that is if it wouldn't be an inconvenience. I believe it's nearby."

"A couple of blocks, but it's a cold night for walking."

"I'm used to cold places. You can smoke your cigar on the way."

"There's nothing I enjoy more than showing off my store."

To the waiter she said, "The check then, please."

"The Cigar Room at Farley's is a club," said Nick. "Only members may pay. That makes this my treat."

"Okay," she said as Nick signed the bill, "but when you come to New York, it's on me."

"Only if you charge it to Melvin Chandler's expense account."

As they made their way from the room, Nick gave a parting wave to Lerch.

"He must be a good friend," said Madeline. "He was truly concerned about the threatening phone call you received."

"Jack has a tendency to see mountains in mole hills."

Descending the stairs, she asked, "Do you really keep a pistol in your store?"

"You never know who might come through the door."

While they claimed their coats from the ground-floor checkroom, he drew a cigar case from his jacket pocket and removed a cigar.

Madeline asked, "Have you ever met Melvin Chandler?"

Nick returned the case to the pocket. "Nope."

"He's quite a character," she said as he helped her on with a long mink coat. "I think you'll find him fascinating."

Slipping into a double-breasted overcoat that Peg Baron

had bought him to replace one that was twenty years old and looked it, he asked, "How long have you known him?"

"Not so very long. Of course, I knew *about* him even before I moved to New York."

Nick clipped and lit the cigar in the vestibule, then opened the door and held it for her.

"Moved from where?"

"I was born in Providence, Rhode Island," she said as they walked briskly along Waterhouse Street toward Massachusetts Avenue. "I'd been studying public relations at Boston University, but dropped out when my mother got sick and became bedridden. When she died, I got a job with a p.r. firm in New York. After a couple of years, I decided to try going it alone."

"You've obviously done very well to have landed Melvin Chandler as a client."

"That was a fluke. I was lucky enough to meet Ben Salter at a party just at the moment Ben had persuaded Mel to find an outside publicist to promote *Smoke Dreamer.*"

"I thought publishers took care of publicizing their books."

"They usually do, but Mel is determined to see his book on best-seller lists, no matter how much it might cost. I told him that money alone can't achieve that goal, but he's forging ahead."

"Was it your idea that he hype the book by giving a million dollars to Harvard?"

She stopped abruptly. "How do you know about that?"

"The fellow who thinks of himself as my Boswell—or my Dr. John H. Watson is a better way to put it—" Nick said as they resumed walking, "sits on the university's gifts committee. He's also on the committee that expelled Chandler from Harvard. How's that for a coincidence?"

"I'm very much looking forward to meeting your Watson. He's a very fine writer."

"Until now Woolley has been dead set against being part of any of the events to publicize the book. But I think he'll change his mind after I tell him about the person who's in charge of Chandler's publicity. Woolley is well into his seventies, but advancing age has not affected his appreciation of those he calls the fair sex."

"Fair sex! How quaint. I'm dying to meet him."

"He lives above my store in the top-floor apartment. I can introduce you if you wish."

"I'm afraid I'd feel rushed. I do have a plane to catch and I've got to pick up my bags at my hotel."

Presently they reached Brattle Street.

Nearing the store, Nick looked toward it and barked a laugh.

Startled, Madeline asked, "What is it?"

Nick pointed ahead. "It's the Indian. Someone's hung another sign on it."

Attached to a yellow ribbon, the white placard bore small print done by hand in black ink that read:

TOBACCO IS A STINKING WEED
HATEFUL TO THE NOSE
LOATHSOME TO THE EYE
HARMFUL TO THE BRAIN
DANGEROUS TO THE LUNGS

Removing the sign, Nick shook his head slowly as he said, "I must tip my hat to whoever took the trouble to do this. It isn't just another person who's against smoking. This guy knows tobacco's history. These words are from an attack on smoking that was called *A Counterblaste to Tobacco* written by the king of England who also authorized a new translation of the Bible into English, James the First. He also had Sir Walter Raleigh's head chopped off. But not because he was responsible for tobacco being brought to England from Virginia. James and Sir Walter just didn't care much for each other."

"Two of these signs, that horrible phone call," Madeline exclaimed. "I must say, Nick, you're being awfully blasé about this. I think you should call Lieutenant Lerch."

"Trust me, Madeline. By now he's into his third Dewars scotch on the rocks as he bores his new sidekick to death with cases from the files of Lieutenant Lerch of the murder squad. You asked to see if the Happy Smoking Ground is suitable for Melvin Chandler's book-signing, and that's what we're going to do. I say to hell with King James and all his present-day spawn!"

PART III

Cordially Requested

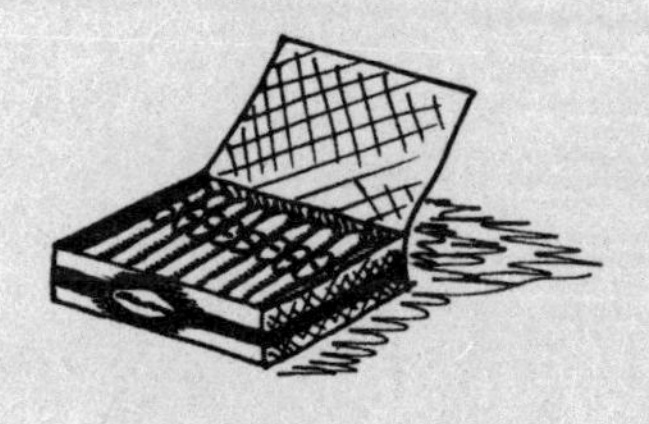

Of all the hearts
That close to mine entwine
None lies so near,
Nor seems so dear
As this cigar of mine.

ANONYMOUS

THE WORDING OF the proposed invitation which Madeline Lewis presented to Melvin Chandler for his approval was embossed in gold ink on a royal blue card:

You are cordially requested to help me celebrate
publication of my memoirs,
SMOKE DREAMER,
as I autograph copies at noon, December 4,
at THE HAPPY SMOKING GROUND,
Brattle Street, Cambridge, Massachusetts,
and with an evening of good drinks and fine cigars
in the Upstairs Cigar Room of FARLEY'S
starting at 7 P.M.

"This is excellent," he said, returning the card. "How many of them are going out?"

"At the moment there are a hundred-fifty, primarily to the press."

"Ben will give you a list of names and a note to enclose for those who aren't living in the Boston area advising them that arrangements will be made for them at a hotel at my expense." He tilted back his head and blew smoke toward the ceiling. *"My enemies list."*

"Why are you inviting enemies?"

"They are the only true measure of success."

Two days later, tall, willowy and red-haired Veronica Redding gazed at Richard Chandler naked on a bed. In soft light formed by a shaft of a weak wintry sunlight, he had the glowing skin, golden hair, and deep blue eyes of a male nude painted by John Singer Sargent.

Glaring at the card in his hand, Richard said, "Whose father but mine would send an invitation to a son *by mail?*"

"Well, you can't expect him to send it by messenger all the way to Cape Cod."

"Ronnie, he knows how to use a telephone."

"Can you take along a guest?"

"You can forget about going, darling," Richard said as he ripped the invitation in half, "because I have no intention of massaging my old man's ego."

Veronica sat on the bed and stroked his chest. "You're just upset about the money."

Richard threw up his arms. "*Of course I'm upset.* It's my inheritance he's giving away."

"You make it sound as if he's about to drop dead at any minute. Your father's as strong as a horse. Besides, what's one million to a man who makes five times that much in a year? By the time he dies, you'll be in line for *hundreds* of millions."

"Oh yeah? What if he gets it into his head to give it *all* to charities? It would be just like him to decide to go out in a blaze of publicity about what a great and good man he was at heart. He wouldn't be the first multimillionaire who tried to get people to forget what a son of a bitch he was in life."

"He would never cut off his only son."

"He's threatened to more than once."

"That was before Donny died. So why run the risk of being disinherited by getting him angry with you for not accepting the invitation to his big party?"

Richard gathered the pieces of the card. "You're right, of course. You always are."

"And please, pretty please," said Veronica, settling back on the bed, "talk to that woman in charge of his publicity campaign and see if you can wangle an invitation for me."

"You hate cigars," said Richard, turning toward her. "Why are you so set on going to a party where there'll be hundreds of people puffing away on them?"

"I want to go because I'm tired of being left out. You and I have been together for more than two years. As far as your father is concerned, he doesn't even know I exist."

"Sometimes he hardly knows I exist! You'll meet my darling papa when I think the time is right. Not a second before."

"And when will that be?" she said with a sulky expression. "When he's laid out in his solid gold coffin?"

Richard kissed her shoulder. "From your lips to God's ears."

Presently he sat up and reached for the bedside phone.

Stirring languidly, Veronica asked, "Who are you calling?"

"Mother."

"Whatever for?"

"To tell her about the invitation, of course."

The call was answered in Anita Weston Chandler's house on Beacon Hill by the maid named Carmelita. "Mrs. Chandler's residence. Who's calling, please?"

"It's me, Carmelita."

He heard a click on the line that meant someone else had picked up.

"Hello, Mother," he exclaimed. "You may hang up, Carmelita."

"Darling," said Anita sweetly, "isn't it rather early for you to be up and about? Where are you calling from? Please don't say you're in Boston. That would be most inconvenient."

"Don't worry, I'm not about to drop in on you. I'm at the cottage."

"Are you alone?"

"You know better, my dear."

"Tell Elizabeth I said hello."

"Her name is Veronica."

"What happened to Elizabeth?"

"She was long ago, Mother."

"Oh, I'm sorry. I liked her. What can I do for you, my sweet?"

"Have you looked at your mail today?"

"Lord, no. I'm still in bed. Why?"

"I've gotten an invitation to one of dear old Dad's cigar extravaganzas. And to an event at a cigar store in Cambridge where he'll be signing his book."

"Your father's written a book? About what?"

"About him, of course."

"How terribly boring. But what's this to do with me and my mail?"

"I thought he might have sent you an invitation, too."

"Darling, if I've been invited it's because someone in his office made a mistake. The only mail I receive from your father is legal papers."

"Anyway, if you've received an invitation, and you're not going to accept it—"

"I have no interest in watching your father autograph his book."

"Good, because if you've gotten one, I'd like Veronica to use it."

"In the unlikely event that there's one in my mail, I'll forward it to the cottage."

"Just call and tell me if you got one. I'll pick it up on my way to the signing."

She sighed wearily. "Very well. When is this ludicrous affair scheduled?"

"December fourth."

"I'll be sure to be out of town."

A moment after hanging up, she placed a call to her attorney. Connected to voice mail, she blurted, "Jonathan, it's Anita Chandler. Please call me immediately. Mel has written a book. It could affect the terms of the divorce settlement."

* * *

In Boston, in an alcove of a book-cluttered one-bedroom apartment on the top floor of a four-story house on Commonwealth Avenue that a hundred years before had been the mansion of a doctor, Charles Appleton opened the mail while having a breakfast bagel with cream cheese at a small desk. At the bottom of the invitation, he read, "For auld lang syne, do come. Yours, M. C."

His mind raced back more than thirty years to three young men talking in Harvard Yard, white with snow. Wearing a stadium coat he'd bought on sale in Filene's Basement, he walked toward Widener Library with Kevin Rattigan, who was outfitted by Brooks Brothers of Fifth Avenue in New York. Awaiting them on the library steps, Mel Chandler had his hands jammed in the pockets of his costly Boylston Street overcoat. Hatless, with long windblown hair, a handsome face creased with worry, and the almost purple eyes looking scared, he begged, "You really have to help me out of this scrape, Charlie. You're the only guy I know who understands how these things are done."

Back then, everyone believed "Good Old Charlie" from Southie could handle anything. Nobody knew the ins and outs better than the likeable guy who'd grown up in Boston's south end and through intellect and having been spotted by an alumnus as a hell of a goalie in the game of ice hockey had landed a Harvard scholarship. Yessiree, if something needed to be done on the quiet, all you had to do was go see Charlie Appleton, the great fixer of Harvard Yard.

Need a paper that's due tomorrow? Tickets to the big game? Where to place a bet on it? Someone to go on a double-date when the girl you were dying to take out insisted that she bring along her dog of a roommate?

Want a little weed? A tab or two of LSD? Cocaine? How to get laid cheap and a room to do it in? Abortionist?

As Kev Rattigan knew, Charlie could even show a guy the bar to go to find companionship with another guy.

The really great thing about having Charlie Appleton for a friend back then was that no matter what you needed, what you did, or why, you could count on him to keep his mouth shut.

Looking at his desk calendar for the date of the events to which he'd been invited, Charlie found no conflict. Wondering if Kevin had also gotten an invitation from Mel, he decided to call him, but remembered that Kev was conducting a seminar at Boston College.

Because Steve Yedenok had spent a long and frustrating afternoon in a conference room of the law firm of Hebert and Eveland, preparing for his deposition in the case of libel on file in the United States Court for the Southern District of New York as *Yedenok vs. Melvin Chandler Enterprises et al.,* he opened his mail in the small, windowless kitchen of his studio apartment on West Ninety-sixth Street well after six o'clock. In almost impossible-to-read scrawl at the bottom of the invitation Chandler had written, "Stevie, I know that if you'll attend we can dispose of all this legal nonsense in less time than it takes to smoke a cigarillo. Mel."

Welcomed with a smile from the greeter in the crowded lobby of "21" at seven o'clock, Dave Selden self-consciously smoothed his multi-colored tie, wondering if it was too splashy for his blue pin-striped suit, and declared, "I'm joining Mr. Whelan for dinner."

The greeter turned slightly and gestured toward the lounge. "He's waiting for you, sir."

Selden found Whelan seated in a big flower-patterned wingback chair. Portly, with a shock of white hair, he looked crisp in a blue double-breasted blazer, white shirt with gold cuff links, muted tie, and slate-gray slacks. He gazed intently at stock market data on a television screen that had long ago replaced the tickertape machine which had kept "21" patrons such as himself informed on the ups and downs of Wall Street since affable Jack Kriendler and his cousin Charlie Burns had opened the restaurant as a speakeasy just two months after the market crash on Black Tuesday in October 1929.

"Good evening, Jack," said Dave. "I trust your portfolio fared well today."

Whelan rose from the chair with the accumulated dignity of his seventy-five years. "Part did, part didn't. It doesn't matter. I'm in for the long haul."

"Thanks for seeing me on such short notice."

"If you hadn't called, I'd be eating alone again," he said, leading Dave from the lounge into the restaurant that had been created by Jack and Charlie from three town houses on West Fifty-second Street. "We'll order a drink and our dinner at the same time, and then you can tell me all about this invitation you've gotten from Mel Chandler."

The captain led them to a table against the west wall. Whelan's regular spot, it afforded a panoramic view of the long curved bar and three distinct dining sections of the noisy restaurant whose tables with red-checkered covers had served everyone who was someone in New York's society, commerce, show business, or literary world for more than seventy years.

Seated beside Whelan, Dave looked around and whispered, "Everytime I come in here I expect somebody to come rushing up to me and ask, 'How the hell did you get in?' "

"I felt the same," said Whelan, draping a huge napkin over his knees, "the first time Bob Benchley brought me here."

"Robert Benchley! What a wit. Such a great writer. God, I wish I could have known him. But when he died in 1946, my future father was nineteen, still in the army in Europe, and a year from meeting the gal who became my mother."

A waiter took their orders, a gin martini for Whelan and Maker's Mark whiskey for Dave. For dinner Whelan chose salmon and Dave, the restaurant's famous chicken hash.

"Now, about that curious invitation you've gotten," said Whelan.

Dave drew it from an inside pocket.

"Having been fired as Chandler's managing editor," he said, handing it to Whelan, "I was more than a little surprised to get it."

Whelan smiled. "It doesn't surprise me a bit. I've known Chandler thirty years. When I was an up-and-comer in the literary department of the William Morris Agency, Mel was looking for someone to handle a novel he'd written. He'd just been expelled from Harvard. It was your typical first venture into fiction, painfully autobiographical and sophomoric. I told him that he should forget about ever being a writer. A few years after that he was in a position to hire writers for his magazines. As you know, I sold him a lot of my clients' stuff through the years. Knowing him as I do, inviting a man he'd cashiered to a party is what I'd expect. My guess is that he needs you again. This is his way of asking you, in a roundabout way that's just like him, to kiss and make up."

"You're saying I should drop everything and go?"

"Yes, but be careful of his kiss. He's got a poisonous tongue. I kind of wish he had invited me. Boston is a great spot in the winter. There are no less than half a dozen ski slopes close by. What are you doing that's so important to keep you from going?"

"I'm trying to finish my own book, which my contract requires me to turn in to my editor by the end of next week."

"What an editor expects," said Whelan as drinks were brought, "is that the manuscript that's due next week is not going to come in anywhere near on time." He sipped the martini and then smiled slyly. "Perhaps Mel's heard that your book is mostly about him."

Dave lifted his glass. Shaking his head, he said, "No one's seen the manuscript but me."

Whelan set down his martini. "However, you wrote a proposal and an outline which made the rounds before I found a publisher willing to pay the advance I demanded. Who can say who might have slipped it into a fax machine or scanned it as an attachment in Mel's e-mail?"

"For what purpose?"

"In the hope of a generous reward, of course. Or it could have been done by someone connected with a publishing house that had to take a pass on my asking price. It would not be the first time one editor passed a proposal to another. It's a small universe. You never know when you might find yourself looking for a job. It's nice if you can do so with a chit or two to cash in."

"That proposal went around quite a while ago."

Whelan shrugged. "It would be totally out of character, but perhaps Mel doesn't have an ulterior motive in inviting you."

"Mel Chandler doing something without an ulterior motive would be a first."

"Whatever his reason, it will probably provide another juicy little anecdote for your book. When are you going to let me see the manuscript, by the way?"

Dave lifted his whiskey. "As soon as I get back from my trip to Massachusetts."

Nine

AT HALF-PAST NINE on a night that felt as if snow might be in the offing, Professor Andrew Reynolds entered a basement apartment in a house on Museum Street opposite Rockefeller Hall. A small man in a puffy gray down coat which concealed spindly arms and legs, he had an angular face with a hawkish nose supporting half-moon pince-nez glasses. The overall effect of these features was that of a character from Charles Dickens, ironically Reynolds' academic specialty.

Acutely aware that Rob Devonshire, chairman of the steering committee of Snuff Out Smoking, had been presiding over the meeting of its four members for more than an hour, he said breathlessly, "I'm sorry I'm late. I became so caught up in the lively give-and-take of my eight o'clock seminar on *Bleak House* that I lost track of the time. However, I'm sure you proceeded quite satisfactorily without my presence."

He pulled off thick yellow woolen mittens and warmed long, bony hands by rubbing them together vigorously as he looked from face to face. To Rob's left sat Marcy Granick. Pert and vivacious, with long black hair and intensely probing green eyes, she was treasurer of the organization. To her left was Randolph Sloan. Thin to the point of gauntness, he wore large black horn-rimmed glasses giving him an owlish look which befitted his position of secretary. Next to him was the vice-president of S.O.S. Small but muscular Vito Antonnuci was an Olympic-caliber gymnast whose speciality was the pommel horse.

"We always welcome your guidance," said Rob.

As Reynolds sat next to Vito, he asked, "What have you come up with?"

"I believe we've devised a plan that covers both Chandler's book-signing at the Happy Smoking Ground and the cigar night at Farley's," Rob answered, "and a little added attraction in the form of a picket line in front of the hotel where Chandler will be staying for the two nights he's in Cambridge."

"Excellent," said Reynolds, eyebrows arching. "How did you discover which hotel?"

Rob smiled at the young woman seated beside him. "Marcy had the idea of calling all the hotels in Cambridge and pretending she was a member of Chandler's staff who was phoning to confirm the reservation."

"Brilliant, Marcy," Reynolds exclaimed.

"I found the right one on the fourth call. He'll be at the Mayflower, staying in the penthouse John F. Kennedy suite."

"Chandler has always been obsessed with J F K. I remember reading in a newspaper article a few years ago that he was incensed at losing out in an auction sale of one of Kennedy's cigar humidors to Marvin Shanken, owner of *Cigar Afficionado* magazine, Chandler's chief rival. He was forced to settle for a pocket cigar case carried by Winston Churchill during the second world war. Foolishness. That money could have been used to aid the homeless."

"All the picket signs for the protest demonstrations are being made by a friend of Vito," said Marcy. "We've ordered two hundred of them."

"Plus a thousand fliers to post along surrounding streets and to hand out," added Vito.

"Have we applied for the required permits?"

"I took care of that at City Hall this morning," replied Randolph Sloan.

"Very good. We must adhere to all the pertinent rules. We must keep the focus on our adversary at all times."

"I had to cut a class to do it, though," said Vito.

Reynolds patted him on the shoulder. "A slight sin, compared to the scarlet one which we are marshaling forces to oppose."

"As to Chandler's plan to speak to members of the club he belonged to when he was a student at Harvard," said Marcy, "Ron and I will be in the audience, prepared to ask him some tough questions."

"Assuming he'll open the meeting to them," said Rob.

"He will," answered Reynolds. "His ego will demand it."

"Finally," Rob continued, "I'll be working up a press release for newspapers, radio stations, and TV news departments. We might get some coverage before the events that will add to the number of people joining the two demonstrations."

Beaming with delight, Reynolds said, "If I didn't know your ages, I'd think that the four of you had been students organizing against the Vietnam war back in the Sixties. You've done a magnificent job of planning. I am very proud of you!"

"So, unless you have something else to bring up, Professor," said Rob, "the chair will entertain a motion for adjournment."

"Offered," said Vito.

"Seconded," declared Marcy.

"Hearing no objections, we are adjourned until the call of the chair," said Rob. "Those who might want some refreshment are invited to stay, but there's a house limit of one beer per member, on account of I was taking care of some business with someone who's interested in our demonstrations so I didn't have time to stop at a store and pick some up."

Reynolds led Rob aside. "Just what was the nature of the person's interest? I inquire only because I vividly remember how our anti-war demonstrations were infiltrated by enemies of the cause in the hope of discrediting them."

"The woman contacted me through our web page. We met this afternoon at a coffee shop near Symphony Hall. She told me she's a cellist with the BSO, which is true. She showed me her name listed in a program. She explained that she's been against smoking since her sister died. She blames the death on the sister's having been a lifetime cigarette smoker. She gave me a check for two-hundred dollars made out to Snuff Out Smoking. It's more than enough to cover the costs of printing the placards and handbills."

"How generous of the lady," said Reynolds. "One does not readily find someone willing to back up a conviction with cash. Perhaps I should drop her a note of thanks. What's her name?"

Rob drew the folded check from his shirt pocket and read, "Margaret M. Baron."

Ten

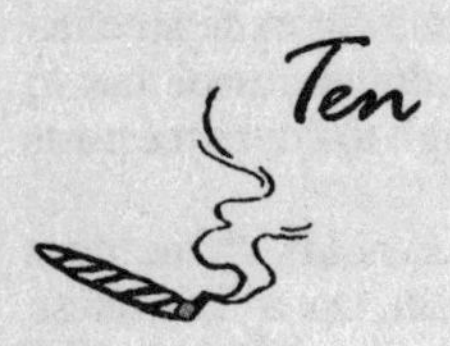

WHILE THE SNUFF Out Smoking committee was convened in Rob Devonshire's basement apartment, the woman whose generosity in support of the cause of stamping out smoking had so impressed Andrew Reynolds sat opposite Nick Chase and beside Professor Woolley at a small table in a corner of Nick's second-floor apartment.

Enjoying a late dinner of spaghetti and meatballs cooked by Woolley in Nick's small kitchen, Nick had listened to Peg Baron's report with both satisfaction that his plan had worked and pride in the woman who had carried it out so effectively.

From the moment fifteen years before when Woolley had introduced Nick to Peg shortly after the grand opening of the cigar store below, Nick had seen her as the embodiment of the colorful history and culture of the city on the other side of the Charles River. Born Margaret Mary Moran, she had grown up almost in the shadow of Old North Church, from which a signal had been sent to an anxious horseman waiting in Charlestown on the opposite side of the river—one lantern if by land and two if by sea—to trigger the midnight ride of Paul Revere on the eighteenth of April in '75. As Irish-rooted as John L. Sullivan, "the boy wonder from Boston" of the world of boxing in the 1890s, and a long-suffering fan of the Boston Red Sox, who'd suffered year after year over not seeing the team in a World Series, Peg had been five years old when John F. Kennedy had shown that a Catholic was not barred from winning the White House. Her studies in Boston University's school of music, gifted fingers on strings and bow of the cello, and personality had so impressed Arthur Fiedler that he had granted her request for an audition. Her brilliant performance in the Vivaldi *Sonata in C Minor for Violin, Cello, and Continuo* had earned her a chair with the Boston Symphony Orchestra. A childless marriage to a violinist of mediocre talent, Everett Baron, had ended in its seventh year when he'd killed himself.

With Peg's report on her meeting with Rob Devonshire completed and the meal over, Nick said, "Coffee in the living room?"

This adjournment meant taking a few steps from the dining table to a cluster of overstuffed arm chairs and the greenish, worn, and slightly sagging couch. Woolley took a chair and lit a black pipe while Nick sat on the couch with Peg and smoked one of the last three of her Almirantes.

"Giving the kid a check was a nice touch, Peg," he said. "In my experience nothing is so convincing of one's sincerity as forking over filthy lucre."

Not a smoker, but liking the mingling aromas of Woolley's pipe and Nick's cigar, Peg smiled appreciatively. "I expect reimbursement."

"From the description of Devonshire," Nick said, glancing at Woolley, "I believe he's the guy I caught hanging the sign on my Indian."

"It seems like a tempest in a teapot," said Peg. "So what if these people from Stamp Out Smoking march around with signs and yell slogans? If December fourth is as cold as today, the whole thing will be over in ten minutes."

Nick took a puff of the Almirante. "Forewarned is forearmed."

"I really don't think those people plan to chuck bricks through your store window, Nick."

"It's not my window I'm thinking about. My concern is for Melvin Chandler's safety."

"He doesn't appear to be worried."

"From what I know of Chandler," said Woolley, creating a cloud of smoke, "an attack on his person would play right into his hands. This well-planned return to Cambridge is nothing but a crass and blatant grab for p-u-b-l-i-c-i-t-y. It's ironic that Andrew Edwards and his followers are playing right into his greedy mitts."

"Passion for a cause is a malady that frequently results in blindness to one's self-interest," said Nick. "May I cite a case in point?"

Peg laughed. "Is there any way we can stop you?"

"When I was promoted to the homicide squad—"

"Ah, this is a tale from ancient history," Peg interjected.

"—I was assigned to partner with a terrific detective by the name of Ricciardo. Even though he'd put in a lot of years on a job that ran on the smoke of cigarettes and cigars, he was a nonsmoker. He was also dead set against anyone else smoking. Knowing this, I promised him that I'd do my best not to light up a cigar when we were riding in the car. But one night when we were on the way back to the office from a drug-related homicide in a garbage-filled and rat-infested cellar on the Lower East Side, where I'd gone about four hours without smoking, I lit one up . . . just to get the smell of that place out of my nostrils. The next day, he went to see the captain and said either Chase went or he would. Well, the captain was a guy who not only enjoyed good cigars, he made a habit of bumming them from me. Ricciardo found himself in charge of the evidence room, the only place in the precinct where regulations banned smoking. Three weeks after Ricciardo's transfer, David Berkowitz started his killing rampage. My new partner, Joey Coggins, who smoked like a chimney, and I were assigned to the Son of Sam Task Force. When Joey and I were in on Berkowitz's arrest and got commendation letters from the chief of detectives, poor old Ricciardo was still stuck in the evidence room. Pretty sad, huh?"

"What's sad in your story," said Peg, "is that your captain squandered the talents of the detective who you say was terrific."

"The point I was hoping to make," Nick replied, "is that if Ricciardo had been as accommodating to me as I was considerate of his views about smoking, and hadn't blown his top over one cigar lit up under very trying circumstances, he'd have been in on the Son of Sam collar."

Woolley asked, "Is Ricciardo still on the force?"

"I believe he took his pension a few years ago and moved to San Francisco, where they have the strictest no-smoking laws of any city in the country."

"So your story has a happy ending after all," said Peg, grinning.

Nick held out his cigar and gazed at it affectionately. Taking Peg's hand, he recited:

> *"Just as a loving, tender hand*
> *Will sometimes steal in yours,*
> *It softly envelops and embraces me,*
> *And memory wakes at its command—*
> *The scent of a good cigar."*

Peg slowly shook her head. "Oh brother! I think it's time for me to leave the two of you to your manly pursuits. Besides, it's late and I've got a very challenging score to study."

"You did good today, Peg," said Nick as he went with her to the door. "And as the man said, 'Look for a check in the mail.' "

Rising slightly on her toes, she kissed his cheek lightly. "Maybe I'll decide to take out the two-hundred in trade."

As Nick returned to the couch, Woolley asked, "What did you expect Peg to learn by meeting with that young man?"

"I had to know for certain that this organization Snuff Out Smoking has its sights set on protesting at my store."

"Surely you expected that from reading Reynolds' letter in the newspaper."

"Don't you find it odd that the Happy Smoking Ground has been in business this long, yet not once has your friend Reynolds targeted it?"

"This is the first time Melvin Chandler announced his intention to be in your store. That's a very alluring temptation. If you're worried about it, cancel your invitation to him."

"Surrender to Snuff Out Smoking? Not on your tobacco pouch, my friend."

PART IV

Flaming Passions

Tobacco, some say, is a potent narcotic,
That rules half the world in a way quite despotic;
So to punish him well for his wicked and merry tricks,
We'll burn him forthwith,
as they used to do with heretics.

ANONYMOUS, 19TH CENTURY POEM

Eleven

"I'M GLAD WE'RE going to Boston today," said Richard Chandler to Veronica Redding on the night of December third as he finished packing a suitcase in the bedroom of the cottage in Hyannisport. "The radio says there's a chance the Cape will get socked hard by a snowstorm sometime tomorrow."

From the bed Veronica asked, "Are you sure your mother won't change her mind about going to the party?"

"She left for Miami yesterday. By now she's enjoying a vodka martini in her South Beach house, probably with a humpy would-be-model she slipped her phone number to while he waited on her table in one of those trendy Ocean Drive restaurants."

"Does that mean we'll be staying in her house on Beacon Hill?"

"Would you prefer a hotel?"

"Hell, no."

"I thought not."

"How are you going to introduce me to your father?"

"It won't matter what I say. His Highness King Melvin won't approve of you."

"Does he know how much you hate him?"

Richard stopped packing and thought a moment. "I doubt he's thought enough about me to have noticed."

"I think it's a case of sibling rivalry transferred to the father. You hate him because when your brother was born—"

"Stepbrother. Little Prince Donny!"

"I think that after the kid was born, your old man paid more attention to him than to you, and that's why you came to hate him. Your father, I mean."

Richard slammed shut the suitcase. "Since when have you become a psychiatrist? Now, hurry and get dressed. I want to be at Mother's house before the bad weather sets in."

Ominous-looking leaden clouds forming a low roof over midtown Manhattan appeared to justify a prediction of heavy snow by afternoon, but limited to regions south of the Connecticut shore. Areas north and east, including Boston, would experience little more than a dusting, unless the approaching storm veered from the path projected by National Weather Service computer models.

Because Dave Selden had been a railroad buff all his life who felt, as did poet Edna St. Vincent Millay, that there was not a train she wouldn't take, no matter where it was going, he experienced growing excitement when he stepped from the down escalator of the Seventh Avenue entry to Penn Station.

With visions of trains pulled by steam engines so vivid that he could almost smell the smoke, he glanced at an electronic board listing departure times of the Amtrak trains which ran on the old Pennsy tracks below and noted he was nearly an hour early for the new high-speed reserved-seating service which Amtrak claimed would cut travel time to Boston almost in half. Since its inception, he'd been wanting to try it out. But writing his book and the cost of the trip had persuaded him to postpone the experience.

Thanks to Chandler's puzzling invitation, he would be doing so today, with the additional pleasure of avoiding a New York City snowstorm. With luck, by the time he was back in town, streets and sidewalks would be cleared. He'd be able to get back to work on his book, curiosity quenched, and, he hoped, resentment of having been fired by Chandler finally laid to rest.

* * *

While Selden waited for his train to be announced, Steve Yedenok was seated in the last row on the left side of a crowded plane awaiting clearance to take off from LaGuardia Airport.

He was there despite advice of counsel. On the telephone the previous afternoon Ray Sheffield of Hebert and Eveland had been emphatic. "Accepting that invitation," he'd said, "was not a good idea. It was a terrible idea. I wish you hadn't done it."

"I see no problem," Steve had replied. "He only wants to talk."

"This firm has dealt with Chandler before. He's slippery as an eel. The notion that we can, in his words to you, 'dispose of all this legal nonsense in less time than it takes to smoke a cigarillo' is practically an admission that he knows you've got him by the short hairs. You've come a long way with this, Steve. We're almost there. Don't give in to him now."

"This lawsuit has been dragging on nearly six years. Frankly, I'm fed up with it. One way or another, it's got to end. If I don't talk to him, he's going to drag this thing out even more. But I want this behind me. I need to get on with my life. I'm nearly broke, Ray."

"What about your reputation? Settling out of court with Mel Chandler for money won't restore it. You can do that only by forcing him into a witness chair in a very public trial that will be embarrassing to him. He understands that. That's why he wants to talk with you. As a friend and your attorney, I'm telling you nothing good will come of you going to Boston. And I'm not sure that Hebert and Eveland can continue representing you if you follow through on this."

Delayed by what the pilot explained over the intercom as "every aircraft in the world in line ahead of us," the plane departed twenty minutes late and rose into a glowering sky.

When Melvin Chandler, Madeline Lewis, and Benjamin Salter arrived at Teterboro Airport in New Jersey in a stretched white limousine at noon, no such traffic jam stood in the way of a prompt take-off of *Cigar Smoker* magazine's twin-engine Gulfstream G-4 corporate jet. The magazine's name was painted in blue and gold on its sleek white sides and depicted on each surface of the tail was a man's hand holding a bandless lighted cigar.

Less than an hour later, the plane made an undelayed approach and flawless landing at Boston's Logan International Airport, where another white limousine stood waiting to carry the passengers to Cambridge and the Mayflower Hotel overlooking the Charles River.

Settled into the seat with Salter to his left and Madeline to his right, Chandler took a long cigar from a pocket case, peeled off the band, trimmed it with a pair of small gold scissors, and lit it with a silver Zippo lighter bearing his initials. As the car moved forward, he puffed an almost perfect ring.

As the smoke ring slowly dispersed, Chandler found himself recalling the last time he'd been in Cambridge—a fateful day almost forty years before the meeting of the committee investigating the missing thousand dollars. Good old Charlie Appleton, mute regarding the motivation of the friend accused of embezzlement. Good old Charlie, too, for the deft manner in which he'd come to that friend's rescue in a related matter. And for being the only one to come to the Greyhound bus station in Boston to see him off.

In those four decades, Chandler mused, as the limousine left Logan Airport, he'd come to Boston occasionally on business, but not until this moment had he been ready to venture into the city across the Charles and chance stirring bad memories. But forty years was enough. The time was right for setting things right, as much as he was able and if the people from back then were willing after so long a time.

Curling an arm around Madeline's shoulder, he said, "You've done a great job setting up this trip, Maddy."

"I'm a little worried about the weather forecast for tomorrow. It calls for snow. I'm afraid it will keep people away, except for the anti-smoking protesters. I have no doubt they'll be there."

"Everything's going to be just fine," said Chandler. "As to

any protesters, I say, bring the bastards on. The more the merrier. I can hardly wait for the fun to start."

As Chandler's limo rolled toward Cambridge, Charles Appleton was at his desk talking on the phone with Kevin Rattigan. He'd been trying for ten minutes to persuade Kevin to accompany him to Chandler's party at Farley's.

Kevin's response was that if Chandler had wanted him there, Chandler would have sent him an invitation.

"I'm sure if Mel had known your current address," Charlie said, "you'd have gotten one."

"I don't think so," Kevin replied. "You're the one who was Mel's college buddy. He put up with me and my faggot ways only because I was your friend."

"That's not true, Kev."

"Of course it's true, but back then you were too naive to grasp it, just as you never were able to see how Mel was constantly using you. Evidently, he thinks he still can."

"Aren't you the least bit interested in finding out what's on Mel's mind?"

"Old darling, I'm *dying* to know. But as it happens, I have a ticket for the theater. You tell me all about your reunion with Mel over lunch. Since you will probably want to sleep late after this mysterious Chandler soirée, shall we get together the day after tomorrow? I'll come by and pick you up at, say, one o'clock?"

"I'd rather have you come with me, but okay, lunch at one, day after tomorrow."

When Andrew Reynolds entered the basement apartment on Museum Street, Rob Devonshire declared, "Everything's ready, Professor. Everybody knows where to be and when."

Standing beside Rob, Marcy Granick added, "They've all been given signs to carry and leaflets to hand out."

"You've both done excellent work," said Reynolds. "What about press interest?"

"I've talked to assignment editors at all the TV and radio stations, and to the city desks at the newspapers," Marcy answered. "None of them said for sure that they'll assign reporters, but unless some really big news story breaks, I'm sure we'll get good coverage. Just in case, Vito Antonucci is bringing a video camera. He'll make copies of the tape available to any news media that want them. And I'll have my camera for shooting still photos to hand out to newspapers."

"How many of our people do you expect to show up?"

"At least fifty at the cigar store," said Rob.

"About the same number will be outside Farley's in the evening," Marcy said.

"That's terrific," exclaimed Reynolds. "Tomorrow will be the day Melvin Chandler will rue having had the audacity to show his face again at Harvard."

A few hours after the meeting in the house on Museum Street, Chandler's stepping from his limousine at the Mayflower, a smooth landing by Steve Yedenok's plane at Logan Airport, and on-time arrival at South Street Station of Dave Selden's train, Lieutenant John Lerch heard a rap on the door of his tiny office on the second floor of Cambridge Police Headquarters. Looking up from a desk cluttered with paperwork related to legal proceedings in the Lilly Foster murder, he was surprised to see in the doorway a figure holding a walking stick.

"Pardon the interruption," said Woolley. "I tried calling you, but your line is always busy, so I took the chance that you'd be here."

"Come in, Professor. To what do I owe this unexpected pleasure? Don't tell me you've run into a brick wall in your writing and Jake Elwell finally needs professional help!"

"I'm deeply concerned about this business of Melvin Chandler's signing books at Nick's store tomorrow," said Woolley urgently as he came in.

Lerch pointed him to a straight-backed chair in front of the desk.

"Why is that?"

Seated with his walking stick across his knees, Woolley answered, "Plans are afoot by a group called Snuff Out Smoking to stage a protest at Nick's store."

"I'm aware of that. The group has a police permit for an hour's rally on Brattle Street."

"I'm afraid it may turn violent."

"Have you a basis for this concern?"

"Some weeks ago," Woolley said, leaning forward, "Nick received a threatening phone call from one of the organizers of this protest rally. It was made by a Harvard student by the name of Rob Devonshire. He is the president of S.O.S."

"Nick told me about the call," Lerch replied, "but he said it was anonymous."

Woolley sat back. "So it was. We've identified its maker."

Lerch's eyebrows arched. "How did you manage that?"

"Peg Baron had a meeting with him. It's a long story."

Lerch presented a patient smile. "I've got time. Let me hear it."

When Woolley finished relating Peg's conversation with Devonshire, he continued, "I'm sure you'll agree with Nick's conclusion that the redheaded young man who put the sign on the Indian is the same one to whom Peg gave the check and who made the threatening call to Nick."

"I'm not sure I can agree with your reasoning, Professor. There are lots of guys with red hair. As to the rally tomorrow in front of Nick's store, he doesn't seem bothered by it. And there will be a police presence to maintain law and order at all times."

"Nonetheless, I'll sleep a great deal easier if I can go to bed tonight with your promise that you'll be at Nick's side during the protest rally tomorrow and the event at Farley's."

"I think it's unnecessary, Professor, but you can count on me."

Fifteen minutes later, Woolley struggled out of the cramped rear seat of the taxi which returned him to Brattle Street from police headquarters. As the taxi departed, he saw Nick Chase bending over the backdrop of the store's display window, stacking several copies of Chandler's book. Already in place was a poster proclaiming that the author of *Smoke Dreamer* would be in the store tomorrow to autograph copies purchased by customers at a twenty-percent discount.

As Woolley entered the store, Nick straightened and turned to him with a smile. "How's the display look from outside?"

"Marvelous. A twenty-percent discount! Not out of your share of the proceeds, I hope!"

"Chandler is absorbing it."

"How generous of him," said Woolley, as he unwound a long, orange muffler. "Of course, he could afford fifty-percent. Hell, he could *give* them away."

"What's brought you out of that third-floor cocoon of yours on this frigid afternoon?"

"I decided to pay a call on an ailing friend."

"To take him a little hot soup?"

"He's ailing, not hungry."

"Speaking of food, I've been invited to partake this evening of some of my daughter's incomparable beef stew. Jean has also extended the invitation to you. She and Mike think their child should have quality time with the old fart she calls 'Uncle Whiskers.' I hope you'll come."

"Why wouldn't I?"

"It's just that lately you seem to be in a mood to stay away from parties."

"If you are referring to Melvin Chandler's shindig tomorrow night at Farley's," Woolley said, fishing a black pipe from a pocket, "I've changed my mind. I'll be attending after all."

"Glad to hear it! A party's not a party without you. Maybe after all these years you'll get Chandler to clear up the mystery of those purloined thousand bucks."

Twelve

AROMAS OF BEEF stew and baking biscuits greeted Nick and Woolley as they stepped from the elevator at five before seven.

On the tenth floor, Jean and Mike Tinney's two-bedroom apartment's windows afforded a spectacular view of a corner of the Boston Public Garden and most of Boston Common. But its chief attraction was proximity to the Boston Police Department's headquarters, only a few blocks south and west on Berkley Street.

When Jean opened the door, Nick exclaimed, "Excuse us, lady, but the word on the street is that a couple of old reprobates can get a free meal here."

Jean turned her head and shouted, "Mike, there are two bums at the door. Call the police."

Mike appeared from around a corner. "Honey, we *are* the police."

Scampering past him from the living room, six-year-old Trish exclaimed, "Grandpop! Uncle Whiskers!"

With dinner over, a reluctant child packed off to bed, her mother clearing the dining room table, and the three men settled into chairs to smoke in the living room, Mike savored a small H. Upmann After Dinner that Nick had given him, blew a column of smoke, and asked, "So, Nick, how are things going in the tobacco trade on Brattle Street?"

"Quite well, thanks."

"Don't be surprised to read in the papers the day after tomorrow," said Woolley, jerking a pipe from his lips, "that there's been a riot on Brattle Street."

"Utter nonsense," said Nick. "There's not going to be a riot."

"If there were to be one," Mike asked with a frown, "who would be rioting?"

"The anti-smoking brigade vows to stage a protest at Nick's store," Woolley answered, setting aside the pipe. "They will be marching behind the banner of a group called Snuff Out Smoking."

"S.O.S. for short," said Nick. "I think that if they wanted to stop codgers like me from smoking cigars, they should have named the group Stop the Old Gasping Galloots, and for short they'd be called—"

"Stogies," said Mike, grinning widely. "That's a good one, Nick."

Looking apprehensive, Jean emerged from the kitchen. "What are they protesting? I don't recall them ever doing so at your store, Dad."

"That's because until now," said Woolley, "the Great Satan of Smoking has not presented himself at Nick's store."

Jean's expression turned quizzical. "Great Satan of Smoking?"

"Woolley refers to the publisher of the magazine *Cigar Smoker*, Melvin Chandler," Nick replied. "He's coming to the store tomorrow to autograph copies of his memoirs. Woolley's got it into his head that the Happy Smoking Ground is in peril of being attacked, sacked, and burned to the ground."

Mike chuckled. "That would make the store the plain Smoking Ground."

"That's not funny," Jean protested, abandoning the kitchen and settling beside Mike on the couch. "I don't like the sound of any of this."

"Everything will be fine," Nick said, turning toward an end table and gently tapping the long gray ash of his cigar into a glass tray with the name of his store in blue around a full-color likeness of the Indian which guarded its entrance. "I'm betting that it will be so cold on Brattle Street tomorrow that no protesters will even show up. There's nothing like a good cold snap to cut down the incidence of misdemeanors. As cops yourselves, you must have noticed how the crime rate plummets in the wintertime. The same is true for outdoor protests. I cannot recall one demonstration against the Vietnam war being staged in freezing temperatures. But if a handful of hardy types manages to show up on my doorstep, I have every confidence that the Cambridge police will keep the situation under control. If not, they can always flash a call for reinforcements from the coppers on this side of the Charles River."

"I'm not happy about this, Dad," said Jean. "I wish this man Chandler had picked some other place to sign his memoirs. A book store, for instance."

Mike removed the cigar from his mouth and nodded his head. "Now that Jean mentions it," he said, "it does seem a bit strange to me that Chandler chose the Happy Smoking Ground. Why not one of the big tobacco stores here in Boston?"

Nick puffed twice and said teasingly, "Is my own family begrudging me and my store a little publicity? I'm so insulted that if it weren't for the fact that I haven't had my dessert, I'd go straight home. What is it to be, by the way, Jean?"

"Devil's food cake."

"On the eve of a visit to my store by the Satan of Smoking," Nick said, chuckling, "that's a most appropriate choice."

About forty-five minutes later on the way back to Cambridge, bundled up as he waited for the heater to come on in Woolley's car, Nick grumbled, "I wish you hadn't brought up the subject of the likelihood of protesters tomorrow, my friend. Jean is just like her mother. She's a worry wort. She'll be lying awake half the night picturing Brattle Street becoming a battleground."

"I'm sorry if I've upset her," Woolley replied, "but in my opinion you are taking all this too lightly. You seem to have forgotten that a threat has been made against you."

"I got that phone call two months ago. If anything were going to happen, I'm certain it would have by now."

Woolley switched on the windshield wipers. "If this snow continues like this, you may prove right about the weather keeping people away."

Thirteen

NICK AWOKE A little before seven in the morning expecting to hear the scraping of snow shovels. But when he went to a window in the living room and drew aside a curtain, he looked down on only a dusting of snow on sidewalks and the roofs of parked cars on Brattle Street.

As he prepared his usual breakfast and listened to news on the radio, a young woman who presented the weather advised, "The storm which dumped from eight to ten inches of snow on New York City overnight is expected to reach us by nightfall. While today will see only snow showers, the National Weather Service has issued a winter storm warning for tonight for all of Massachusetts and southern New Hampshire and Maine. If this powerful storm follows the track predicted, heavy snow will begin to overspread all of Cape Cod by noon with the leading edge reaching the greater Boston area around eight o'clock. Driving conditions during the homebound rush should be all right, but by this time tomorrow the accumulations should exceed a foot or more along the coast and close to that in Boston proper. Greater depths are likely farther inland. Temperatures that are now in the high twenties will plummet toward the teens this afternoon with increasing winds, resulting in a windchill factor well below zero. As a result of this storm to the south, airports have been forced to close from New York to

Washington, so if you have plans to go to those cities today, you should check with your airline regarding likely cancellations."

Listening to the same broadcast in a spacious second-floor bedroom of Anita Weston Chandler's house with a commanding view of the gold dome of the Massachusetts State House and the sweep of Boston Common, Richard Chandler said to Veronica Redding, "It's good that we came up yesterday. We might have been snowed in."

"Maybe the events your father has planned will have to be cancelled."

"The storm's not due here till much later. Mother Nature wouldn't dare to interfere with a party at which Melvin Chandler is guest of honor, self-appointed. Once this unpleasantness with the old man is over with, we'll head up to his place in Vermont."

"I didn't know he has a place in Vermont."

"He calls it his *chalet*. The deal with Mother in the divorce was that she'd get this house, the cottage on the Cape and the South Beach condo. He wound up with the Sutton Place house, an apartment in Washington, a house in Beverly Hills, and the chalet."

"Since he's this close to Vermont," she said, "maybe he'll decide to use it."

"Trust me, he won't," he said, sliding closer to her. "He hasn't been there since he had a scare over his heart condition two years ago. We'll definitely have the place to ourselves . . . and if all goes well today, for as long as we wish."

During a restless and fitful night, Charles Appleton found himself going between bed and his desk. Finally, he'd sat for hours watching Commonwealth Avenue attain a thin coat of snow and trying to decide what to do.

One minute he was holding Chandler's invitation and pondering skipping the signing and cigar night. In the next he thought about showing up at Farley's and waiting for the propitious moment in which to confront Chandler. Around four o'clock, resolved upon the latter, he'd put down the invitation and taken pen and paper to write several versions of how to tell Mel to his face, in front of everyone, that he would not be dragged into Mel Chandler's life again.

But in the bleak light of dawn with snow tapering off and then stopping, his mind raced back in time to the snows of another winter. Suddenly, resentment about having been taken for granted and then ignored for more than thirty years gave way to the curiosity he had felt on the day he'd received the invitation with its maddening plea scrawled at the bottom: "For auld lang syne, etc., do come. Yours, M. C."

Picking up the invitation, he muttered, "Okay, Mel. I'll see you one more time. But never again. Never, never, never!"

As requested, a room service breakfast of poached eggs, toast, and coffee was delivered to Dave Selden's room on the seventh floor of the Mayflower at eight o'clock.

Giving the young waiter a five-dollar tip, he asked, "Do you know how the weather's going to be today?"

"There's a lot of snow coming this way, sir, but not till tonight."

"I've got an appointment tonight at a restaurant. Will I be able to find a cab?"

"The doorman will be happy to do it for you. But you should arrange for a cab to pick you up after your appointment, as well."

"Thanks," said Selden with a smile as he thought ahead to the evening and what he was planning to do, "but I'm not sure if I'll need one."

Four floors above Selden's room, Steve Yedenok was still asleep.

Taking advantage of his unexpected invitation from Melvin Chandler to come to Boston, he had passed a delightful evening at Symphony Hall enraptured by the BSO's peerless performances of Dvorak's *Carnival Overture,* the Liszt *Hungarian Rhapsody No. 2,* and Vivaldi's *The Four Seasons.* The concert had been followed by drinks in the hotel lounge until the bartender had cut him off.

Falling into bed around two o'clock, he drifted to sleep with the pleasure of having gotten drunk at the expense of that libeling son of a bitch Mel Chandler.

What might happen between them later on would depend on how much drinking he'd be doing at a place called Farley's.

Looking at the clock on the night table next to Madeline Lewis's bed, Ben Salter said, "I should get back to my room and get dressed for the day's festivities."

"It's only eight-thirty," said Madeline, making a little circle with a fingertip on his bare chest. "Mel's not expecting us to join him at breakfast until nine-thirty."

"He's an early riser. It wouldn't do to have him phone my room, would it? Or, heaven forbid, *go there looking for me,* and find my bed's not been slept in."

She yawned and said in a sing-song voice, "All your trials will soon be over."

"I'm not sure of that. I might find that I've jumped from the frying pan into the fire," he said, bending to kiss her. "But ah, such tempting flames."

Spanning half the top floor of the hotel, the John F. Kennedy suite was decorated with an array of black-and-white photographs of a president whose life had been cut short by an assassin on a day when the current occupant of the rooms was a pimpled, trouble-making kid in his first year of high school.

Nearly forty years later on a cold and cloudy morning, Melvin Chandler was seated at an antique writing table and looking out a huge window affording a view of the Charles River. In the distance beyond it he saw through dull gray light the towers of the city of Boston. In racks of newsstands there, all around Cambridge and across America, a man could, if he wished, buy a copy of the latest issue of a magazine which, for more than a decade, had extolled the finest things life offered a man in the way of sensory pleasures, without being pornographic.

Now anyone interested in how Melvin Chandler had gone

from a teenager in trouble in school to create *Cigar Smoker* magazine would find the answer in his book. He'd labored hard on it, describing not only the successes he'd achieved, but spelling out all the ambition, the soaring ego, the ruthlessness.

It was all there. The kid with promise in school. Discovering sex. Harvard and the bad scrape he'd gotten into. Marriage to Anita. The disappointment of how Richard had turned out. The second marriage that might have lasted had a hit-and-run driver not killed Norma and Donny. Men who had started as friends but become enemies.

Many sins were recounted on the pages of *Smoke Dreamer,* but anyone hoping to find a word about him feeling a need for repentance would be disappointed.

Fourteen

AWAITING THE ARRIVAL of Chandler at his store, Nick stood in the doorway with Professor Woolley, Lieutenant Lerch, and Peg Baron. On the other side of Brattle Street, three TV news cameramen and two newspaper photographers flitted like bees around a crowd of about fifty protesters gathered behind several gray steel police barricades.

"The red-haired kid in the front," said Peg, pointing to the crowd, "is the one I met with."

"He's definitely the guy I chased away from the Indian," Nick said.

"The man next to him in the orange cap with the hate in his face," Woolley said, "is Andrew Reynolds."

As Nick peered at the protesters, a roar went up from them.

This caused police officers and the cameramen to jerk to attentiveness and look anxiously toward Brattle Square.

"It appears the man of the hour is about to arrive," said Lerch.

Four officers in front of Nick's store moved briskly across the sidewalk to the curb as a white stretch limousine glided to a stop in front of the store.

With a roaring of jeers and catcalls exploding behind the barricades, Chandler emerged from the rear of the car and turned to face the crowd. Grinning, he thrust up his arms in a

V as though he were a hero acknowledging a reception by admirers.

"What nerve," Peg said with a half laugh. "Who the devil does this guy think he is, President Eisenhower?"

"It's not from Ike that he's borrowed that gesture," replied Woolley as the noise of the crowd increased with each taunting wave of Chandler's upthrust arms. "He's a product of a later generation. This is in-your-face Sixties sock-it-to-'em-baby Richard Milhous Nixon."

"You ought to know, Professor," Nick gibed.

Woolley stroked his beard. "As a matter of fact, I do feel a twinge of nostalgia."

As he spoke, the jeering crowd chanted, "S.O.S., S.O.S., S.O.S., Snuff Out Smoking, Snuff Out Smoking, burn the books, burn the books."

Someone shouted, "Let's get the author!"

Another screamed, "Death to Chandler!"

Surging forward, the crowd broke through the barriers and shoved aside the handful of vainly resisting police. In an instant the protesters flooded across the street. With waving signs and fists, they rushed the limousine.

"Oh hell," exclaimed Lerch, rushing from the doorway.

Racing after him, Nick reached the limousine as a picket sign carried by Rob Devonshire grazed Chandler's head.

As Nick and Lerch each grabbed one of Chandler's arms to pull him away, Nick heard the shattering of glass as a brick crashed through the store's window.

In the next moment, police sirens wailed as several patrol cars sped from the direction of Brattle Square. Scrambling from them, police officers with helmets and plastic shields protecting their heads and faces plunged into the crowd with night sticks flailing.

As the battle raged, Nick and Lerch shoved Chandler into the store. By the time Nick had the door shut and locked, the protesters were in full retreat in both directions of Brattle Street. Several who had not been as swift in fleeing found themselves being arrested and shoved into the back seats of police cars. Only when the crowd had been dispersed did police let Madeline Lewis and Ben Salter exit the limousine.

As they entered the store, Lerch declared breathlessly, "This book signing is off!"

"What nonsense," Chandler exclaimed as blood trickled from a shallow gash in the center of his forehead. "Of course the signing will go on."

"You could have been killed," Lerch said angrily as he shook his head. "After this riot, there is no way that I'm going to allow anyone to walk into this store and then maybe pull out a gun or a knife."

Peg Baron used her handkerchief to blot blood from Chandler's face. "He's right," she said. "It's much too dangerous."

"What alarmists," Chandler said. "I'm certain I was hit with that sign accidentally. It's a mere scratch. As you can see, the bleeding has stopped. I am not in the least concerned for my safety." He gazed fiercely at Lerch. "And who the hell are you to be giving orders?"

Nick answered, "This is Lieutenant Jack Lerch of the Cambridge Police Department's homicide squad."

Chandler's eyes went wide "Homicide?"

"Yeah, homicide," said Lerch. "And you're not the only person in this store whose safety I've got to think about."

"If you mean me, Jack," Nick said, "you can set your mind at ease. I'm capable of taking care of myself."

"Famous last words!"

"Jack is right, Nick," said Woolley. "Why run the risk?"

"As to the signing," Madeline interjected, "Mr. Chandler can go ahead and autograph the books. Anyone who desires a copy can come in and purchase one at another time."

"Good idea, Maddy," said Salter.

As he spoke, Chandler studied Woolley's face. "Do I know you, sir?"

Woolley beamed with pride. "Back in 1968 I had the distinct privilege and pleasure of voting to toss you out of Harvard."

Chandler beamed. "Of course, Professor Woolley! I thought you were dead long ago."

"You're free to sign all the books you want to, Mr. Chandler," Lerch blurted, "but I'll be giving my man at the door orders not to let anyone in to get one autographed in person. If I must, I'll have the door sealed with Crime Scene Do Not Enter tape. It is actually a crime scene, you know. People have been arrested. Property has been damaged. There's no telling how long the investigation's going to take. It's within my authority to order all of you to clear out until then."

"Very well, Lieutenant," said Chandler grudgingly, "I'll do as you wish, but I think you are making too much of this."

"This was a very close and nasty occurrence, Mr. Chandler," Lerch continued gravely. "It's also my advice, but strictly unofficially, that you cancel the event I understand you've planned for this evening at Farley's."

"That is out of the question," Madeline protested. "Hundreds of people have been invited. Subscribers to the magazine. Advertising people. The press! Some people have been brought here at considerable expense from New York."

"As I said, I can't prevent it. I'd need a court order to do that, and I don't have enough time to get one. But I will be there in my capacity as a homicide detective to start in right away on my investigation, in the event one of the anti-smoking nuts you've met this morning manages to crash your party and succeeds in murdering you."

"Your concern for me touches me deeply, Lieutenant," Chandler said, sitting on a stool behind the counter where the books were stacked. "I welcome your attendance at the affair at Farley's this evening. You look to me like a man who appreciates good cigars."

"A good cigar to the lieutenant," Nick said, "is the one someone gives him."

"Should I be murdered while in the police precincts of Cambridge," said Chandler as he began autographing, "you should look for suspects not among people who are against smoking, but among those whose names are listed in the index of *Smoke Dreamer*."

Fifteen

ANIMATED DRAWINGS OF snowflakes drifted from gray clouds which blanketed a map of New England on the TV screen as Nick lounged on his bed watching the six o'clock news.

Because the Happy Smoking Ground had been forced to close by Lerch's edict and the broken window, now covered with a huge slab of plywood, he'd said goodbye to Chandler and his two assistants a few minutes after Lerch had decided they could leave the store in safety.

Tuned in to the news to see what would be reported about the riot, Nick was disappointed to find the newscast starting with the weather.

An attractive young woman with blond hair and a grave expression stood in front of the map and asserted, "A winter weather warning is in effect for the entire region. Although the snow is just beginning in Boston, by the time this storm has moved out to sea, accumulations will range from eight inches in the city to a foot or more across Cape Cod and areas south and west."

Nick grunted. "Hey, what do you expect in December in Massachusetts?"

When he was married, directing comments to a TV screen was a habit which had at first amused and then irritated his wife.

"You're talking back again," Maggie would chide, emphasizing her displeasure with a nudge of an elbow or rebuking scowl. "They can't hear you, you know!"

"Winds may cause blizzard conditions," the weather woman continued sternly as Nick missed Maggie's teasing. "Because of the storm's severity, travel has already been impacted. Airports have been forced to shut down as far south as Washington, D.C. These disruptions have forced many flights out of Logan Airport and others in the region to be grounded.

"That's okay with me," Nick said to her, "I'm not going anywhere."

Onto the screen came pictures of people battling their way through blowing snow on the sidewalks and streets of New York City, Baltimore, and Washington, D.C.

"All right already with the weather," Nick said impatiently. "Show me the damn riot!"

Fearing that if he changed the channel he would miss the pictures of the altercation on Brattle Street and that other stations might have already shown them, he remained tuned to the channel he preferred for local news. Coverage of the riot did not appear on the screen until the very end of the half-hour.

"Things got pretty hot outside a cigar store in Cambridge at noontime today," an anchorman said over a picture of the store's green sign. "It was anything but a happy smoking ground when protesters demonstrated against smoking in general and one man in particular."

The screen showed Chandler grinning while surrounded by angry faces.

"The demonstration was organized by a group called Snuff Out Smoking. Its target was cigar magazine publisher Melvin Chandler," the narration continued. "He'd gone to the store to sign copies of his autobiography."

In a close-up, Chandler was shown as he was struck by the picket sign.

"He was not seriously injured, and he went ahead with signing the books, even though police kept customers away," the voice said over a picture of the yellow Crime Scene Do Not Enter ribbon across the door.

This was followed by a shot of the cigar store Indian.

"When asked about the near-riot," said the anchorman with a chuckle, "this eyewitness maintained a wooden expression and refused to comment."

"Cute," said Nick in disgust as he pressed the Off button on the remote control.

When the phone rang, it was Peg Baron calling. "Did you see yourself on the channel four news?"

"I always watch five."

"Oh, too bad. You looked wonderfully heroic rescuing Chandler from that mob. He was lucky to get away with just that little scrape. But the reason I called is to suggest that because of the snow, instead of you and Professor Woolley walking to Farley's, I come by and pick you up."

"It's snowing already?"

"Yes, and pretty hard. I don't want the professor trying to navigate slippery sidewalks. I can be in front of the store at ten to seven."

"Since the weather's only going to get worse as the night goes on," Nick said, "maybe you and Woolley should forget about going to the Farley's soirée."

"Woolley may choose to stay at home, but a little snow isn't keeping this gal from finding out about these so-called cigar nights that have been such a rage with all you macho types."

"My dear," Nick replied, "you are going to be awfully disappointed."

As he hung up the phone, he heard Woolley descending the stairs.

Gazing at the cigar in his hand, he wondered what Peg would say if he told her that in it a man could see the nature of life itself. As it was enjoyed, the wisps and eddies of the rising and drifting smoke could be seen to represent the path through life toward death, or simply an escape from present troubles. As a poet of old, Francis Miles Finch, had written:

A cheerful cigar, like a shield will bar
The blows of care and sorrow.

The door swung open and Woolley barged into the room, bundled for the storm.

"Nick, you look lost to the world," he exclaimed. "Time to get a move on!"

"We've got a few more minutes, Professor," said Nick, getting off the couch. "Because of the snow, Peg is picking us up in her car."

Sixteen

"I THINK WE should forget about going to the party," declared Veronica Redding, as hard-falling snow obscured the view of the State House from the bedroom window of Anita Weston Chandler's house on Beacon Hill. "The way it's snowing, it's probably been called off anyway."

"My father is like Santa Claus, but without the charm," Richard replied as he buttoned his shirt. "Nothing ever keeps him from his appointed rounds."

"Maybe that crack on the head he got this afternoon will keep him away."

With a grin, Richard recalled observing the riot while walking toward the cigar store from Brattle Square. "That was quite a sight," he said, "but my father's head is the least vulnerable part of his anatomy, except for his heart."

"I'd hate to go all the way through a snowstorm and get there and find out everything has been canceled because of what happened, or because of the weather the restaurant's closed."

"We're in Boston! Nothing closes on account of a little snow. It would take a blizzard."

Veronica peered anxiously through the window. "It sure looks like one to me."

"You may do as you wish," Richard said, putting on a necktie, "but I'm going. And if it turns out that he's playing the martyr by staying in his hotel, I'll just have to go to the Mayflower and settle the matter there. Are you coming to Farley's or not?"

"Well, I'm certainly not staying in this big old house by myself!"

Richard went to the window and assessed the snowfall.

"Wear sensible shoes, if you've got any, darling," he said, turning from the window. "I'm leaving the car in the garage. We'll probably have to take the MBTA."

"What the devil is that?"

"The Massachusetts Bay Transit Authority, dear. The subway."

Because Charlie Appleton had decided at the last minute not to go to Mel Chandler's book signing, he'd missed witnessing Mel under attack. Now, coming up out of the MBTA Harvard station just before seven o'clock to attend the party at Farley's, he felt that during the trip from Boston time had raced in reverse.

Looking at the old red brick walls girding Harvard Yard and feeling the sting of windblown snow on his face, he was again watching Mel artfully dodging and stopping traffic as he made a mad dash across Massachusetts Avenue. Breathing hard and with deep blue searching and worried eyes, he'd bounded onto the sidewalk in front of the Coop and blurted "So how did it go, Charlie? I've been on pins and needles all day."

"Everything's fixed."

Visibly relieved, Mel let out a laugh. "Of course it is! I never doubted for a second that it would be. Charlie, you are the absolute best!"

Thirty-plus years later, as Charlie walked briskly toward Waterhouse Street, he was again transported in time, but to the Democratic Party convention in New York City in 1976. Attending as an alternate delegate from Massachusetts, he had gone to Jimmy Carter's headquarters at the Americana Hotel.

He'd run into Mel Chandler in the lobby.

In retrospect the meeting seemed as surreal as the ferris

wheel scene in the movie *The Third Man* with Mel taking the role in a post-war Vienna of a blackmarketeer, Harry Lime, chillingly played in the film by Orson Welles. Like Lime addressing Joseph Cotten in the part of western novelist Holly Martins, Mel had constantly called him "Old Man," as if that was his name.

Plucking a cigar from his mouth, Mel had startled the crowd in the lobby by bellowing, "Charlie Appleton. What the fuck are you doing here? This is one hell of a pleasant surprise running into you, Old Man!"

Feeling embarrassed, he'd muttered, "It's been long time no see, for sure, Mel."

"What brings you to Gotham, Old Man?"

"Politics."

"That always was your bag, as we used to say. Tell me, Old Man, what have you been up to all these years?"

"I've been teaching."

"At our old alma mater?"

"No, at Boston University."

"I've not forgotten what you did for me in the bad old days, Old Man," Mel said, looking at his watch. "I've gotta run now, but do give me a call. We'll have drinks and a long chin wag about auld lang syne. If there's anything I can do for you while you're in town, don't hesitate to let me know, Old Man. How's Kevin Rattigan? Are you still banging him?"

With that, he'd hurried out to Seventh Avenue, a trail of cigar smoke in his wake, not to be heard from again until the arrival of the invitation that now sent good old Charlie Appleton out into a snowstorm.

Waiting for an elevator, Dave Selden watched the indicator as it showed the elevator start its descent at the top floor of the hotel. When it stopped at the seventh and the door slid open to reveal a tall, thin man in a loose-fitting charcoal gray overcoat, Dave gasped and exclaimed, "Steve Yedenok. You're the last person I expected to see in this hotel."

Steve smiled wanly. "I was thinking the same thing about you, Dave."

"Are you in Boston because you got an invitation from Mel Chandler?"

"Apparently he's called a meeting of the Mel Chandler Haters Club," Steve replied as the door closed. "Shall we share a cab to Farley's?"

"If we can get one."

"You're looking good, Dave. What have you been doing since you were shown the door at *Cigar Smoker?* I assume you've landed on your feet."

"My contract required that should I ever get the door, I'd also get a golden parachute," Dave answered. "That's allowed me to take all the time I wish to write the great American novel. Please don't tell me you've already done it, Steve!"

Yedenok shrugged. "I haven't been writing much lately."

Detecting the odor of liquor on Steve's breath, Dave supposed why. "Sorry to hear it."

"I assume you know about my libel suit against Mel and the magazine."

"When I got word of it, I was afraid you might also sue me."

"Mel's slander campaign against me began after you and *Cigar Smoker* parted ways."

The elevator reached the lobby.

As the two men stepped from the car, Dave said, "I think Mel has invited us to this big party because he's working some kind of angle."

"He wrote a note on my invitation to the effect that he was interested in settling my lawsuit against him. My lawyer is dead set against it. But I would like to get on with my life, without Mel Chandler in it, so here I am. Why did you come?"

"I talked about what to do with my agent, Jack Whelan," said Dave as they crossed the lobby. "Jack figures that Mel's heard that he's in a novel I'm writing."

"Is he?"

"He's the main character, and not so thinly veiled. Jack thinks that Mel will probably try to sweet-talk me out of finishing it."

"And if that ploy doesn't work," Steve said as they waited under the hotel's canopy for a doorman to summon a taxi, "he'll attempt to buy you off."

Several yards away from the entrance to the Mayflower, with coat collars lifted against the blowing snow, two young men and a young woman carried picket signs that declared, "Snuff Out Smoking."

Steve nodded at them. "I saw on the news that some of those people caused such a hell of a ruckus at the cigar store where Mel was to sign books that the signing was canceled."

"I was there," said Dave with a chuckle as a taxi pulled up. "One of them clobbered Mel on the head with one of their picket signs. Little damage was done. Unfortunately."

THE FIRST SUCH gathering known as a cigar night, Nick recalled for the elucidation of Peg Baron and Professor Woolley as Peg drove slowly through the snow toward Farley's, had been in May 1992. Held in a ballroom of the sumptuous Ritz-Carlton Hotel in seaside Laguna Niguel, California, its purpose was to raise money for a memorial foundation in the name of Ruth Berle, the late wife of cigar-smoking comedian Milton Berle. To accompanying music of Bach, played by a string quartet, 157 men in tuxedos and three elegantly dressed women feasted on lobster rivoli, filet mignon, and ripe cheeses and champagne, followed by cognac and cigars.

Since that pioneering event, cigar nights had been encouraged by new magazines such as *Cigar Aficionado* and Melvin Chandler's *Cigar Smoker* and supported in their efforts to fashion a comeback in cigar-smoking by cigar manufacturers and distillers of whiskies and brandies. The men who flocked to them had been described by journalists and other observers of the phenomenon as overachieving males who were born during and after the second world war. Grown up, successful, and wealthy, these "baby boomers" decided to complement expensive cars, showcase homes and wine collections with costly premium cigars.

Other analysts of the passion for cigars at a time of widespread disrepute surrounding smoking found rebellion in the upsurge in men who took up cigar-smoking. As cigar-friendly restaurants opened and clubs dedicated to the cigar appeared, they sat in butter-soft leather chairs away from daily stresses and learned or rediscovered that a cigar was made for all the senses, for all the pleasures, for the nose, palate, fingers, and eyes.

"The point being made," Nick concluded, as Peg miraculously discovered a parking space less than half a block from the restaurant, "was that to light and smoke a cigar was to engage in comforting rhythms and establish communication with the self. The true pleasure of the cigar is found in the slow movements, the measured pace of a ceremonial act."

"I get it," Peg exclaimed, "it's like having sex, but without the partner."

"What a coarse person you are," Nick said while Woolley cackled a laugh.

Walking as quickly as caution in ankle-deep snow allowed, they reached the door of the restaurant with their hats and the shoulders of their coats speckled with large, heavy, wet snowflakes. After handing the garments to a young man whom Nick did not know, they ascended the stairs to the second floor. A small table at the top was stacked with press releases.

Peering into the cigar room, Nick found the space changed. Wall lamps which normally burned low had been turned up. Huge blow-ups of the cover of Chandler's book decorated the walls. Dozens of tables in the middle of the room had been removed in order to accommodate several buffets offering a bewildering selection of food.

The crowd surrounding the tables, Peg noted, was predominately male.

Assaying a surprisingly large turnout in a snowstorm, Woolley declared, "The weather does not appear to have put a damper on things. I was afraid we'd be the only ones here."

"Where better to spend a winter nor'easter," said Nick, "than in a cozy place to eat and drink and savor fine cigars with a group of kindred souls?"

"At home in bed," Peg replied, "curled up with a good book."

"When I feel the need to read a good book," Woolley said, "I write one."

A waiter appeared with a tray of flutes of champagne. "If you prefer something else," he advised, "there's an open bar at the other end of the room."

As Peg took a glass of champagne, Benjamin Salter appeared in the doorway. In his tuxedo he resembled a headwaiter. Spotting Nick, he made his way around a knot of guests.

"Good evening," he said cheerily. "I'm glad to see a little snow didn't keep you away."

"I may be retired from the police," Nick replied, "but I still live by the three main rules of the copper's handbook. Never pass a men's room without using it, never stand when you can sit, and never turn down free food and drink."

"Especially," Peg interjected, "if someone's also giving out cigars."

Salter looked at her quizzically.

Nick introduced them.

"I notice the absence of our host," he said, looking around. "I hope that knock Mel got on his head isn't going to keep him from his own party."

"He's feeling fine," said Salter. "When I left the hotel a few minutes ago, he was lying on his bed, smoking and talking on the phone about a business problem that suddenly came up."

"I'll wager that the true reason he's late," Woolley said, "is that he's planning to make a grand entrance."

Salter smiled thinly. "You may be right, Professor."

"I also note," said Nick, "the absence of the woman who set up all this."

"Maddy is downstairs settling the bill with the manager," said Salter, turning away. "Now, if you'll excuse me, I should circulate."

"Of course," said Nick.

"In the meantime, free food and drinks await you. And, of course, plenty of free cigars."

The aroma of many of them being smoked richly scented the air.

As Salter plunged into the crowd, Woolley said, "There's a man who is just right for his job. Unctuous and uppity. In short, a snob."

"What did you expect in a man who works for a snobby magazine?" asked Peg.

Nick demanded, "Since when is Peg Baron an expert on the contents of *Cigar Smoker?*"

"Know thine enemy!"

"Did you note," said Woolley, "that Salter is the only man at this soirée, except the waiters, who is wearing a tuxedo?"

"I'm afraid I don't have a novelist's eye for picking up such details," said Nick. "Now, if you don't mind, Peg and I are going to visit the bar. She looks thirsty and I am in dire need of a Bushmills neat."

"The hell you didn't notice," Woolley replied as Nick and Peg left. "Bring me an Armagnac. In a giant snifter."

While Woolley lingered near the door, Madeline Lewis arrived wearing a blood-red dress. Pausing a moment, she surveyed the room. Noticing Woolley, she went to him.

"I'm so glad you're here, Professor," she said. "Where's Nick?"

Woolley pointed toward the bar. "He's wetting his whistle."

"And who's his very attractive date?"

"Her name is Peg Baron."

"Of course!" Madeline exclaimed. "I should have recognized her from the descriptions of the woman who was at Nick Chase's side in Professor Woolley's account of the murder of the antique dealer."

"To paraphrase a shopworn pick-up line from the days of my youth," he said, stroking his beard and looking at her with flirting eyes, "what's a nice gal like you doing in a place like this?"

"I'm just trying to earn a living, Professor, and I've found no better way to do so without working hard than being a publicist. Or, as a hard-bitten character in one of your very charming Jake Elwell thrillers would put it, working as a flack."

Woolley beamed. "I'm flattered that you're familiar with my little opuses."

"I'm constantly amazed by your ability to come up with so many interesting characters and such baffling mysteries. In reading your books I have yet to spot the villain."

"The abiding dread of an author of mysteries," Woolley said, "is that the reader will solve the puzzle ahead of the detective."

Returning with Peg's and Woolley's drinks, Nick interjected, "The abiding dread of the detective in real life is that the puzzle won't be solved at all."

"Good evening, Nick," said Madeline. "And it's a pleasure to meet you, Miss Baron."

"I was beginning to think you wouldn't be here," Nick said, handing Woolley his glass.

"Just for the fun of it, Professor Woolley," said Madeline, "which of the people at this party would you choose to make suspects in a murder mystery?"

"As I said, that would depend on who's the victim."

"Suppose someone murdered . . . me."

"I can not imagine anyone wanting to kill someone as beautiful as you," said Peg.

"How about Melvin Chandler? He's got plenty of enemies."

"Evidently," said Peg. "After the riot outside Nick's store he told Lieutenant Lerch of the Cambridge police that if he's ever murdered the killer's name will be found in the index of his new book."

"Did he really? Some of those people are here. His son Richard, for instance. He's the handsome young man at the bar with the overly dressed blonde. The murder motive for Richard would be impatience in collecting a very large inheritance."

"The tried-and-true motive in most mystery novels! Where there's a will," said Woolley with a chuckle, "there's always somebody looking for a way to cash in on it."

Madeline nodded toward the middle of the room. "If Richard is too obvious a suspect for you, I recommend Dave

Selden. He was the managing editor of *Cigar Smoker* from its very beginning. They had a huge fight a couple of months ago that ended with Mel telling Dave to clear out his office and ordering security men to escort him from the building. Yet Dave is here, big as life. Interesting, don't you think?"

Woolley sipped the Armagnac. "Quite."

"And there's Steve Yedenok," Madeline continued. "Thin man. Far end of the bar."

Nick asked, "Why should he be a suspect?"

"If someone filed a million-dollar slander suit against you, Professor Woolley, would you invite him to a party? Of course you wouldn't. But there's Steve, drinking Mel's liquor as though nothing ever happened between them."

"Perhaps the two have patched things up," said Nick.

"I know for a fact that they haven't. But that's the sort of thing Mel does all the time. He thumbs his nose at the people he's turned against, or at the people who hate him. It's like a sport to him. You saw how he made a point of taunting those protesters this afternoon."

Woolley shook his head disapprovingly. "He was damn lucky Nick and Lieutenant Lerch managed to extricate him with no more than a slight scrape of the forehead. I'd expected to find the Snuff Out Smoking folks picketing here at Farley's."

"When I left the hotel, that red-haired Devonshire kid who struck Mel with the sign was there with a girl and another boy, marching back and forth and shouting their crazy slogans. The kid ought to have been arrested, but Mel refused to make a charge."

"It wouldn't have held up," said Nick. "I was standing next to Mel when it happened. It was so clearly an accident that I would have been obligated to say so to the police. Besides, I've got a feeling that Mel is probably grateful that it happened. It guaranteed TV coverage in which he looked like a martyr. It made me wonder if Mel had set up the whole thing. Or is that sort of gimmick more likely to be the brainchild of a publicist?"

"Pay this man no attention, my dear," said Woolley. "He's teasing you."

"As delightful as it's been talking with you all," Madeline said, "I see Ben Salter waving at me. I appear to be needed. I hope we can resume our chat later."

Watching her as she wove between knots of men smoking, eating, and drinking, Woolley declared, "A remarkable woman, wouldn't you agree, Nick?"

"And you," said Nick, noticing the approach of Dave Selden, "are a shameless old flirt."

Woolley swirled Armagnac in the huge snifter. "Age does have its privileges."

"If you can take your eyes off Madeline Lewis for a moment," Nick said, "maybe you'll be able to tell me who's the man in the back of the room wearing a tan corduroy jacket with elbow patches who for the past several minutes has been staring your way. A fan of your Jake Elwell books, perhaps, trying to summon the nerve to approach you for an autograph?"

Peering through a haze of cigar smoke, Woolley exclaimed, "Well, I'll be damned! I do believe it's Charles Appleton. If so, these past thirty some years have not been kind."

"A former student of yours?"

"Your memory must be slipping, Nick. I told you about Charles Appleton in connection with the theft of the thousand dollars by Mel Chandler from his club."

"Yes, I recall now. Appleton was its president. You thought he knew why Chandler did it, but Appleton refused to cooperate with the investigation."

"I'm surprised to see him here."

"Why not go over and say hello?"

"If Charles Appleton is interested in speaking with me, he'll have to make the move." Woolley turned to Peg Baron. "Come with me, my precious. It's time to explore the buffet."

As they left, Dave Selden approached Nick timidly.

"Excuse me, but aren't you Nick Chase?"

Nick lifted his Bushmills as if to offer a toast. "I plead guilty."

"My name is Dave Selden."

"I know."

Selden looked at Nick quizzicallly.

"Madeline Lewis pointed you out to me," Nick explained.

"She did?"

"What can I do for you, Mr. Selden?"

"Do for me? Nothing. I came over to say hello because I remembered your face from the cover of the first *Cigar Smoker* that I edited on my own. Of course, you were in a policeman's uniform back then."

Nick patted his belly. "I wish I could tell you it still fits."

"Congratulations on the continuing success of your store. There was one owner in a small town in California whom we featured on the cover as our tobacconist of the year who closed his shop a few months later. He got fed up with being constantly harassed by anti-smoking forces. I gather that you've been spared their venom."

"I'm glad to say it's been pretty much live and let live on Brattle Street," Nick said as he helped himself to a Partagas cigar from a lidless box on a nearby table.

"Until today, apparently."

"Today was an aberration. My store and I have been left alone by the anti-smoking crowd. It may have something to do with it being known that I keep a pistol in a drawer behind the sales counter. I guess that Chandler being there today was just too tempting."

"I hope your store came through the riot safely."

"Except for a broken front window," Nick said, clipping the cigar with a plastic cutter bearing the name of Chandler's magazine, "I'm pleased to report the Happy Smoking Ground is still in business."

"I saw the riot on TV in my hotel room. What a disgrace. I was very worried about Mel, and now I see that he's not here."

Nick lit the cigar with a box of *Cigar Smoker* wooden matches. "I'm told he's fine, but delayed by a business matter. He'll join us soon."

"Have you read his book?"

Nick blew a column of smoke. "I was sent an advance copy."

"And immediately opened it to the index to look for your name?"

"Actually, the first thing I read was the introduction. Having no expectation that I'd be in the book, I didn't look at the index until a good deal later. That I was in there came as quite a nice surprise."

"Mel could hardly omit a *Cigar Smoker* tobacconist of the year who later found time to solve a couple of murders, one of them in which the victim was a movie superstar."

"What have you been doing since leaving *Cigar Smoker?*"

"Ah, you know about that."

"It happened to come up in a conversation between Madeline Lewis and my old friend Professor Rogcr Woolley."

"Why would I figure in their conversation?"

"This will sound silly, but they were discussing who should be considered a suspect if Melvin Chandler were to be murdered. It was a ridiculous discussion."

"It's not ridiculous at all. In the event someone killed Mel, I'd expect to find myself on the list of suspects. I doubt anyone on the planet could have a more compelling reason to be suspected. Except for his ex-wife and ne'er-do-well son, I've been associated with Melvin Chandler longer than anyone."

Nick took a puff of the Partagas. "In the light of your being abruptly fired, may I ask why you're at this party?"

"I suspect that Mel invited me to ask me to take back my job. My guess is that he thinks if he makes me editor again, I'll quit writing a book about my years with *Cigar Smoker.*"

"A kiss-and-tell?"

"You could call it that."

"Will you stop writing it if he takes you back?"

Selden smiled. "Maybe. Maybe not. It depends on how I feel at the moment. There are many ways to get even with somebody you believe has wronged you. Murdering him is one. Making him grovel could be good. But even better is laughing in his face and telling the ungrateful son of a bitch to go fuck himself."

"I can see how that would work," Nick said, looking toward the entrance at Lieutenant Jack Lerch.

In snow-flecked hat and overcoat, he stood in the doorway, eyes sweeping the room.

"Whichever option I choose, you'll soon know," Selden said, abruptly walking away. "It's been a pleasure meeting you, Nick."

Raising the hand holding the cigar and waving it, Nick sought to catch Lerch's attention. Instead of responding by entering the room, Lerch gestured for Nick to come to him.

When Nick did Lerch said softly, "I want you to very nonchalantly slip away from this party, get your coat, and come with me."

"I don't like this, Jack. You're wearing your 'There's big trouble' face. What's up?"

Lerch whispered, "I was on my way here in my car when I got a call from Sid Goldstein at the office. There's been an incident at the Mayflower Hotel."

"That's Mel Chandler's hotel. What's happened?"

Lerch drew Nick from the room. "All I know is that Chandler is dead."

PART V

Up in Smoke

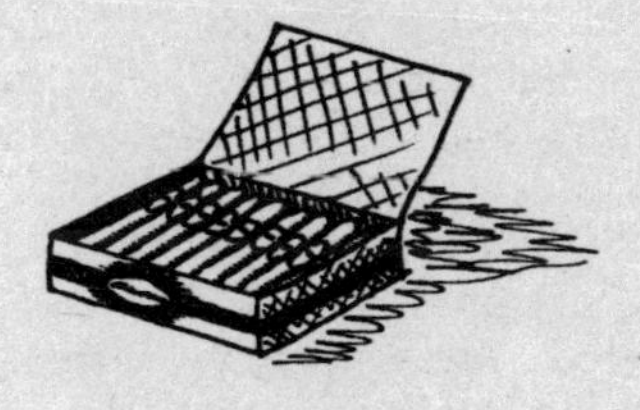

We travel like a comet wild
On which some distant sun had smiled
And from his orbit thus beguiled
With a long tail of smoke.

"A Brief Puff of Smoke"
Eclectic Magazine, 1892

Eighteen

CLUSTERED IN THE middle of the snowy street when Lerch's car stopped in front of the Mayflower Hotel were three police cars, an ambulance, and two fire trucks whose crews appeared to be preparing to leave.

Puzzled, Nick asked, "There was also a fire?"

"All the information I have is very sketchy," Lerch replied as they strode to the entrance. "Goldstein said it looks as if he had a heart attack while he was smoking a cigar. He was found on the bed. When he died, his cigar set the bed covers burning."

"If that's what happened," said Nick as Lerch pushed through a revolving door, "why are you here? And why me?"

When he stepped out of the revolving door, he found the lobby decorated for Christmas and crowded with milling, grumbling, and frightened guests, many in robes and pajamas, who had been driven from their rooms by the fire alarm.

"We're here in case this wasn't an accident," said Lerch grimly while striding toward the elevators, where a police officer held open the door of one of them. "Chandler's room is on the top floor," continued Lerch as they entered the car. "Goldstein's up there waiting for us."

"Are you thinking it's possible that Chandler didn't have a heart attack?"

"I'd be remiss in my duty if I didn't consider the possibility, especially since that mob at your store today looked damned determined to do him bodily harm."

When the elevator stopped at the top floor and the door opened to a small lobby, Nick noted a burnt smell pervading the air, but saw no smoke.

"This is the penthouse level," said Lerch, turning left from the elevator. "There are two suites. Chandler's is the John F. Kennedy."

Finding its door open, they entered a large foyer decorated with a life-size bust of J F K and a few photographs of him as president. They were met by another police officer in uniform. "Hello, Lieutenant," he said as he offered a gesture of salute. "You'll find Detective Goldstein in the bedroom at the end of the short hallway to the right."

A spacious room, it had a wide window affording a dim view through the snow of the Charles River and the silhouette of the Kennedy Library. Like the foyer, the walls were festooned with Kennedy photos. To Nick's right as he surveyed the room from the doorway was a low bureau. On top of it were a handsome brown leather traveling cigar humidor, a gold cutter, a small box of cigar matches, a bottle of cognac, and two brandy snifters. Against the opposite wall and beneath a reproduction in oils of the official White House portrait of Kennedy was the king-size bed. Fully clothed, Melvin Chandler lay on his back in its center. The right hand holding a half-burned Cohiba lay in a small circle of fire-blackened yellow bedspread and underlying sheet.

"It wasn't much of a fire," said Nick, moving to the scorched bed.

"Fortunately, a maid showed up to get the suite ready for the night," said Goldstein. "She told me she traced the smoke, saw the flames, and ran into the corridor to hit the fire alarm. Then she went in the bathroom to wet some towels. By the time the firemen got here, she had the fire put out."

"I'll want to talk to that maid," said Lerch while Nick bent over Chandler's body.

"If she hadn't gotten the fire out," Nick said, "Chandler would be toast and we'd have no way of knowing that this bed wasn't set ablaze by his cigar."

Lerch's eyes went wide. "What's that?"

"Chandler wouldn't have a lighted cigar in his hand when he lay on the bed. If he'd been having a heart attack, he would have dropped it. Also observe that the band is on it. Chandler always removed the band from his cigar. He believed that people who leave the bands on are not only unsophisticated in the art of cigar smoking, but uncouth. He wrote editorials on the subject in his magazine and devoted two and a half pages of his book to a tirade against keeping bands on cigars. When a man removes the band of a cigar, he does so *before* he lights it. His humidor is on the bureau, along with his pocket cutter and a box of matches. That's where he would have taken off the band. I also call your attention to the tip."

Lerch bent close to look. "What about it?"

"It's not trimmed. You can't smoke an untrimmed cigar. He would have clipped the cigar and lit it with a wooden match from the box on the bureau. Chandler was as steadfast on using wooden matches as he was about a band on a cigar being proof that someone was probably a bounder. Now note how he's holding the cigar between two fingers, as if it were a cigarette. In all the pictures I've seen of Mel Chandler smoking, he holds his cigar the way I do, between the thumb and the tips of the first two fingers. I believe that someone put him on the bed, stuck the cigar in his hand, and started the fire in hopes of covering up the fact that Chandler was murdered."

Lerch turned abruptly to Goldstein. "Sid, phone headquarters and order up a crime scene unit. Then put in a call to the coroner's office and tell whoever answers that the services of Dr. Awini are required here immediately. When that's done, find the manager of the hotel and get his ass up here, too. We'll need to get the register of the hotel's guests and talk to the entire staff that's been on duty since Melvin Chandler moved into this suite. For starters, bring in the maid."

"Her name is Millie," Goldstein said as he left the room. "She's very shook up."

Middle-aged, short, and stout, with black hair pulled back into a bun, she trembled slightly as she related smelling smoke, finding Chandler on the burning bed, sounding the fire alarm, and putting out the blaze with wet towels.

"Going to the fire alarm box and coming back to put the fire out was very resourceful and brave of you, Millie," said Lerch. "You've been a big help."

"Thank you, sir, but what I don't understand is why the boy I saw out in the hallway and going into the fire-escape stairway didn't do it. I mean, he must have known about the fire, else why was he using the stairs and not the elevator?"

With a look of astonishment, Lerch said, "You saw someone going into the fire stairway?"

"Yes, sir. A boy, nineteen or twenty years old, stocky, with red hair."

Nick asked, "You're certain of the red hair?"

"I sure am, mister."

"Thank you, Millie," said Lerch with a quizzical glance at Nick. "You may go."

"The redhead could have been Rob Devonshire," said Nick. "Madeline Lewis told me that earlier this evening three members of Snuff Out Smoking were picketing the hotel. I assume that when they saw police cars pull up, and then an ambulance and fire engines, they took off. Madeline says she recognized the kid who hit Chandler with the sign."

"How in hell do *you* come to know his name?"

"Obtaining that bit of information happens to have cost me two hundred bucks."

"Did the C notes also buy you his address?"

"He should be easy enough to locate. He's a student at Harvard."

"This is great info, Nick," said Lerch, turning to Goldstein. "See that this kid is found and brought in for questioning."

"I hope that you're not going to rush to judgment in this case," said Nick, "and ignore the advice of the victim that if he was murdered you'd find names of suspects in the index of his autobiography. I can provide a copy of *Smoke Dreamer.* I have plenty on sale at my store, all of them signed by the author."

"Most of the indexes in biographies that I've read have hundreds of names."

"Then I suggest you start with a much shorter roster, the invitation list for Chandler's party, now in progress in the cigar room at Farley's."

"Excuse me, Lieutenant," said Goldstein, "but if we're going to be talking to people at that party, shouldn't we send someone to Farley's to detain them? If the murderer is from out of town, he could slip through our fingers."

"No one's going anywhere in this weather," Lerch replied, "unless he's like Santa Claus and has a sleigh with eight tiny reindeer and a red-nosed one named Rudolph to guide it."

DURING THE NEXT HALF-HOUR, Nick observed why Lieutenant John Lerch had risen to second-in-command of the Cambridge Police Department's Investigations Division and chief of the homicide squad. Calmly and efficiently, he summoned into action all the human and technical components required at a suspected crime scene to discover and eventually collect everything that might turn suspicion and theory to proof.

In the hope of determining scientifically that someone had killed Melvin Chandler and set the bed afire in an attempt to make his death appear accidental, three men and a woman in white jumpsuits with "Crime Scene Unit" in large black letters on their backs moved into the bedroom.

"Take care removing the cigar from his hand," Lerch said anxiously. "That stogie may be the key to this mystery."

With a team of criminalists at work, Detective Goldstein entered the John F. Kennedy suite in the company of a tall, elderly man in a blue blazer. A picture of the Pilgrims' ship *Mayflower* was embroidered on the left breast pocket. Pinned to the coat on the left side was a nameplate: "Bernard Wolf, manager."

Lerch asked, "Did you bring the list of the hotel's guests?"

Presenting a computer print-out, Wolf said, "I can't believe that one of our guests could be in any way involved in this terrible tragedy."

"It's just a routine police procedure," Lerch answered. "Was Mr. Chandler one of your regular guests?"

"I'd have to check on that, but I believe this is—was—his first time with us."

"Do you know if he had visitors?"

"If Mr. Chandler were expecting someone, that person would just take an elevator."

"I understand that there had been people picketing in front of the hotel," Nick said, "the group calling itself Snuff Out Smoking."

"Yes, I was upset about that. I reported it to the police, but I was told that thc group had a constitutional right to be there."

"Could one of the group have gotten into the hotel and onto an elevator to this floor?"

"My lobby staff had orders from me to keep an eye on those kids. The last thing I wanted was them bringing their noisy protest and their signs into the hotel."

"But in a busy lobby," said Nick, "one of them, or even several, could have left their signs outside and come in, quietly?"

"The lobby was especially crowded earlier this evening. Because of the snowstorm many guests whom we expected to check out found themselves with no place to go. We had to scramble to accommodate them and to take care of the people who work in town and were looking for rooms so they wouldn't have to drive home in a blinding snowstorm."

"Thank you, Mr. Wolf," said Lerch. "I'd appreciate it if you'd see to it that members of your staff are available to be interviewed by my officers."

"Why is it that necessary? It's my understanding Mr. Chandler fell asleep smoking."

"That does seem to be what happened," said Lerch with a reassuring smile, "but we in the police department have our routine procedures. Thanks again for your cooperation."

As the manager was leaving, the medical examiner arrived.

Among hundreds of hopeful recruits in the class of 1952 of the New York City Police Department training academy, Nick had been taught that in the relatively brief history of the detection and solution of murder cases, the detective's indispensable ally and best friend was the forensic pathologist. On the honor roll of individuals known first in the annals of criminology as coroners and later as medical examiners, he had learned, was Great Britain's Bernard Spilsbury. In 1910 he'd found a scar from an old hysterectomy on a scrap of human flesh which had proved that Dr. Hawley Harvey Crippen had murdered his wife. In 1949, English pathologist Keith Simpson had cracked the case of the "Acid Bath Murder." He'd done so by poking around in the slime of liquified animal fat and proved murder by finding gallstones because he knew they'd be there.

In later annals of American forensic pathology were New Yorkers Dr. Milton Helpern, Dr. Michael Baden, and Dr. Yong-Myun Rho. In Los Angeles there had been Dr. Thomas Noguchi, made famous by his investigations of the questionable deaths of movie stars.

Americans had been introduced to the most famous of the current forensic pathologists during the O. J. Simpson trial. Born in China, Dr. Henry Lee was head of the crime laboratory of the Connecticut State Police. In that capacity he'd proved a case of murder by finding bits of the body where the killer had used a wood chipping machine to dispose of it. He became involved in the case by Simpson's defense lawyers, who challenged a prosecution case largely based on blood evidence. While watching the trial on TV with Nick and hearing Dr. Lee testify in his Chinese-American accent, "Something wrong here," Professor Woolley had exclaimed with enormous delight. "Good lord, they've brought in Charlie Chan!"

Now, on a snowy night, into the Kennedy suite on the top floor of the Mayflower Hotel strod Middlesex County's version of such an illustrious pathologist. Bundled up in a three-quarter-length car coat with an uplifted fur collar and a bulky red scarf looped around his neck, Dr. Hossain Awini had on a gray deerstalker cap that gave him the appearance of a short, stocky Sherlock Holmes. Carrying a small black leather physician's bag that was so old and worn it might have been toted by Dr. Watson, he went straight to the body.

"No frontal bullet holes," he declared, studying it visually. "No stab wounds. No ligature marks. No blood except that which has dried around a fresh contusion of the forehead, which was not the cause of death. May I touch the body, Jack? Are your criminalists done?"

"For the moment, Doc. Help yourself."

Awini drew latex gloves from the bag, put them on, and turned the body onto its left side.

"No noticeable wounds in the back."

He eased the body into its original position.

After a moment of pondering, he muttered, "He's of the age to maybe have had a heart attack." Bending over the body, he plunged a hand into Chandler's right coat pocket. "If he was being treated for coronary artery disease," he said, "it's likely he carries—"

The hand rummaged in the pocket.

"Ah ha, here they are," Awini exclaimed as he withdrew his hand and held up a small, round brown bottle with white label. "A coronary patient's constant companion! Nitroglycerine."

"That's very interesting, Doc," said Lerch impatiently as Awini slipped the bottle into a small plastic evidence bag, "but we have good reason to believe this is a murder case."

Awini handed Lerch the bag, frowned, and looked again at the body. "Do you also have a theory," he said in a grumpy tone, "regarding cause of death?"

"If I did, I wouldn't have dragged Middlesex County's best m.e. out in a snowstorm."

"It's letting up a bit, actually. But weather is of no concern to the Grim Reaper and those of us who follow in his wake. We're both like postmen. Neither snow nor rain, et cetera, shall stay us from successful completion of our appointed rounds. If you want an offhand opinion as to the manner of death, assuming it was not natural, I'd venture the p-word."

"Poison! That's what I've been thinking."

"My definitive word will be forthcoming after autopsy

and preliminary toxicological screening, which I suppose you want me to perform immediately."

"You know me, Doc," said Lerch with a shrug. "Impatience is my only flaw."

Awini left the bed and went into the bedroom. Returning a few seconds later, he gave a nod. "This man was under treatment for both coronary artery disease and diabetes. You'll find three containers with medications on the bathroom sink. One of them is the nitrates prescribed for c.a.d." Gazing toward the bureau, he exclaimed, "Cognac!"

Lerch asked, "What about it?"

Awini moved to the bureau. "The cognac suggests death by misadventure. If he'd had a glass or two and suffered angina spasms, then taken several nitroglycerine pills, the combination could have resulted in severe hypotension, tachycardia, bradycardia, heart block, palpitation, or death due to circulation collapse."

Nick stepped forward and asked, "Could the nitro have been put into the cognac without him detecting it?"

Awini turned to him. "I was wondering when you'd stop lurking in the background and put in your two cents by asking the pertinent question. Where is your faithful companion and chronicler of your recent adventures in crime detection, Professor Woolley? He's well, I hope."

"Woolley is going to keep you waiting to claim his body for many more years."

"As to your question," Awini said, "both cognac and nitroglycerine pills produce a tangy sensation in the mouth and throat. Nitro in cognac would not be noticed."

"If he'd been slipped this lethal cocktail," asked Nick, "how long would it have taken him to die from it?"

"If he suffered circulatory collapse and did not receive immediate help, he'd be dead in very short order. Mere minutes."

"In addition to how he died and the approximate time of death," Nick said, "it's important for us to know if he died on the bed or was put there. And if he died before the fire was set."

"If he was moved after death or was still breathing when the fire got started, he'll tell us," Awini replied. "The sooner I'm allowed to take the body and ask it some questions, the sooner I'll have answers for you."

Lerch said, "Haul him away at your convenience, Doc."

With that, Lerch beckoned into the room a young woman wearing white coveralls. She carried a large black valise containing the tools of her trade. The crime scene kit, known in Britain as "the murder bag," had been introduced to criminology in 1924 by Bernard Spilsbury after he'd seen a detective at a murder scene handling chunks of decaying and putrid human flesh and pieces of evidence with bare hands. Were Nick to open the black bag carried by the young woman, he would find rubber and white cloth gloves, evidence-collection envelopes and sealable plastic bags of varying sizes, an array of glass tubes, swabs and swatches for collection of bloodstains, and modern versions of the oldest implements in the detectives's tool bag—a kit for finding and preserving fingerprints.

"Hello, Norma," said Lerch to the young woman as she opened her bag. "I want the cigar that was taken from the victim's hand checked for fingerprints and for any DNA material. Right now, I need you to dust every item on top of the bureau for prints—the bottle, the glasses, the matchbox, the cigar case, and the cutter. And dust and collect the medicine bottles in the bathroom."

Soon after, Dr. Awini supervised two burly young assistants wearing black coveralls in the removal of the body.

"Yes, Jack," he said on his way out of the bedroom, "I have your cell phone and beeper numbers and I'll use them to alert you immediately of my findings. Nice to see you again, Nick. Please give my regards to Woolley. And while you're at it, tell him to give me a call so I can rib him unmercifully about the truly unforgivable blunder he committed in his latest Jake Elwell novel on the use of the Dillie-Koppanyi Test for the presence of barbiturates."

Looking round the suite as Norma dusted for fingerprints, Lerch said to Nick, "That's all we can do here. It's time we headed to Farley's to break this news to the guests at Chandler's party. If the redheaded kid didn't do it, maybe one of them killed Chandler. Perhaps we'll get lucky and the killer will be waiting for us, eager to confess."

Twenty

TRAFFIC ON THE streets had kept the snow from accumulating deeply, Nick noticed as he got into Lerch's car for the short drive to Farley's. But at the density and rate of the snowfall, he judged, and with traffic subsiding later in the night, the city's snowplows might have difficulty keeping all but the main roads open.

Following Lerch's car in his own vehicle was Detective Goldstein. In three patrol cars were a total of eight officers in uniform, needed to assist in collecting names and addresses of the guests at Chandler's party.

When Nick, Lerch, Goldstein, and the eight officers entered Farley's cigar room, Woolley and Peg Baron rushed to meet them.

"There you are, Nick," Peg exclaimed. "Where did you disappear to?"

"Something came up."

"Obviously so," said Woolley, looking at Lerch, Goldstein, and the eight policemen. "It must be big if you've called out a regiment."

As he spoke, they were joined by Madeline Lewis and Benjamin Salter.

"Why all the cops?" Salter said with a nervous smile as he looked at them. "Are we being raided? Has one of those anti-smoking nuts phoned in a bomb threat? Is there a bomb?"

"I'm afraid I've brought bad news," said Lerch.

Madeline took a deep breath and blurted, "Something's happened to Mel!"

"*That's* why he's not here," said Salter "What's happened? Was he attacked again by those S.O.S. people as he left the hotel?"

Lerch replied, "Mr. Chandler is dead."

"Oh no," said Peg.

"My word," exclaimed Woolley. "Was it because of that blow he took to the head? Was it worse than it seemed?"

"It wasn't from that," Nick said. "There are indications of heart attack."

Madeline gripped his arm. "Oh, that can't be right."

"He didn't tell you he was being treated for heart disease?"

"No. He always seemed to me to be in top physical condition."

"And you, Mr. Salter?"

"He had a heart problem, but it was under control. His only difficulty was that he had a circulatory problem that affected his, uh, ability to, uh, perform with a woman."

"Before we announce his death to everyone here," Lerch said, "we need to tell Chandler's son. Nick told me he was here earlier. Is he still?"

Madeline pointed to the rear of the room. "Richard and his girlfriend have been at a table in the back since they arrived."

As Nick and Lerch approached the table, Nick declared, "Mr. Chandler, I'm Nick Chase."

Richard rose and extended a hand. "I know! You're the owner of the Happy Hunting Ground tobacco shop, scene of this afternoon's unpleasantness."

"The Happy *Smoking* Ground," Nick said as they shook hands. "This is Lieutenant Lerch of the Cambridge police."

Richard gave Lerch a puzzled look, then grinned. "I can't be parked illegally, officer. I left my car in the garage. This is Veronica Redding. We came by taxi."

"Mr. Chandler, I'm sorry to have to report," said Lerch grimly, "that your father's been found dead."

Veronica gasped. Richard dropped into his chair.

"It happened in his hotel suite," said Lerch, "probably close to a quarter to seven."

After a pensive moment, Richard asked, "Have you got the person who murdered him?"

Lerch's eyes opened wide. "Why do you suppose he was murdered?"

Richard shrugged. "Why else would a policeman be sent to tell me? I mean, if he'd just died naturally from a heart attack or something, somebody at the hotel or a hospital would have notified me, right?"

"Did your father have a bad heart?"

"He's had ticker problems since he was a young man. He told me that's what saved him from being drafted into the army during the Vietnam war. But I thought the condition was well under control long, long ago."

Nick asked, "Was the fact that he had a heart condition widely known?"

"If you were the publisher of a magazine that exalts smoking and leading the rich life of steaks and booze, would you advertise that you had a disease that was blamed on those things and that your doctor had told you to give them up? Besides, he held and espoused the view that heart problems, cancer, and other diseases aren't caused by smoking and diet, but are hereditary. How would it look and what would it do to sales of *Cigar Smoker* if Melvin Chandler announced that he was giving up on stogies?"

"What about you?" Nick said. "Are you a smoker?"

"That I'm not is just one of the things about me that disappointed my father. Where have they taken his body? I'll have to make funeral arrangements. He always insisted on being buried. He said that he preferred to be cremated, but he didn't want late-night TV comedians making jokes about the great guru of the cigar revival going up in smoke."

Lerch grimaced and answered, "The body is at the morgue. Before you can claim it, there will have to be an autopsy. The law requires one in deaths where no physician was present at the time of death, or when the cause of death is uncertain."

"When will the body be released?"

"I'll see that you're notified. What's your phone number and address?"

"Ronnie—Veronica—and I will be spending the weekend at my mother's house in Boston, on Beacon Hill."

"I can send an officer to tell her."

"Mother's in Miami Beach. I'll take care of informing her."

"This is an awkward question," Nick said, "but since you think your father has been murdered, is there anybody you suspect could have done it?"

"I can think of several candidates," Richard replied as he looked around the smoky room, "some of whom are at this party." His eyes returned to Lerch. "It's such a nice one," he went on, "which I suppose you are, like the police captain in *Casablanca,* about to declare over?"

"Afraid so."

"That's too bad. Father would have wanted it to continue."

"There are a few routine matters to be taken care of first. Before I can permit anyone to leave, we'll be needing their names and addresses."

"So you *are* treating my father's death as a murder?"

"It's routine procedure. I'm sorry about your loss, young man. The Cambridge Police Department is at your service if you need help in making the arrangements."

"That's very kind of you."

"Is there anyone else at this party," said Lerch, "who should know of your father's death before I make the announcement of it to the entire group?"

Richard nodded. "Yes, father's assistant who set all this up, Madeline Lewis."

"She knows."

"And Ben Salter."

"He's also been informed."

"I do have one request, Lieutenant Lerch."

"Of course, son."

"Can you hold off telling everyone until Veronica and I have gone?"

"No problem at all."

"I don't feel up to being surrounded by a crowd of gloomy faces and hit with a barrage of condolences," said Richard as he and Veronica left their table. "I'm certain some of them will be as phony in their sincerity as the concession speech by a loser on election night congratulating the guy who beat him."

As the couple found their way through the throng and out the door, Lerch said to Nick, "What do you think?"

"About what?"

"Do you see the grieving son as a suspect?"

"Not enough data to say."

"What do you think of the woman with him?"

"If Veronica Redding is anything, she's a possible conspirator."

Lerch groaned. "I meant what do you think of her *as a woman?*"

"Very pretty. Way too young for you."

"I'm not too old to look and admire."

"A woman like that is like a fine cigar. Look at it and admire all you like, but to be fully appreciated, it has to be smoked. And shame on you, a married man, for looking at her like that."

"You're missing my point, Nick."

"Which is what?"

"Isn't it possible that Melvin Chandler was intent on enjoying the company of just such a woman, but on account of his weak heart he departed this mortal coil before he could climb into the saddle?"

"That doesn't explain the fire."

"The dame he was with could have been a high class hooker. When he croaked, she panicked and started the fire to make it look as if he died smoking in bed. You must admit that it is a possibility."

"Until we hear from Dr. Awini, anything's a possibility," said Nick. "In the meantime, I leave it to you, Goldstein, and your intrepid murder police to figure out who done it. Unless you consider me, Woolley, and Peg suspects, while you and your men conduct your interviews with the guests at this aborted shindig, I'm getting out of here before we're snowed in. If you need me, we'll be having a cozy nightcap at my place."

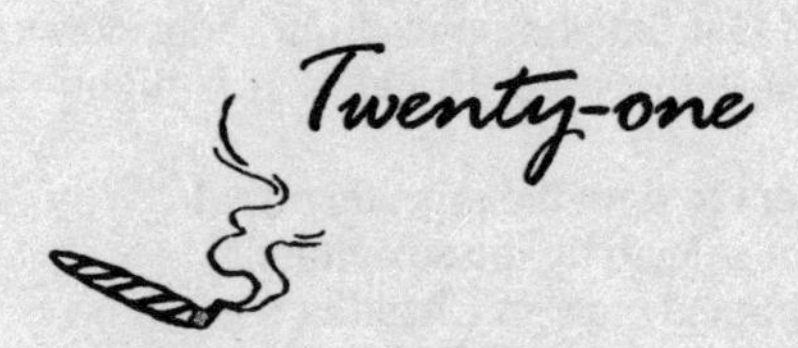

Twenty-one

IN THE SNUG warmth of Nick's apartment Woolley held a glass of port as he slouched in the embrace of an overstuffed arm chair. Peg grasped a cup of black coffee as she nestled beside Nick on the green couch.

They listened intently as Nick described the scene in the hotel suite and shared Awini's opinion that Chandler had died as the result of a lethal cocktail containing nitroglycerine.

Finished with the narrative, Nick looked quizzically at Woolley. "So what do you make of all this, Professor? Was it a tragic happenstance? Or murder?"

"You mentioned Rob Devonshire," Woolley answered as he fished a pipe from a pocket. "I believe it's possible that he left the S.O.S. picketers, went up to Chandler's suite, and confronted him. Chandler became so agitated that he took the nitro with a sip of cognac without realizing there could be fatal consequences."

"This caused Devonshire to panic and start a fire to conceal what happened?"

"Exactly."

"Jack Lerch sees a similar scenario, but the person in Chandler's suite was a prostitute."

Peg shook her head. "I can't picture Chandler carousing with a prostitute a few minutes before he was due at Farley's. *After* the party, maybe."

"Neither theory makes sense to me," Nick said. "If Chandler had a hooker in his suite and dropped dead, the lady would have been out of there in a flash. As to him letting in someone from the Snuff Out Smoking picket line, considering what happened outside my store, I think that is highly unlikely."

Woolley took a moment to light the pipe, then said, "Why don't you buy into Awini's death by misadventure?"

"Because of the untrimmed cigar in Chandler's hand."

"Perhaps he was about to trim it," Woolley interjected, "but before he could do so, he felt chest pains. He took a nitro pill, washed it down with a swig of cognac and then lay down on the bed."

"There are two flaws in that explanation, my friend. No one washes down nitroglycerine. The pill is put under the tongue to dissolve. Taking a drink would prevent the nitro from taking effect. But even if Chandler did as you say, I believe he'd have put down the cigar. However, that said, if he did carry the cigar to the bed and lie down with it, there is no way the cigar could have set the bed on fire. It wasn't lit."

"Chandler could have been about to light the cigar when he had a fatal seizure."

"Impossible!"

"Explain."

"Two reasons," Nick said. He raised a finger. "The cigar wasn't cut." A second finger went up. "The box of matches was on the bureau." The fingers came down and folded into a fist. "The only explanation for the cigar in Chandler's hand is that it was put there after he was dead," he continued, pounding the fist on a knee. "If the killer had let it go at that and not started that fire, the verdict of an autopsy would have been as Dr. Awini first surmised, that it was death by misadventure in the form of an accidental combination of Chandler's nitrate heart medication, cognac, and an excessive dose of nitroglycerine."

"Without the fire," said Woolley through a billowing puff of pipe smoke, "this could have been a perfect murder."

"I've been thinking quite a lot about that fire," Nick said

as he took a cigar from the humidor. "Running through my head has been, 'Why the fire?' " Using a plastic clipper that operated with two fingers, he cut the cigar neatly. Picking up a box of wooden matches bearing the logo of Farley's cigar room, he pointed the cigar at Woolley. "How do you explain the fire, Professor?"

"It's obvious," Woolley answered. "The person who set it wanted to make it appear that Chandler died smoking in bed and thereby dispel suspicion of foul play."

"But the method used to murder him guaranteed that his death would have been attributed to an unwitting mixture of medication, nitroglycerine, and alcohol."

Woolley fell silent as Nick's questioning gaze darted between him and Peg.

Striking a match, he asked, "Why not let it go at that?" He studied the glowing end of the cigar and blew on it to be sure it was burning evenly. "Why the embellishment?"

Peg gave Nick an exasperated look "Okay, you've teased us long enough with your 'I'm about to show you dunderheads what a smart sleuth I am.' Tell us why, why, why."

Nick puffed once. "This is conjecture, of course."

"Noted."

"Suppose the killer wanted to be sure that Chandler's death would not be seen as having occurred accidentally."

Peg let out long sigh. "Why on earth would someone who went to an extraordinary length to make the death appear accidental want to raise a suspicion of murder?"

"I want to hear this," exclaimed Woolley, jerking the pipe from his mouth. "I may use it in my next Jake Elwell book."

"Okay, try this on for size, Mr. Mystery Novelist," Nick said, gently placing his cigar in an ashtray. "It was done in order to set up somebody as the murderer."

Woolley chuckled derisively. "A frame job? It's a cliché, old boy."

Nick retrieved the cigar. "It's an explanation for setting the fire."

"Assuming your theory is right," said Peg, "whom do you suspect?"

Nick glanced at Woolley. "Pardon another cliché, Professor, but at the moment I suspect no one . . . and everyone. Solving a murder is a matter of determining three elements: the means, who had the opportunity, and who had a motive. We know the means, the nitroglycerine pills slipped into Chandler's cognac. I believe the means rules out Devonshire. How could he know about Chandler's heart condition? If Devonshire didn't do it, all Jack Lerch has to do is find out which of the people on Melvin Chandler's invitation list knew, and had motive and opportunity."

"There must be at least a hundred people at that party," said Woolley.

"Most of whom are members of the Boston area press," Nick said. "This case comes down to how many of the other guests at the party knew where Chandler was staying, and which of them was familiar with Chandler's medical history, had a reason to want him dead, and was clever enough to set the fire as a ruse to deflect the attention of the police from the real killer to a fall guy, if you will allow me another cliché."

"You are also just the man to keep Lerch on the right track," Woolley said as he looked at his watch. "And now, children, it's way past this old man's bedtime, so I'm bidding you both a pleasant night's rest."

As he rose from the chair, Nick said, "I know you didn't have much use for Chandler, but I was hoping that you and he could have put the past behind you. Was that foolish on my part?"

"The older I get, the more things that troubled me in the past have a way of becoming less and less important. But I regret to say that I found nothing in Chandler to alter my opinion of him."

"Perhaps if you'd had time to talk with him," Nick said, accompanying him to the door, "you would have changed your mind."

"From the little I saw of him, I believe he was as much a schemer as he was when he pilfered money from a club that embraced him when no others would. I do regret that he was murdered, but I confess I'm amazed it didn't happen long ago. Of course, if he had been murdered sooner, you wouldn't have been on hand to find out who did it. I'm sure you'll get to the bottom of this delightful mystery before Lerch mucks it up."

"I know you'd like nothing better than me providing fodder for another book by getting involved in this murder," Nick said, opening the door, "but you'll have to look for inspiration elsewhere. I have no intention of sticking my nose in this case."

Woolley grinned. "We shall see about that!"

As Nick turned from the door and found Peg putting on her coat, he demanded, "Where do you think you're going?"

"Home, of course. I have no intention of staying here and waking up to find my car's been towed so snowplows can clear Brattle Street," she said, donning her coat. "I'm putting the old heap in its garage and these bones of mine into my own bed, and leaving you alone to figure out who killed Melvin Chandler." She kissed the tip of his nose. "No matter what you say about not getting involved in this murder, your handsome schnozzola is already stuck in it. You're like a thoroughbred racer who's heard the bugle-call to the post. Or to choose a metaphor that's more appropriate to this case, you're the dalmatian in the firehouse whose keen nose has detected a whiff of smoke."

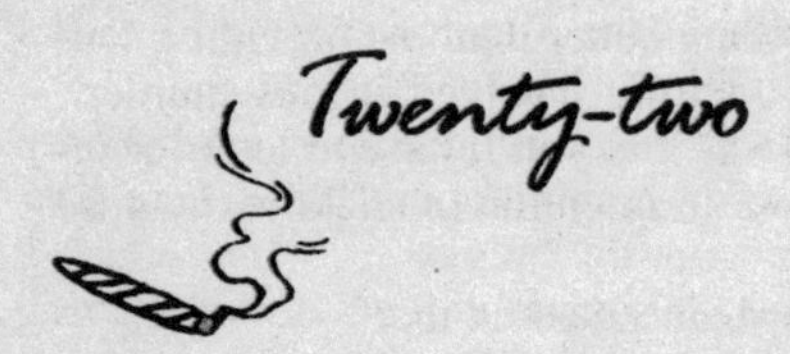

Twenty-two

CLOSE TO MIDNIGHT, Lieutenant Lerch looked up from his desk to find Goldstein entering his office with a tight grip around the right arm of a sleepy, scared-looking, stocky red-haired youth in sneakers, blue jeans, and gray sweatshirt under an unzipped blue jacket with gold sleeves and H-A-R-V-A-R-D in red across its front.

"Well, well, well," said Lerch, tipping back in his swivel chair. "May I assume, Detective Goldstein, that this gentleman's name is Rob Devonshire?"

"It is indeed, boss."

"If I'm under arrest, I'd like to know why," Rob demanded. "If this is happening because of what occurred at that cigar store, I hit Chandler with the sign by accident. I was told no charges would be filed."

"If you were arrested," said Goldstein, "you'd be in handcuffs."

"Then why am I here?"

"Have a seat, Rob," Lerch said, indicating a straight-backed chair in front of his desk, "and you'll soon know why. If what you say in answer to a few questions I have for you is satisfactory, you'll be free to leave."

Rob sat. "Shouldn't you be advising me of my rights?"

"Only if you're under arrest. You aren't. But I'm hoping that you'll cooperate with us in our investigation."

"What are you investigating?"

"I regret to say," Lerch answered, "that the man you *accidentally* hit with that picket sign today—yesterday—is dead. He was found in his suite at the Mayflower Hotel. It looks like it's a case of murder."

"Hey now, just a minute," Rob protested, rising halfway off the chair. "I don't know a thing about that. There's no way you're going to pin a murder on me."

"You were seen at the Mayflower around the time Chandler died."

"I was out in front," Rod said, sitting again. "I was picketing."

"You were also in the hallway outside Chandler's suite."

"Says who?"

"The person who saw you going into the fire stairway."

"She's mistaken."

Lerch came up straight. *"She's* mistaken? Who said that the person who saw you was a woman? I didn't. Did you hear me say any such thing, Detective Goldstein?"

"No, sir."

Rob gulped a breath. Shifting nervously on the chair, he nodded. "I was there. But I was never in Chandler's suite."

"You were sightseeing? Thinking about booking a penthouse suite?"

"I knocked on the door a couple of times but got no answer. Then I got a whiff of smoke from under the door. I tried the door latch. When the door swung open, I saw a light to my right in a room at the end of a corridor. The door was open. I saw smoke in the room, so I went to the door and saw Mr. Chandler lying on the bed, not moving. It was burning. I got the hell out of there as fast as I could."

"Why didn't you report all this? How come you didn't pull the fire alarm?"

"I was going to pull it. Believe me, I was," Rob pleaded, "but the elevator door opened. I was afraid that if I was found up there, after what occurred earlier in the day, I'd be accused of killing Mr. Chandler. Which apparently is what's happening."

"Why were you up there?"

"I went to see Mr. Chandler."

"For what purpose?"

"I went because he asked to see me."

Lerch tilted back again. "Chandler asked to see you? When?"

"I got a phone call from him at my apartment late this afternoon—yesterday afternoon. He said he wasn't angry that I'd hit him with the sign and that he wanted to talk with me about the whole issue of smoking, my right to be against it, and his right to do so. He asked me to come up to his room at a quarter to seven. I thought the least I could do was apologize for hitting him on the head. I was really sorry. I'm not a violent person."

"Can anyone verify that you got the phone call? Was anyone with you at the time?"

"No. But wouldn't there be a record of some kind at his hotel that he called me?"

Upright again, Lerch asked, "Where do you suppose he got your phone number?"

"I have no idea. The call was a huge surprise."

"Did you tell your fellow members of S.O.S. about this huge surprise, and that you'd been invited to meet with the enemy?"

"Mr. Chandler asked me not to tell anybody."

"Did that surprise you?"

"When he asked me not to tell anyone in S.O.S. that he and I would be meeting, he said he was afraid I'd be talked out of it. He said he really wanted to talk to me."

"Ever been arrested, Rob?"

"Certainly not. You can check."

"I can and I will. Ever been fingerprinted?"

"Of course not."

"Would you volunteer to be printed now?"

"What for?"

Lerch smiled benignly. "Your cooperation would go a really long way toward persuading me that you're not a murderer. But if you don't care to be helpful, then I'll have to order Detective Goldstein to place you under arrest on a charge of suspicion of murder, in which case I won't need your cooperation to get a set of your fingerprints."

"If I agree, you promise I won't be arrested?"

"I can't promise you that, Rob, simply because I don't know if the prints you give us will match the fingerprints found in Chandler's bedroom. If you were not in there—"

"I wasn't. I just stood at the door looking in."

"Then there's no reason why you shouldn't volunteer to be fingerprinted, right?"

"I guess not."

"Fine. Now, go with Detective Goldstein and when the printing's done, you'll not only be free to go home, but Detective Goldstein will arrange for a patrol car to take you."

Rob smiled nervously. "Really? That would be great."

"In this snow there're probably not going to be any taxis on the street," said Lerch as he turned his attention to papers on his desk, "and it's certainly not a fit night out for walking, even for a man of your youth and obvious physical fitness. Being a heavy cigarette smoker and with a heart condition, if I tried trudging through snow like this I'd be popping nitroglycerine pills under my tongue every other minute and praying I'd make it home to a warming glass of cognac."

"The worse thing you could do in a situation like that is drink alcohol, Lieutenant."

"Are you also against drinking, Mr. Devonshire?"

"No, but it's been shown that alcohol doesn't warm the body. It's a depressant. It lowers the blood pressure. The best thing to do if you're cold is to drink coffee. It's a stimulant."

"You're in medical school, Mr. Devonshire?"

"Pre-med. I hope to start med school next year."

"I was hoping you could offer some advice concerning my heart condition."

"Maybe in a couple of years, but at the moment I know next to nothing on the subject of cardiology, except that smoking cigarettes is bad for it. Give 'em up."

"What about drinking?"

"I have a feeling, Lieutenant," Rob replied as he and Goldstein departed, "that no matter what a doctor says, you're going to continue with both."

Twenty-three

AT THE TIME Rob Devonshire answered a knocking on the door of his basement apartment on Museum Street to find a detective, Dave Selden and Steve Yedenok had been seated at the bar of the Plimouth Rock Lounge for better than an hour. Except for making deploring comments on New England's winter weather, they'd trudged together in silence for more than a mile since Farley's.

Crusted with snow and ice, they entered the lobby of the Mayflower Hotel and found its chairs and sofas littered with unhappy-looking and uncomfortable people who'd been stranded by the storm and left without rooms in a hotel filled to capacity.

Selden was not surprised when Yedenok said, "I propose that we warm ourselves up with a couple of stiff drinks."

Although the lounge was also crowded with other marooned people, they found a booth with a window affording a rare view of Memorial Drive without a flow of traffic. Snow stung the window as a stiff wind off the Charles River whipped it almost horizontally. Light from windows of the lounge sparkled from the iced surface of a broad, snowy lawn stretching between the hotel and the highway. Evergreens dotting the lawn resembled ice cream sundaes with thick dollops of whipped cream.

"Now that we're inside," Selden said, "the snow looks pretty."

Yedenok looked anxiously toward the crowded bar and said, "This place will never get an award for speedy service." He shifted eyes to the view. "God knows when the airport will open and planes will be flying again so we can get the hell out of this town. I was nuts to have come up here."

"Why did you?"

"Mel wrote on my invitation that if I came, between us we might be able to settle my lawsuit against him and the magazine. Why are you here?"

"My agent thought I was invited because Mel was having second thoughts about letting me go and wanted to kiss and make up. I hope that when you saw him this evening, you and he worked it out to your satisfaction."

"Saw him this evening? I haven't seen him. Where'd you get the idea that I saw him?"

"When I was waiting for the elevator, I noticed it coming down from the penthouse floor. Since it didn't stop anywhere and you were in it, I assumed you'd been up there to see Mel."

"You're mistaken," Yedenok replied sharply as he watched the approach of a waitress. "I got on the elevator on my floor, the eleventh."

The waitress asked, "Good evening, gentlemen. How may I serve you?"

"Double gin martini, extra martini," said Yedenok. "I mean, extra *dry.* And you might as well make it two doubles, in case this place gets even busier."

"Scotch for me, on the rocks," said Selden.

"Yes, sir. One or two?"

"In snowstorms," Selden said, "one's my limit."

As she departed, Yedenok flashed a nervous smile. "I wonder if anyone has ever told the people who own this place that they misspelled its name. It should be 'Y,' not 'I.' "

"I think 'I' is the way the Pilgrims spelled it," Selden replied. "But I'm pretty sure they'd disapprove of the name being applied to a bar, no matter how it's spelled."

A silence fell and remained until the returning waitress

placed their drinks before them and said, "One scotch on the rocks, two double gin martinis extra dry."

Yedenok drank half of the nearer martini quickly, set the glass down gently, and said, "There's nothing so good as the first."

Selden took a sip of the scotch. "To take liberties with a great line from Charles Dickens about Jacob Marley in *A Christmas Carol,*" he said, putting down the glass, "Mel Chandler is dead as a doornail. Between you and me, Steve, who do you think murdered him?"

"*Murdered* him? Why do you think he was murdered?"

"All those cops showing up at the party. Taking down our names and addresses. Telling us they might have to contact us later. I think they'd do that only if Mel had been murdered."

Yedenok finished the first martini in a gulp.

Selden lifted his scotch. "A toast! If it is murder, here's to whoever did it! And if it was you who polished the bastard off, I salute you with a line from my favorite film, *The Maltese Falcon,* when Bogart said to Ingrid Bergman, 'Here's looking at you, kid.' "

"I did not murder Mel Chandler, and I resent you thinking I did," said Yedenok angrily.

He reached for the second martini.

Selden raised his hands. "Okay, okay."

"And the line is from *Casablanca*. The woman in *The Maltese Falcon* was Mary Astor, and what Bogart said to her was, 'Yes, precious, I'm sending you over.' "

"Just once in a movie with a murder," Selden said, "I'd like to see the killer get away with it. Shall I tell you why? Because most of the time, people who are murdered get exactly what they deserved. That doesn't happen much in real life. Too bad." He lowered his voice to a whisper. "And just between you, me, and the snow, Steve, it's about time that Mel Chandler has gotten what *he* deserved. A dose of sudden death! I just hope nobody calls on me to deliver the eulogy at his funeral, because I just might say things about him that he left out of his book."

"Have you read it?"

"I got a copy of it months ago," Selden replied with a proud smile. "A friend of mine who works for the publisher sent me a set of the galleys. You haven't seen the book yet?"

"I'd planned to buy one at the signing at that tobacco shop. When I arrived and saw that angry crowd, I turned right around and came back to the hotel. Were you there?"

"I wasn't about to queue up and give him the satisfaction of me buying his book. My plan was to see Mel at tonight's party."

"Am I in the book?"

"You weren't in the galleys when I read them, but that was before you slapped him with your libel suit. Now that he's dead, I assume it's been made moot."

"Oh no. I'm also suing the entity that owns the magazine. Whether I can legally sue his estate is a matter I'll take up with my lawyer when I return to New York."

Selden gazed out at unrelenting snow. "From the looks of things," he said as Yedenok consumed the second martini, "we may be stuck here till spring."

At that moment, fourteen floors above the Plimouth Lounge and one below the John F. Kennedy suite, Ben Salter was following Madeline Lewis into her room. Like Selden and Yedenok, they'd been forced by the lack of taxi service to walk from Farley's.

"Thank goodness Mel decided on the Mayflower and not a hotel across the river. I'd hate to have had to hike to Boston in this blizzard."

"These conditions are nowhere near a blizzard," Madeline replied as she took off her wet coat. "If our hotel was in Boston," she continued, seated on the bed and taking off the half-boots she'd had the foresight to pack, "we would have just hopped on the subway. It's a short walk to the MBTA station in Harvard Square."

"No matter where they are, I hate subways," said Ben, red-faced from the cold and still breathing hard from the exertion of trudging through deep snow. "I'm always getting lost in the damned things. I'm like the man named Charlie in the funny song from the Fifties that Mother used to sing, who got lost in the system and spent his life riding the MTA."

"By the time I got to Boston University," she said, smiling, "the 'B' had been added to the name. Instead of the Massachusetts Transit Authority, it was the Massachusetts *Bay* Transit Authority."

Salter rubbed his cold hands together. "What did you think when all those cops barged in? I almost laughed."

"It looked like one of those raids on speakeasies in the Prohibition era."

"Some cop boss probably figured that as long as the party was going to be broken up," Ben said, taking off his coat, "why not send a bunch of his men to see that no food went to waste by getting thrown out?"

"You're such a cynic. You always were."

"Heaven only knows how many cigars they helped themselves to when they were taking names and addresses."

Madeline looked at him thoughtfully.

"Nick Chase said it looked as if Mel had a heart attack. If that's what they think, why did they come to the party and take names and addresses? I think so many cops came because that detective decided that Mel was murdered."

"If Nick told you it looked like Mel had a heart attack, there's no way the police could have determined so quickly that he didn't."

"They could have found a clue of some kind that points to murder."

"Babe, you've been watching too many detective shows. If the cops believed Mel was murdered, they'd have said so. And they'd have done more than take down a bunch of names and addresses. They'd have been asking everybody questions. How long have you been at this party? What were you doing before got here? What was your relationship to the murdered man? Stuff like that."

"They did spend a lot of time talking to Richard."

"He's Mel's son. It stands to reason they'd talk to him longer than the others, especially if they suspected he had killed Mel."

"If they'd have thought that, he'd been under arrest."

"Not necessarily."

The moment Richard Chandler and Veronica Redding had left Farley's, she turned up the collar of a full-length mink coat and declared, "I must say that I think you handled that scene in the worst possible way."

Buttoning a chesterfield overcoat, Richard retorted, "Do you now?"

"It was stupid of you to come right out and ask that detective if he had the person who'd murdered your father in custody when he'd said nothing about murder."

The door to Farley's opened and several people stepped outside.

Richard took Veronica by the arm and led her toward the street. "I think it best, darling," he said quietly and sternly, "if we wait to talk about this until we get back to the house."

A trip which should have been swift required nearly an hour. Because snow continued to come down hard and sidewalks had not been cleared, they'd found the walk from Farley's to the MBTA station in Harvard Square slow going. Effects of the storm also delayed the arrival of a train to Boston. Riding in silence, they'd left it at the Washington Street stop and faced another walk on unshoveled sidewalks to Beacon Hill.

As they entered the house and were taking off their coats in the foyer, a woman's voice called from the living room, "Is that you, Richard?"

With an astonished expression on his face as his mother stepped into the foyer, Richard exclaimed, "I thought you were in Miami."

"I was, but only long enough to pick up my luggage and put it and me on the next plane back to Boston."

"Why did you do that?"

"On the way down I changed my mind about not seeing your father. Excuse the state of my clothing. It's the suit I wore during the entire trip. I'm sure it looks horrible. My flight was the last one they let land at Logan Airport before they closed it because of the snow. God only knows where my luggage is. I had a devil of a time finding a cab. I wound up sharing one with a very nice man who's in the cigar business in Miami. He'd been invited to Mel's big party. How's that for a small world? He's staying at the Palmer House. I hoped to reach home in time to catch you before you left for Farley's. But the snow was so bad by then that I decided not to go."

She paused in her narration to look at Veronica.

"Is this beautiful young woman the one you mentioned on the phone?"

"Yes, this is Ronnie," said Richard.

"Veronica Redding," she said. "I'm pleased to meet you, Mrs. Chandler."

"Please call me Anita. You and Richard make a lovely couple."

"Mother, there's something I've got to tell you about Mel."

"Tell me in the living room," she said, turning away. "I'm eager to know everything that went on at Farley's. I'm especially keen to hear Veronica's impression of the great Mel Chandler."

Richard caught her by the elbow and blurted, "Mother, he's . . . dead."

Stepping away from him, she asked, "He had a heart attack?"

"There's going to be an autopsy. I think the police suspect murder."

"Why do you say that?"

"A detective came to tell me about Dad's death."

"What detective?"

"His name is—"

"Lerch," said Veronica.

"When he came to inform me of Mel's death," said Richard, "I immediately assumed he suspected murder. Why else would so many police swoop into Farley's and begin taking down names and addresses of all the guests?"

Anita crossed the large living room slowly and sat in a chair next to a window that was coated with blown snow.

"Did this detective question you?"

"He asked me if Mel had a history of heart trouble."

"And you answered—"

"I told him yes. Then he asked me if a lot of people knew about the condition. I told him no, that only the people closest to him knew, because if word got out that the publisher of *Cigar Smoker* magazine had heart problems, it could be bad for business."

"When Richard asked Lerch if Mel was murdered," said Veronica, "Lerch told Richard to assume that he was, and asked if there was anyone Richard knew of who might have done it."

Anita frowned. "What did you say, Richard?"

"I said I could think of several candidates."

With a slight smile Anita said, "Merely several?"

Richard shrugged. "I could be wrong about Mel being murdered. Maybe he did suffer a heart attack. He might have stopped taking his medication."

"Did the detective tell you where and when Mel died?"

"He said he was found in his suite at the Mayflower around a quarter to seven."

"Where were you at that time?"

"Ronnie and I were trying to find a taxi."

"Is there anyone, other than Veronica, who can verify it?"

"Sure. The cab driver."

"What's his name?"

"How should I know?"

"The cab number?"

Richard looked at her blankly. "Mother, do you think that I killed him?"

"What I might think is irrelevant. But if Mel was murdered, you are going to be the prime suspect. As the principal beneficiary of his will, you're bound to be at the top of the list."

"Richard *was* with me," Veronica insisted.

"I doubt that Detective Lerch will lend much weight to an alibi offered by a woman who is romantically involved with a young man who stands to inherit several millions of dollars and a successful magazine publishing enterprise. He is more likely to suspect you were in on it."

Richard sobbed, "As God is my witness, I did not kill my father!"

"Unfortunately, my darling," Anita said, picking up a gold-trimmed white antique-style telephone, "the Almighty can't be subpoenaed to testify."

"Who are you phoning?"

"My lawyer, of course. If a defense is required, he'll know how to assemble a group of attorneys who will make the O. J. Simpson dream team look as though they were a bunch of first-year law students."

Charles Appleton's route after leaving Farley's took him by foot to Harvard station and the subway to a change in lines at Park Street in Boston. Off the train at the Boylston Theater stop, he faced a strenuous snow-impeded walk straight up Boylston Street. A right turn onto Exeter took him to Commonwealth Avenue and his apartment house. The trip had been vexing not only because of the beastly weather, but because he'd been nagged all the way by questions.

The most frustrating concerned what had been on Mel Chandler's mind when he'd sent the invitation with its surprising handwritten post-script: "For auld tang syne, do come. Yours, M. C."

Chandler's death had made getting an answer to that puzzler impossible. But if Mel had died from a heart attack, why had police come to Farley's in such numbers? And why had they detained everyone and taken names and addresses?

Among the police he'd noticed a short, pudgy man by the name of Lieutenant Lerch. He'd recognized him because his face was frequently seen on television news programs and in newspaper photos at the scenes of murders. Why was a homicide detective bothering with a death from a heart attack?

Accompanying Lerch had been the owner of the tobacco shop on Brattle Street at which Chandler had been attacked by anti-smoking protesters. He, too, was a familiar figure and a well-known name from the news.

For some reason, the ex-detective who now ran a tobacco shop had left Chandler's party at Farley's soon after it began, only to return in the company of eight policemen in uniform led by a homicide detective. Why?

Yet none of these questions tantalized him more than an impression that came over him soon after his arrival in the cigar room at Farley's.

In that crowd of faces, one had looked very familiar. During the journey from Farley's, he had racked his brain trying to place it.

As he reached home and climbed the stairs to his apartment, he remembered.

When he opened the door to a welcome rush of warm air, the purpose of Mel's invitation seemed clear. And wildly fantastic.

The words of "Auld Lang Syne" asked, "Should auld acquaintance be *forgot* and *never* brought to mind?" Evidently, after all this time Mel had decided the answer was "no," and he needed to face his past, own up to it, and set things right.

From a bookcase he took a scrapbook. Carrying it to his desk, he found himself hoping that in the unexpected final hours of Mel's life he'd managed to do the right thing. But what if he hadn't? Perhaps Mel had chosen to wait and do it at the party. What a terrible irony it would be if at such a long overdue moment, a heart attack had prevented Mel from correcting a wrong.

Remembering his own role and his long years of silence on the matter, he leafed through the scrapbook and wondered what obligation now rested with him, if any.

After pondering the question a long time, he closed the scrapbook, took a deep breath, and with trembling hand, picked up the phone.

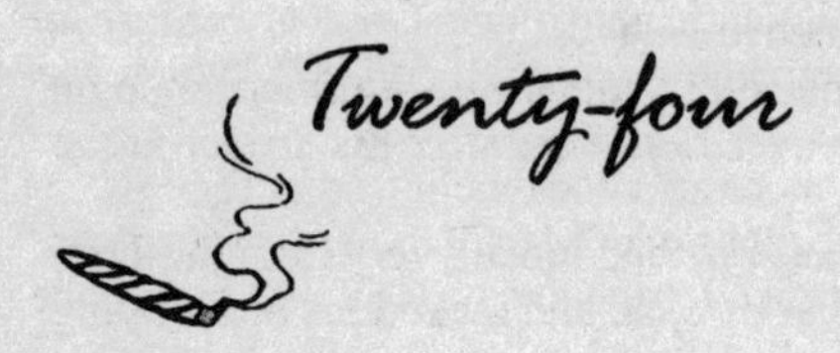

AFTER WORKING ALL NIGHT, Dr. Hussain Awini left the autopsy room and went into his office. On the wall behind his desk, displayed side by side in black frames, were two expressions of verities of his profession.

The one on the left was from the Book of Job:

HE DISCOVERETH DEEP THINGS OUT OF DARKNESS,
AND BRINGETH TO LIGHT THE SHADOW OF DEATH.

The other copied an inscription in the office of the New York City medical examiner:

THIS IS THE PLACE WHERE DEATH
DELIGHTS TO HELP THE LIVING.

Before booting up a computer to formalize his findings in a written report, Dr. Awini flicked through his Rolodex and found Jack Lerch's beeper number. When Lerch phoned, the caller ID display on Awini's phone showed that Lerch was in his office at police headquarters. Answering the call, the doctor skipped amenities and blared, "As a taxpayer, I'm glad to see that someone on the public payroll besides me works nights."

Lerch replied, "What have you got for me, Doc?"

"Melvin Chandler had quadruple coronary artery bypass grafting. As a result, he was being treated with a nitrate. Preliminary tests indicate he'd ingested the required combination of the nitrate, alcohol, and a substantial overdose of nitroglycerine to precipitate circulation collapse, which was the cause of his death."

"So the means of his murder was the nitroglycerine."

"Whether someone other than Mr. Chandler was responsible for the overdose is not for me to say. He could have done it by mistake."

"It's murder, Doc. The proof is the fire."

"My written report will be on your desk today, weather permitting."

"The snow's over, Doc. It stopped about three hours ago. Thanks for the quick answer."

As Lerch hung up, Awini noted the time: Six-thirty.

When Lerch looked at his watch, he decided to wait a while before phoning Nick Chase.

Shortly before seven, Nick awoke and heard the sound of a snow shovel at work. That the snowfall was over was confirmed when his clock radio went on.

"With a foot of snow on the ground in Boston," the voice of a male newscaster asserted in an annoyingly jolly tone, "the big cleanup of the white stuff is getting under way."

"White stuff," Nick repeated grumpily. "What a worn-out cliché."

The newscaster continued, "Most of the main thoroughfares are passable, but opening up the side streets is expected to take a while. Logan Airport remains closed, but limited service may be restored early this afternoon."

Nick got out of bed, went into the living room, and looked through a window to assess the status of Brattle Street. He found it unplowed and both sides bounded by parked vehicles turned into huge, graceful mounds of snow. The only snow shovel at work was attacking a small stretch of the opposite sidewalk in front of the Brattle Street Theater.

With no idea when, or if, the young man with whom he had contracted in the summer to undertake such work on behalf of the Happy Smoking Ground would appear, and remembering that yesterday a sheet of plywood had been put in place of the display window because an anti-smoking zealot had heaved a brick through it, Nick decided not to open the store.

As he returned to the bedroom with the intention of getting another hour's sleep, the man on the radio had moved from the effects of an overabundance of white stuff to reporting other news. After two items on political subjects and one concerning a two-alarm fire in an abandoned house in the Roxbury section of Boston, he continued, "And in the Mayflower Hotel in Cambridge last evening, a hotel maid discovered and quickly put out a small fire in the John F. Kennedy suite. Found dead in the room was the controversial publisher of the magazine *Cigar Smoker.* Police say that Melvin Chandler suffered a heart attack. Chandler had come to Cambridge to promote his newly published autobiography because he was a student at Harvard University in the 1960s. Ironically, the fire was apparently caused by his smoking in bed. It was a cigar, of course."

Nick grunted. "Cute," he said, turning off the radio and pulling up the bed covers. "Very cute and snide."

As he drifted to sleep, the bedside phone rang.

Grabbing up the receiver, he answered irritably, "What?"

"Nick, it's Jack Lerch."

"Right. What's up?"

"I just talked to Awini. The man's a genius. Just what he figured might have happened to Chandler is what happened. Someone slipped a lethal Mickey Finn of nitroglycerine tablets into his cognac. I'm going over to Boston to inform Chandler's son that his father's death is officially a murder case."

"I wish you the best of luck in solving it."

"What's that supposed to mean?"

"It means I wish you the best of luck in solving it, because I'm officially declaring myself out of it."

"Oh no you're not."

"Oh yes I am."

"You can't do that."

"I just did."

"This is your murder case, Nick. It belongs to you whether you want it or not because you're the guy who spotted this as a murder. I didn't notice the cigar in Chandler's hand hadn't been clipped and so couldn't have started that fire, you did. You've also got an obligation as the friend of the victim to see that his killer is brought to justice."

"Melvin Chandler was not my friend. I barely knew him."

"You also have an obligation to him because of the honor he bestowed on you when his magazine named you tobacconist of the year."

Nick laughed. "Jack, that was more than fifteen years ago."

"Listen to me, buddy. In tackling this murder I'm probably going find myself up to my ass in cigar people."

"*Cigar* people?"

"You know what I mean."

"No I don't, Jack. Who are *cigar people?* You make them sound like creatures out of a bad science fiction movie. 'Attack of the Cigar People.' 'The Cigar People From Outer Space.' "

"Laugh all you want, Nick," said Lerch, "but whoever killed Mel Chandler is likely to be part of his world, and that world is the world of cigars. No one I know has your expertise in that world. I really need your help, Nick. I *want* your help."

"I really don't see what I can do to contribute to the investigation."

"You can be with me at every step along the way. You can start by sitting in when I talk to the suspects."

"You've got suspects already?"

"Come on, Nick, you know damn well that the person who killed Melvin Chandler was in the cigar room at Farley's last night. You and I probably talked with him. Fortunately, on account of the storm and Logan Airport being closed down, the ones from out of town are stuck here. They're all staying at the Mayflower. Goldstein's there making sure they don't check out. I plan to go to the hotel around nine o'clock to talk to them. I can swing by and pick you up in my all-weather goes-anywhere sports utility van."

Nick thought a moment. Remembering that he'd decided he would not be opening up the store and feeling the stirring of an outrage against those who broke the law that long ago had made him want to be a detective, he replied, "Okay, Jack, I'll see you at nine at the Mayflower. Since it's close by, I'll hoof it over there."

"The snow's pretty deep."

"I'll manage."

"If you make it there at half past eight, I'll treat you to breakfast."

PART VI

Ashes to Ashes

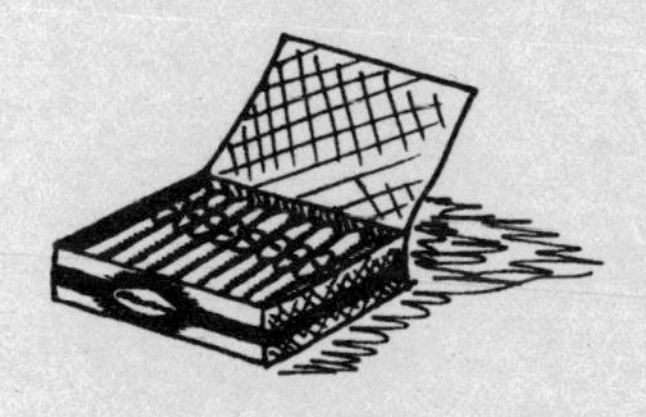

Life's review in smoke goes past—
Fickle fortune, stubborn fate,
Right discovered all too late,
Beings loved and gone before,
Beings loved but friends no more,
Self-reproach and futile sighs,
Vanity in birth that dies,
Longing, heart-break, adoration—
Nothing sure in expectation
Save ashes-to-ashes at the last.

IRVING BROWNE
The Smoke Traveler, 1895

Twenty-five

WITH A PALE blue cloudless sky and warmthless sunlight glaringly reflected off the deep snow, Nick found his footing difficult and the going hard as he made his way toward the hotel. The predominant sounds were the scraping of metal shovels against pavements and the roaring of car engines as whirring tires strained to get traction on unplowed streets.

When he entered the Capt. Miles Standish coffee shop, he found it crowded and noisy as excited hotel guests anticipated the imminent ending of storm-imposed confinement. Looking around, he saw Lerch and Goldstein at a table for four in a corner near the kitchen.

"I trust you agree," said Lerch as Nick joined them, "that Dr. Awini's findings limit the number of suspects in this murder to the people who knew him well enough to be able to get into his suite and slip that overdose of nitro in his cognac. That means it has to be someone who is staying at this hotel."

"Or someone from outside whom Chandler let in," Nick replied. "The son, Richard, for one. There was also an old college friend of Chandler's at the party, name of Charles Appleton."

Goldstein said, "There are four people staying here who were at the party: Lewis, Salter, Steve Yedenok, and Dave Selden. I called them and told them we'd be interviewing them this morning. I also told the people at the front desk that none of them is to be allowed to check out until I give the green light."

"Excellent work, Sidney," said Lerch.

"The only questions now are which of the four you want to talk to first and where."

Lerch looked at Nick. "Any preference on your part?"

"It's always been my policy never to keep a lady waiting."

"That's very gentlemanly, Nick, but I promised I'd buy you breakfast. The questioning can wait till after we've had it. This place happens to serve the best waffles in town. Unlike those my wife whips up now and then, which you could use for base pads at Fenway Park, the ones you get here almost float off the dish."

Lerch and Goldstein ordered two each with sides of sausage and coffee.

When Nick asked for only orange juice, coffee, and toast, Lerch pleaded, "Have more than that, Nick. It's the city that's paying."

"I've been having the same breakfast for forty years. If my stomach suddenly gets waffles it will think I've either gotten married again or died and gone to heaven."

"When are you going to?" asked Lerch. "I mean get married again, not go to heaven."

"Who would have me in either place?"

"Peg Baron."

Nick grunted. "What a circus that would be. Peg's as settled in her ways as I am."

"Man isn't meant to be alone."

"I'm not. I've got my kids. The grandkids. And I've always got Woolley."

"What's his take on Chandler being murdered?"

"The professor expressed surprise that it didn't happen long ago."

"Really? Why would he say that?"

"The Woolley-Chandler connection dates to the late 1960s when Chandler was a student at Harvard. Woolley was on the committee that kicked him out."

"Chandler was expelled? What prompted that?"

"According to Woolley, it was a matter of embezzlement. Chandler helped himself to a thousand dollars from a club he belonged to. That he did it was never in question. The only mystery was why he needed the money. Chandler wouldn't say, and the only person who might have known was such a steadfast friend to Chandler that he refused to cooperate in Woolley's investigation into the affair."

"Maybe Chandler and the steadfast friend were in on the theft together."

"I don't believe there was ever any suspicion of that, but it's a friendship that's managed to endure. His name is Charles Appleton. He was at last night's party."

"There you go," exclaimed Lerch. "It's because of your possession of just that kind of information that you should be working with me on this case. Without you coming up with that little tidbit, how could I have known about this Appleton's connection with Chandler?"

A waitress brought their breakfast. When she was gone, Goldstein said, "Maybe there was something between Chandler and this Charles Appleton guy that was eating away at one or the other all this time and it came to a head last night."

Drenching his waffles with syrup, Lerch asked, "Such as what?"

"Maybe it wasn't Chandler who stole the money. Maybe he was covering for Appleton."

Lerch cut a chunk of waffle with the edge of a fork and lifted it, dripping syrup, toward his mouth. "Chandler took the fall? Why would he do that?"

Goldstein shrugged, "Maybe back then the two were more than friends."

With the waffle poised at his mouth, Lerch said, "Sid, are you suggesting Chandler and Appleton were gay?"

"It was just a passing thought."

"Not an unreasonable one, Sid," said Nick. "It's certainly possible that Appleton refused to testify against Chandler because he had feelings for Chandler. But according to Woolley, Mel Chandler was a committed womanizer. Woolley thought Chandler might have needed the grand to settle clothing bills. He said that Chandler was more interested in having expensive clothes to dazzle women than in pursuing his studies. Another argument against your theory that Chandler was homosexual is the fact that he was married."

"A lot of gay guys marry."

"Whatever there was or wasn't between Chandler and Appleton," said Lerch impatiently, "we'll find out when we question Appleton."

While Lerch and Goldstein devoted their attention to their waffles, Nick sipped coffee and watched Benjamin Salter enter the coffee shop, look around, and thread his way between tables toward them.

Putting down his cup, Nick said, "Gentlemen, I think the matter of who gets talked to first is about to be settled."

Arriving at the table, Salter was red-faced as he demanded, "What the hell is going on? I called the front desk to tell them to prepare bills for me and Miss Lewis and was informed that by the order of the police we are not being allowed to check out. Lieutenant Lerch, this is an outrage. I demand that you revoke that order immediately."

Lerch stood. "I can't do that, Mr. Salter. The death of your employer is now officially a murder case and I have no choice but to regard you and Miss Lewis, at the very least, as material witnesses. Whether you become suspects—"

"Suspects? That is ridiculous!"

"Whether you or Miss Lewis will be considered suspects," Lerch continued, "depends on the outcome of interviews that I intend to have with each of you. That is why I can't permit you to check out at this time. Go back to your room. We'll be up to interview you presently."

"You can damn well do it here and now."

"The middle of a crowded and noisy coffee shop is hardly the place for it. You can go back to your room and wait for us, or Detective Goldstein can handcuff you and escort you to police headquarters to be questioned there. Which shall it be, sir?"

"I'm not answering any questions without my lawyer present."

Lerch resumed his seat. "If you had nothing to do with

Chandler's death, you've got nothing to worry about. You can talk to me now in your room, or wait for your attorney to get here. If he's in New York, you'll have quite a wait. Meanwhile, you'll be occupying a cell at headquarters. I think you'll find accommodations a good deal more comfortable in your room. We'll be there in fifteen minutes."

"Very well, but this is outrageous," Salter exclaimed, turning abruptly and striding away.

Spearing a triangular slab of waffle, Lerch said, "I hope we find out that snotty son of a bitch is the one who did it."

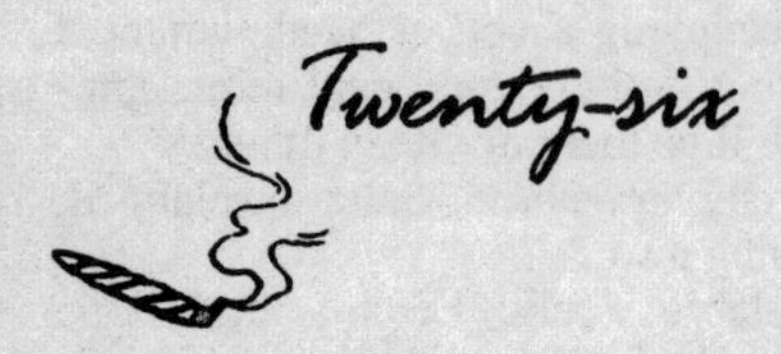

Twenty-six

HALF AN HOUR LATER, when Salter opened the door to his room, Lieutenant Lerch peered beyond him and discovered Madeline Lewis seated by the window.

"This won't do," he exclaimed, as Nick and Goldstein followed him into the room. "Miss Lewis, I can't allow you to be present during my questioning of Mr. Salter. I'll talk to you next."

She looked pleadingly at Nick. "Surely, Nick, you and these men can't be thinking that Ben and I had anything to do with Mel's death?"

"It's routine questioning," Nick replied. "If Lieutenant Lerch is going to find out who is responsible, he has to speak in strict confidence with everyone who might be of help to him in the investigation of Mel's death."

"I assure you that when we left the hotel to go to the party," she said in an offended tone, "Mel was alive and well in his suite."

Lerch shook his head. "This is exactly why you can't be here, Miss Lewis. I insist that you leave at once, or I'll have no choice but to order Detective Goldstein to remove you."

Madeline threw up her hands in anger and bolted out of the chair. "All right, Lieutenant, I'm going."

* * *

When she was gone, Lerch addressed Salter.

"Miss Lewis said that before you left for the party, you saw Chandler in his suite."

"Correction, Lieutenant," Salter replied, occupying the same chair by the window. "She did not say we saw Mel."

"She stated that he was alive and well in his suite."

"Yes, but she didn't mean that *she* saw him. She spoke on the basis of what I told her."

"Which was what?"

"I told her that Mel had told me he was waiting for an urgent phone call, that Maddy and I should go on ahead of him to the party, and that he would follow shortly."

"Do you know who he was waiting to hear from?"

"Yes, it was to be a call-back from his attorney in New York. You see, when I was with him earlier in the day, Mel had gotten a call from his son Richard. The conversation got pretty hot. Richard was yelling so loudly I heard him from the other side of the sitting room. I was kind of embarrassed, so I got up to leave. But at that point Mel slammed down the phone. Then he told me to put in a call to his lawyer in New York. When he wasn't in, Mel got on the line and told the person on the other end that the lawyer was to call him back as soon as possible."

"You said you could hear the son yelling on the phone?" Nick asked.

"Yes. However, I couldn't make out what Richard was saying."

"But you had no trouble making out what Chandler was saying?"

"No trouble at all. I was in the same room."

Lerch asked, "What was the topic of this heated conversation?"

"It concerned Mel's plan to give a million dollars to Harvard. I gathered that Richard was quite upset about it. I specifically remember Mel saying to him that as long as he was alive—that is, as long as *Mel* was alive—he could damn well do whatever he wanted to with his money. And that if Richard didn't watch his mouth, he'd find himself—Richard would find himself—with no inheritance at all."

"What happened then?"

"That's when the conversation ended and Mel immediately ordered me to get his lawyer on the phone." After taking a deep breath, he continued, "Mel was extremely upset by what had happened. I'd never seen him so outraged."

Lerch asked, "That was the last time you saw Chandler?"

"Yes."

"What time was it when this happened?"

"I'm not sure. Around six-thirty, I believe."

"Did you tell Miss Lewis about the phone conversation?"

"I told her Mel was waiting for a phone call, but not why. We then left for the party. I'll live out my days regretting that I didn't send Maddy on ahead without me."

"Why is that?"

"If I'd stayed with Mel while he waited for the phone call from his lawyer, no one could have gotten into the suite. Mel would still be alive. But what's done is done. I can only comfort myself with the thought that Mel has been reunited with Donny and is happy."

Lerch jerked with surprise. "Donny? Who's Donny?"

Nick answered, "He was Chandler's young son, from his second marriage."

Lerch turned to Nick and blurted, "How the devil do you know that?"

"I read about Donny in Chandler's book. The kid died in a hit-and-run accident."

"Mel was devastated. He adored that child," said Salter. "Donny and his mother were killed while vacationing at Mel's cottage on Cape Cod. I always suspected—"

Lerch took a few steps toward him. "Suspected what, Mr. Salter?"

"No, I'm sorry. I mustn't say."

Lerch leaned down and jutted his face close to Salter's. "*Suspected what?*"

Salter sighed deeply. "After Donny was born, there was a lot of jealousy on Richard's part. Over the years, the jealousy grew into resentment. Or so it seemed to me."

Lerch came up straight. "What you *suspected,*" he said,

"was that Richard Chandler might have been driving the car in the hit-and-run that killed the kid and his mother?"

"Richard couldn't have been driving the car," Salter replied. "He was in New York at the time. But I do believe he could have arranged with one of his numerous nefarious friends from Boston to run them down."

With hands clasped behind his back, Lerch paced as he asked, "His motive being what?"

"Money, of course. Donny's death restored Richard to the position of sole beneficiary of Mel's will. Richard will inherit a very sizable fortune. Many, many millions."

Leaning against a bureau, Nick said, "Yet you say Richard was upset about Chandler's plan to give just one million of it to Harvard University."

"All I know is that the million was the subject of the phone conversation that I overheard between Mel and Richard last evening. When I learned that Mel was dead, my first thought was, 'Oh God, Richard killed him.' Later, when I heard that it appeared Mel had died of a heart attack, I felt terribly ashamed of myself for harboring such an idea. But now I'm thinking it again, and it all makes sense to me."

Nick asked, "In what way does it make sense?"

"I can't prove this, of course, but I believe that after Mel and Richard engaged in that horrible telephone conversation, Richard came here to settle the issue once and for all."

"By killing his father?"

"It is known that sons kill rich fathers. I cite Lyle and Eric Menendez."

"There's a slight flaw in your theory, Mr. Salter," said Lerch. "It might be plausible if Richard Chandler had been staying in this hotel, but he was staying at his mother's house on Beacon Hill. If that's so, how could he come here in the few minutes between the end of the phone conversation and when you and Miss Lewis left for the party, leaving Mel Chandler alive and well in his suite?"

"You assume, Lieutenant," Salter answered, "that Richard made the phone call from his mother's house on Beacon Hill. But what if he wasn't there? What if he made that call from this hotel, or from a phone booth nearby? What if he hoped to make it appear that he'd called from Beacon Hill in order to set up an alibi?"

"How long have you been working for Chandler, Mr. Salter?"

"About ten years."

"Obviously you and he got along very well."

"I believe we did. This is not to say Mel couldn't treat me as badly as he did others."

"Since you've been working for him all that time, which of the people who were close to him and he treated badly might have wanted to kill him, other than Richard?"

"I'm not keen about casting aspersions, Lieutenant."

"You had no problem doing so regarding Richard."

Nick moved away from the bureau as he asked, "What do you know about Mel drawing up a special list of people whom he wanted invited to the book-signing and to Farley's?"

Salter smiled. "Evidently Maddy told you about the enemies list."

"Do you recall the names that were on it?"

"There were three: Dave Selden, Steve Yedenok, and Charles Appleton. Mel wrote a note at the bottom of each of their invitations."

"Why did Chandler consider them enemies?"

"I think his use of the term 'enemies list' was a joke he directed at Maddy because she'd told him how much she'd detested Richard Nixon."

"It's my understanding," said Nick, "that Selden and Yedenok had grievances against Mel. He'd fired Selden, and Yedenok was suing him for libel."

"That's right. But I had the impression that Mel wanted to patch things up with them."

"Do you know why Charles Appleton was on the special list, call it what you will?"

"All I know is that Mel and Appleton had been in college together."

"Was there bad blood between them?"

Salter shrugged. "I haven't the slightest idea."

"This question may seem to come from out of left field, Mr. Salter," said Lerch, "but it's one that I have to ask for the record. The medical examiner's report noted that a few years ago Chandler underwent heart bypass surgery."

"That's right. A quadruple. He recovered from it fully. As I told you last night at Farley's, his health problems were under control, except for his, uh—"

"Impotence," said Lerch. "I'm surprised he wasn't taking the new drug for that problem."

"I believe that Richard once suggested that Mel give it a try, but when Mel inquired about it with his cardiologist, he was told it was contraindicated for other drugs he was taking. Mel was terribly disappointed."

Lerch cracked a smile. "What man wouldn't be, especially one who published a magazine glorifying not just cigars, but all the pleasures of attaining the completely fulfilled masculine lifestyle, eh?"

"Mel Chandler certainly delighted in his cigars, Lieutenant," said Salter, "and in all the manly pursuits." Smiling as he rose from his chair, he asked, "Will that be all, Lieutenant?"

"For the moment, Mr. Salter."

"When will I be allowed to check out?"

"I'll let you know."

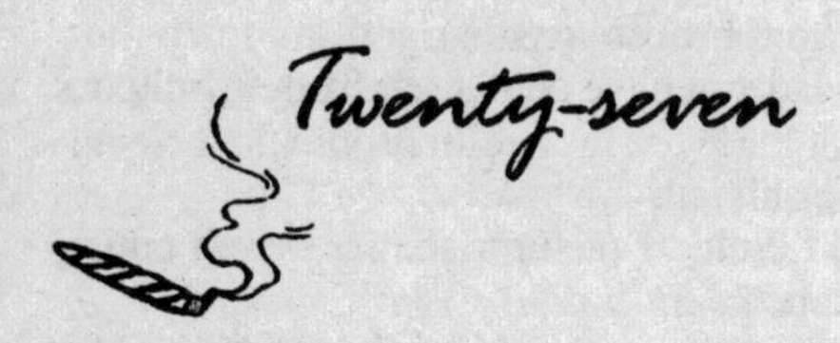

"THIS SHOULDN'T TAKE LONG, Miss Lewis," Lerch declared when she opened the door.

"I find your questioning of me and Ben insulting," she said, stepping aside to let him, Goldstein, and Nick into the room. "The idea that Ben Salter or I would have cause to kill Mel is perfectly ridiculous."

"No one has accused you of anything, Miss Lewis. At this stage of the investigation all possibilities must be considered."

She sat on the bed. "It seems to me that your attention should be focused on the red-haired kid who struck Mel with the sign. He was picketing outside the hotel at the time Mel was murdered. He could have easily sneaked up to Mel's suite."

"Actually, Rob Devonshire says Chandler *invited* him up," said Lerch, "but when he got there, he looked into the bedroom, found Chandler dead, and scrammed."

"Mel would never have asked to see a kid who not only ruined the signing at Nick's store but assaulted him."

"Maybe Chandler had decided to forgive him."

"Oh, I doubt that very much."

"Why's that, Miss Lewis?"

"Forgiveness is not a Mel Chandler trait that I'd ever noticed. If you'll read his book you will see that Mel was a man who carried a grudge and savored his enemies."

"I have read the book," said Nick, "and it's true that he seems to have enjoyed accumulating enemies. Yet he invited at least two of them to the book signing and the festivities last night at Farley's. Do you have any idea why he would do that?"

"It's called rubbing salt in the wounds."

"One of them, Dave Selden, thought that Mel was going to ask him back as managing editor of *Cigar Smoker.*"

She let out a laugh. "What a pipe dream. Or should I say smoke dream? Did Dave Selden offer any evidence that Mel wanted him back?"

"No."

"Of course not, because the idea never crossed Mel's mind."

Goldstein asked, "How can you be sure?"

"Mel would have told me."

Lerch asked, "He was in the habit of discussing his business plans with you?"

"It's not unusual that a relationship between publicist and employer eventually includes all aspects of the affairs of the employer. What the publicist doesn't know can and often does result in nasty surprises. My duty as a publicist is to anticipate possible problems. In that sense I'm like the physician who practices preventive medicine. Better to keep an illness from arising than to have to treat it."

"That's an interesting analogy that I'd like to pursue," said Nick. "You told me last night at Farley's that you weren't aware that Chandler had a heart problem."

"I didn't. He always looked as fit as a fiddle."

"So your relationship as his publicist," said Lerch, "wasn't as all-encompassing as you believed it to be."

"Obviously not."

"I'm interested in Chandler's relationship with his son," said Lerch. "What can you tell me about that?"

"I don't know what you mean."

"Did Chandler and Richard get along?"

"The word I'd use in describing Mel's attitude toward Richard is 'disappointed.' Richard was the prodigal son, but unlike the one in the Bible, Richard showed no evidence of mending his hellion ways."

Nick asked, "If Richard had shaped up and returned to his father's arms, would Mel have ordered that the fatted calf be slain in celebration?"

Madeline shrugged. "We'll never know, will we?"

Lerch asked, "What do you think of Richard?"

"I rarely do."

"Give it a try now."

"He's a grown-up spoiled brat."

"Doesn't the fault for Richard turning out that way lie with the father?"

"Richard also has a mother. In Richard's case, like mother, like son."

"Meaning?"

She got off the bed and went to a window. "Richard was closer to Anita than to his father," she said, looking down at the snowy lawn between the hotel and the river. "According to Mel, Anita was always a spendthrift, so it's no wonder that Richard turned into one."

"If Richard was so much like his mother," said Nick, "why was he living with Mel?"

"Really, Nick," she said, facing him. "Mel was the one with the money. And after the divorce, Anita decided to live in Boston. She's Beacon Hill. Richard's a New Yorker. His heart is in Sutton Place. He inherits it and everything else, you know."

"I don't know," said Lerch. "How is it that you do?"

She settled into a chair. "I told you that there's little about Mel's life which he did not share with me."

"In addition to Richard and Rob Devonshire," said Lerch, "is there anyone who comes to your mind as a likely suspect in Chandler's death?"

"There's a man who was suing him and the magazine for slander. Steve something."

"Steve Yedenok," said Nick. "Yet Mel also put him on the guest list."

"As I said, salt in the wounds."

"Getting back to you, Miss Lewis," said Lerch impatiently. "When was the last time you saw Mr. Chandler?"

"I believe it was about an hour before I left for Farley's."

"When did you leave?"

"About six-thirty."

"So that last time you saw Chandler would have been around—"

"It was around five-thirty. I was in his suite going over the plan for the cigar night event. He was looking forward to making a grand entrance, so he wasn't going to leave the hotel until half past seven. As you know, the time for the party on the invitations was seven o'clock. He wanted to allow for late arrivals. He thought that if he got there around a quarter to eight, everybody would be there."

"As I recall," said Nick, "Ben showed up in the cigar room ahead of you."

"Because of the snow, I stopped for a few minutes in the ladies' room to have a look at myself in a mirror. I wanted to make sure I was presentable. Vanity, thy name is woman."

Nick said, "Ben told me you were delayed because you were settling the bill."

"And so I'd intended. But after I'd checked myself out in the ladies' room mirror, I went to the office to see the restaurant manager and found he wasn't there at the moment. I was told he was in the downstairs dining room, checking to see how many customers had dared the storm by going out to dinner. Because of what happened, I never did see him. I'll pay it sometime today on my way to the airport to return to New York. When will I be allowed to do so, Lieutenant?"

"Not quite yet, Miss Lewis."

She shot out of the chair. "Why the hell not?"

"First of all, Logan Airport is still closed. Second, you're not leaving town until I tell you that you can go."

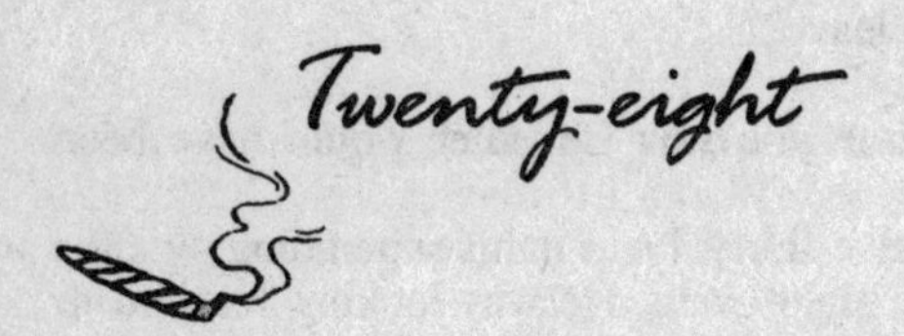

Twenty-eight

STANDING BY THE ELEVATORS, Lerch said to Nick, "Have you noticed and docs it seem strange to you that neither Lewis nor Salter seems particularly upset or surprised by the fact that their boss has been murdered?"

"People react to sudden death in different ways. Neither of them strikes me as being the type to don sackcloth and ashes and wail like banshees over a grave. Besides, as you noted, Mel was their boss. As to not being surprised that Chandler was murdered, neither am I. Having read his book, I'm kind of amazed someone didn't bump him off long ago."

"Maybe it was a spur-of-the-moment thing."

Nick shrugged. "Possibly."

Lerch sighed. "Oh geez, there you go again."

"Here I go again doing what?"

"I've known you a long time, Nick, and I've come to learn that when I ask you about an aspect of a murder and you say 'possibly,' you're thinking, 'Not a chance.' Let me have it."

"The murder could have happened on the spur of the moment, but such killings usually involve a weapon of opportunity. A whack on the head with the nearest heavy object. A quick thrust of a knife that's lying around. If a gun happens to be handy, it's a shooting. Slipping nitroglycerine pills into a glass of cognac doesn't strike me as an impulsive, heat-of-the-moment act. Chandler's killer had to know about his heart problem and what the effect would be of mixing alcohol and nitroglycerine. That necessarily narrows the field in terms of suspects. And it certainly rules out the Devonshire kid."

"I'm not quite ready to strike his name from the list," Lerch replied. "He told me that he's taking pre-med courses in hopes of becoming a doctor. He also said he knows little about the heart, but if he'd killed Chandler, you'd expect him to say that. Agreed?"

"Agreed."

"There were two brandy glasses sitting on that bureau. That means Chandler expected to have a guest."

"Not necessarily."

"I'm listening."

"I'm assuming that Chandler did not bring a bottle of cognac with him. If he ordered the bottle through room service, it would have been delivered with a pair of brandy glasses."

"But you can't say for sure that Chandler didn't order the cognac because he was expecting to share it with a guest."

"No I can't."

"We know that Chandler invited Devonshire to the suite for a talk, so the kid could have seen the nitro pills and dropped a few into Chandler's cognac."

Nick smiled. "No he couldn't."

"Why not?"

"The bottle of nitro pills was in Chandler's pocket."

"Devonshire put it there."

"Why?"

"For the same reason he set the bed on fire, in order to conceal the fact that Chandler had been murdered."

"It doesn't wash, Jack. In your scenario, Rob Devonshire would have to have known that Chandler had heart problems. *And* that he had been prescribed nitrates. Because Chandler was the owner of a magazine in which editorials scoffed at the contention of the health police that cigar smoking is unhealthy, very few people knew that Chandler had undergone bypass surgery and was taking medications for coronary artery disease. The people who knew were a very small group. The circle narrows even more in light of the fact that his killer had to have knowledge of Chandler's coronary artery problems, be aware that he was being treated with nitrates, know that a combination of nitrates in the blood with alcohol and nitroglycerine would be fatal, *and* be in this hotel last evening."

"That's four people," said Goldstein. "Lewis, Salter, Selden, and Yedenok. It's five if you include the son. As Salter suggested, Richard Chandler could have been here when he made that phone call that Salter overheard. The only others on the party's guest list staying here are Selden and Yedenok. What do you suppose is the likelihood that one or both knew about Chandler's heart trouble?"

"There's only way to find out," said Lerch. "What floors are their rooms on?"

"Selden's on seven, Yedenok on eleven."

"Since seven's my lucky number," said Lerch, pressing the call button, "we'll start with Selden. Maybe my luck will hold and he'll save us all a lot of time and trouble by confessing."

Looking at the floor indicator above the elevator door and watching an arrow indicator moving upward, Nick asked, "What do you see as Selden's motive, Jack?"

"Chandler canned him."

"That happened quite some time ago."

"Selden probably figured that if he killed Chandler right away," Lerch said as the elevator arrived and the door slid open, "he'd be a prime suspect, so he decided to bide his time."

Nick smiled. "That is certainly a possibility."

Lerch pressed the button for the seventh floor.

"Go ahead, Nick. Knock the possibility down."

"I was just thinking that if Selden waited so as to not be considered a prime suspect, he picked a time and place to kill Chandler that guaranteed the finger of suspicion would point in his direction."

"That's why Selden set up the scene after the murder to make it look as if Chandler died while he was smoking in bed. He might have gotten away with it if the maid hadn't shown up to put out the fire."

The elevator stopped at the seventh floor.

"If she hadn't doused the flames," Lerch continued as they stepped into the corridor, "a sharp-eyed guy named Nick Chase wouldn't have observed that Chandler couldn't have been smoking in bed. We'd all be at home and in bed. Instead, we're going around this hotel knocking on doors."

Twenty-nine

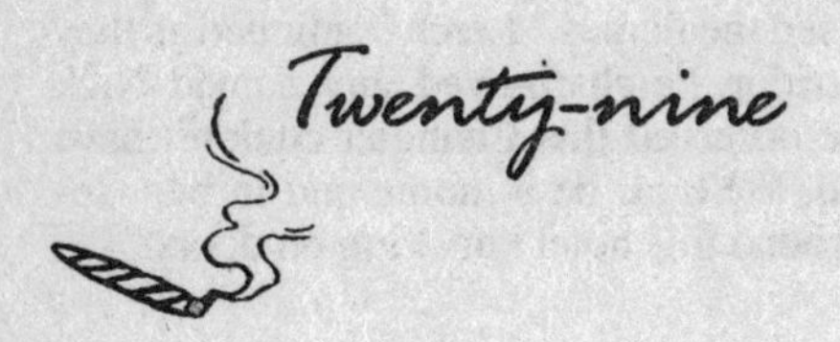

WHEN DAVE SELDEN opened his door, he greeted the men in the corridor with a look of surprise. "Lieutenant Lerch! Nick!"

"We need to talk to you, Mr. Selden," said Lerch.

"Is this why the hotel won't let me check out? Why am I being kept here?"

"You're being detained," said Lerch, "because I'm conducting an investigation of the death of Melvin Chandler."

"What's to investigate? I thought Mel's heart condition caught up with him."

"You were aware of his ticker problem?"

"Of course I knew. I drove him to the hospital for his bypass surgery. For a few years, until Ben Salter came on board, I saw to it that Mel took his medications." As if a light had been turned on in his head, his expression of surprise changed to one of sudden realization. "Ah ha! That's why everyone had to give their names and addresses at the party at Farley's! Mel didn't die of a heart attack!"

"That's right," said Lerch, entering the room and noticing Selden's packed suitcases. "He was murdered."

"Murdered. Holy cow," said Selden.

As he moved to the center of the room, he smiled.

"I can't believe that somebody finally got up the nerve to

actually put an end to the long reign of His Highness King Melvin. I'm . . . flabbergasted."

"We're hoping you can be of assistance in the investigation," said Lerch.

"I'll try, but I fail to see how I can be of help."

"Suppose you start by explaining why you believe Chandler's *end* was deserved."

The smile froze.

"If you think I meant Mel deserved to be *murdered,* you misunderstood."

"Really? It sounded pretty straightforward to me."

"What I meant was that because of the flamboyant Melvin Chandler style, when it came time for him to depart this mortal coil, he deserved an end in keeping with the way he'd lived. He said he wanted to go out in a flurry of headlines. He said it would be a perfect ending if he were found dead in mysterious circumstances."

"Did he really?"

"I'm not making this up, Lieutenant. Mel was always telling me that when he kicked the bucket—his phrase exactly—he hoped to go out like President Kennedy. He said that J F K being assassinated was the best thing that could have happened to him because Kennedy was at a peak of popularity that could only diminish. Mel thought that if Kennedy had lived, his image would inevitably have been tarnished. By being killed in his prime, J F K secured himself an honored place in history. Mel was right."

"You also said that you couldn't believe someone actually got up the nerve to put an end to the long reign of His Highness King Melvin."

"I suppose that phrasing does require some explaining."

"I think so."

"That's what Mel's son calls him. Not to Mel's face, of course. Take my word on this, Lieutenant, Richard did not bestow that title on his father out of respect."

"How did he mean it?"

"Richard saw himself as the Prince waiting in the wings, eager to grab the crown from the fallen monarch's head. The relationship was straight out of Will Shakespeare. Richard could hardly wait to hear the eulogies, 'Let us sit upon the ground and tell sad stories of the death of kings,' as the Bard of Avon wrote about another royal Richard."

"I can't help but notice that you're not exactly weeping over the fact that Chandler was murdered. You haven't even asked how."

Selden shrugged. "Why should it matter to me how he was killed?"

Nick said, "It seems to me that since you've been writing a book about Chandler, you'd be especially interested. Perhaps grateful."

"Grateful?"

"Sure. Now your book will have a juicy ending."

"For the record, how *was* he murdered? Shot? Stabbed? Strangled?"

"He was poisoned."

"There's a clue for you, Lieutenant Lerch," said Selden. "I understand that poison is the traditional woman's murder weapon."

"It's also had an appeal to men."

"Have you looked into the whereabouts at the time of the murder of his ex-wife? Anita lives in Boston. Beacon Hill. If anyone had a motive to kill Mel, it's her."

"That reason being what?"

"Anita has always been convinced that Mel pulled a fast one in the divorce settlement by concealing assets."

"At the moment, Mr. Selden," said Lerch, "I'm more interested in your motive."

Selden laughed. "Mine? I had none."

"Try this one on for size. After giving years of your life to editing his magazine, Chandler gave you the heave-ho."

"Why would I kill Mel when he was about to come crawling to me on his knees, begging me to save *Cigar Smoker* by taking back my job?"

Nick asked, "To save the magazine? Why, was it in trouble?"

"You're in the cigar-selling business, Nick. Surely you've noticed that the cigar boom is petering out! You need no more evidence than to look at the granddaddy of the cigar magazines, *Cigar Aficionado*. The masthead has been altered so that *Cigar* is now in very small letters. The emphasis is on the magazine being for all kinds of *aficionados*. Because of the shift in attention being given to cigars these days, sales of Mel's magazine have been declining. I tried to get Mel to see that changes like those in *Cigar Aficionado* were needed. Ben Salter agreed with me. I tried to convince Mel that the book needs a fresh slant. But he wouldn't hear of it. He and I had some knock-down-drag-'em-out battles over it. Finally, he got fed up, handed me my head, and ordered Salter to call the lawyers and have them draw up my walking papers. It was a very generous payoff, so don't think I killed Mel because he robbed me in the way he cheated Anita."

"Why do you believe Mel had a sudden change of heart and was ready to ask you back?"

"I wouldn't say it was my belief. I was hoping."

"What do you suppose will happen to the magazine now that Mel's dead?"

"I assume that Richard will take over. Whether he'll choose to keep it going, or sell it, I have no idea."

"If Richard asked your advice, what would you tell him?"

"With the right changes in direction, and eventually a new name, the magazine has a good chance of continuing."

"Should Richard want to hire you to run the magazine, would you accept?"

"Absolutely."

"This is all very fascinating," said Lerch, "but what I want to know, Mr. Selden, is where you were between half-past six and seven o'clock last evening."

"If that's when Mel was killed, Lieutenant," Selden replied, "you can exclude me. I'd left for Farley's by then."

"Can anyone verify that?"

Selden moved abruptly from where he had been standing in the center of the room and leaned against a tall cabinet containing a television set.

"As a matter of fact, yes," he replied to Lerch. "You can ask Steve Yedenok. When the elevator came down to my floor, he was on it. We shared a cab. Steve's room is on eleven."

"We know where to find him, thanks."

Selden thought a moment.

"Wait a minute! I just remembered something. While I was waiting for the elevator, I watched the arrow that shows what floor it's on. I didn't make anything of it at the time, but the elevator started at the top floor and came straight down to seven. The top floor is where Mel was staying, in the Kennedy suite."

"We're also aware of that."

"Don't you see, Lieutenant? Since the elevator didn't stop till it got to seven, and Steve Yedenok's room is on eleven, Steve must have gotten on the elevator at the penthouse level."

Nick asked, "Are you sure the elevator didn't stop on eleven?"

"I was watching the arrow. My eyes never left it."

Lerch asked, "How is that you know Steve Yedenok?"

"Steve's a freelance writer. As managing editor of *Cigar Smoker,* I bought a lot of his submissions. I even asked him to do a few pieces."

"If Yedenok was a regular contributor," said Nick, "why was he suing Chandler?"

"In the past couple of years Steve was not as reliable as he'd been. His work was sloppy and often late coming in. Unfortunately, Steve had a problem with booze that was getting worse and worse. Mel finally decided he'd had enough and banned him from the magazine. Steve heard that Mel was also bad-mouthing him to the trade as a hopeless drunk. When Steve couldn't get anyone to take his stuff, he blamed Mel. Then he let some shyster lawyer sue Mel and the magazine for defamation."

"Yet Yedenok was invited to come to the party."

"Steve told me that he expected Mel to talk with him about settling the suit. Judging by the smell of liquor on Steve's breath in the elevator, I think it would have been in Steve's best interests to do so. He could never have won his case in court. The defense against a libel charge is truth. For

Mel's lawyers, proving Steve's a drunk would have been as easy as shooting the proverbial fish in the barrel."

"In your opinion, based on knowing Yedenok," said Lerch, "if he was on that elevator because he and Chandler had a meeting up there on the penthouse floor, and the meeting didn't go the way Yedenok had hoped, might he have settled his grievance against Chandler another way?"

"If you're asking whether Steve is capable of murder, I couldn't say. I suppose anyone can be driven to murder. *However,* I hasten to add that I was not in such a state of mind last evening. I repeat, in case you didn't get it the first time around, I did *not* murder Mel Chandler."

Nick asked, "How did Yedenok seem to you on the elevator?"

"He was as surprised to find me getting on it as I was to see him."

"Could you tell if he'd been drinking?"

"With the very first word from his mouth."

"The odor was that strong, eh?"

"Powerful!"

"You're a man of experience regarding drinks. What do you think he'd been quaffing?"

"One of the brown spirits. Bourbon, probably."

"Brandy?"

"Possibly. But I wouldn't say he'd had enough to be drunk."

"Did he appear excited?"

"Not at all. Judging by the liquor smell, I'd say he was probably feeling fairly mellow."

Lerch gave a quick nod. "Thanks for your time, Mr. Selden."

"Does that mean I'm free to get the hell out of this burg?"

Nick smiled and gave Selden a squeeze of the shoulder. "If I were you, Dave, I wouldn't let a Harvard man hear you call Cambridge a *burg.*"

Selden chuckled. "Don't be concerned about me, Nick. I'm perfectly capable of defending myself against Harvard men. I got plenty of experience handling them four at a time on the ice hockey rink when I was a goalie for Princeton."

"You can leave this burg," said Lerch with a grumpy tone and look as he walked to the door, "when I tell you that you may."

"Am I a suspect?"

"Should you be?"

"I assure you that I'm as interested in your finding Mel's killer as you are, Lieutenant."

Outside Selden's room, Lerch said, "Very well, gentlemen, what shall we make of Mr. David Selden? Credible or not?"

Goldstein answered, "He's a very cool cucumber."

"Selden is right about one thing," Nick replied. "There has been a downturn in the cigar market. A lot of entrepreneurs who jumped onto the 'cigars are back' bandwagon just a few years ago by opening cigar bars and launching magazines are seeing the boom deflating. I don't get nearly as many of the Johnny-come-latelies these days. Of course, the old timers who have been the basis of my business are holding fast."

"Thanks for the sociological and economic analysis of the tobacco trade," Lerch retorted, "but I want to know if you think Selden is credible in terms of this murder case."

"In other words, do I think he did it?"

"Not to put too fine a point on it," said Lerch, striding toward the elevators, "yes."

"He's certainly in a far better position professionally now than when Chandler was alive. With Mel dead and Richard inheriting the magazine, Selden is likely to be brought back to run it. From what I've heard about Richard Chandler, I'd venture the opinion that he's not going to be as interested in the day-to-day operations as his father was. Selden will have pretty much a free hand. As long as *Cigar Smoker*'s bottom line stays in the black."

"Your answer to my question, then, is—"

"He had motive. He had opportunity. He's familiar with Chandler's medications and so would know about contraindications. As the managing editor of a magazine that constantly runs articles on the subject of liquor, he knows about spirits. Therefore, it's possible that Selden is the one who put nitroglycerine in a drink that would mask its taste. On the other hand—"

"Okay, on the other hand he didn't do it because—"

"If Selden's motive was to take revenge for being fired, why, as Selden himself asked, would he kill Chandler when Mel was prepared to kiss and make up and give him back his job?"

"*Assuming* that was Chandler's intent," said Lerch as he pressed the elevator call button, "which we'll never know."

"YEDENOK'S ROOM IS to the left," said Goldstein as he preceded Lerch and Nick from the elevator. "Number eleven-fifteen."

Finding the door open, they entered and found a maid tearing apart the bed. Beside it on a table stood an empty bourbon bottle and a tall glass. A small room service table was littered with a breakfast that appeared to have been barely touched. A coffee-cup saucer from the service was on the bedside table, full of cigarette butts.

Unfurling a fresh sheet, the maid studied the men coming into the room and asked, "Are you gentlemen from the poh-leece?"

Startled, Lerch said, "What makes you think we're the police?"

"Mister, I been workin' in hotels long enough to spot a cop. The man told me that if the poh-leece came lookin' for him, to tell 'em he'd be waitin' down in the bar."

"The bar is open at this hour of the morning?"

"On account of so many people were stranded by the snow, it stayed open all night."

Lerch turned to leave. "Thank you."

"When you talk to him," said the maid, "tell him there's no smokin' allowed in rooms unless you're in one that designates smokin' is permitted, which this one ain't."

Nick followed Lerch from the room and chuckled as he said, "Jack, if you were from the smoke police, I'd say you've got plenty of circumstantial evidence to slap a pair of cuffs on Yedenok for smoking in a no-smoking room. Of course, that's not a capital crime like murder. But who knows? Someday it probably will be."

"I find the cigarettes interesting," Lerch replied as they walked to the elevators. "You'd think a guy who wrote articles for a cigar magazine would smoke stogies."

"Maybe he didn't have any," ventured Goldstein, pressing the Down call button.

"I enjoy a cigar now and then," said Lerch, "and if I was a guest at a party like the one last night where there were boxes of them free for the taking, I would have stuffed my pockets."

"You therefore deduce," said Nick, "that Yedenok did not do so."

"I do indeed."

"The conclusion you draw from this," said Nick as the elevator arrived, "is that if Steve Yedenok is not a cigar smoker, he might not know that to light one up you have to clip the end. Therefore, he could have planted the untrimmed cigar that we found clutched in Mel Chandler's cold, dead hand."

Lerch entered the elevator. "The possibility crossed my mind."

"There is a way to find out if Yedenok is an *aficionado,*" Nick said, patting his left side. "If Yedenok is, in fact, waiting for us in the bar, at some point I'll take my trusty pocket cigar case from my pocket and offer him one."

"That's good, Nick," said Goldstein, "but maybe he won't take it."

"If he's a cigar man, he will. To my knowledge, Sid, no cigar smoker in history has ever turned down the offer of a free one. If Yedenok declines, odds are that he doesn't smoke them, lending credence to his having killed Chandler. If he accepts the offer, the odds turn against his being the murderer. This conclusion is based on the uncut cigar."

Leaving the elevator at the lobby, they found it still crowded with the stranded.

Lerch asked, "Nick, have you considered the possibility that the killer didn't bother to trim the cigar because he expected it to be destroyed in the fire?"

"I have. That could well have happened," Nick said, as they walked toward the Plimouth Lounge. "But for a cigar smoker, the act of trimming one is an ingrained habit. Smoking a cigar is ritualistic. If it's wrapped in cellophane, you unwrap it. You give it a gentle squeeze to judge freshness. If you're a band-offie, you remove the band. You put the cigar under your nose and sniff the delightful aroma. Most men will put the end in the mouth to moisten it. And then you take out your clipper and trim it."

"What if you don't have a clipper?"

"Sidney, a cigar smoker without a clipper in his pocket is as unlikely a creature as a cop walking his beat without a book of parking tickets."

"I guess you could just bite off the end."

"Uncouth, Detective Goldstein. Terribly uncouth. Uncivilized in the extreme."

Standing in the entrance to the lounge and surveying several customers seated in booths and along the bar, Lerch asked, "Nick, do you happen to know what Yedenok looks like?"

"As a matter of fact, he was pointed out to me at the party. He's the thin guy with a glass of bourbon at the far end of the bar."

Lerch walked quickly to him.

Gazing at the reflections of the three men in a mirror behind a display of liquor bottles, Yedenok gulped the last of the whiskey and said, "I was wondering when you guys were going to show up this morning."

"Why was that?"

Yedenok signaled the bartender for a refill. "The kid from room service who brought my breakfast told me a man was murdered in one of the penthouse suites last night. He didn't know who, but I had no doubt that it was Mel Chandler. Or that I'd be questioned about it."

"Why did you expect to be questioned?"

"I figured that someone would tell you that Mel Chandler

and I were on the outs and that I was suing him for slander."

The bartender stepped forward and refilled the glass.

Nick seized the moment to draw the case from his inside pocket. "Are you a cigar man, Mr. Yedenok?"

"Thanks," he replied, taking one. "I've been dying for one all morning. I smoked all I had when I was drinking late last night. I asked for some from room service this morning when I ordered breakfast, but all they had was cigarettes. The funny thing is, there were hundreds, maybe thousands of them at the party at Farley's last night, but what with police taking names and addresses, I stupidly left without taking some."

As Goldstein watched intently, Yedenok went through the cigar ritual Nick had described.

After removing the band from the cigar and wetting the tip, Yedenok patted his pockets, frowned, and asked Nick, "May I use your cutter?"

Nick took out a gold one with his initials, a Christmas gift from Peg Baron.

"Very nice," said Yedenok admiringly as he took it.

"Thanks."

As Yedenok neatly clipped the cigar, Lerch asked forcefully, "What were you doing up on the penthouse floor last evening, Mr. Yedenok?"

He fumbled in a pocket for a box of matches, found one, and then took his time lighting the cigar. Grabbing the bourbon, he answered, "I'm ashamed to admit that I went up there fully prepared to engage in a pitiful exercise in abject cowardice by groveling at Mel Chandler's feet."

"Explain what you mean, please," said Lerch.

Yedenok drank half the liquor. "I was hoping that Chandler would propose that my suit be settled out of court. I figured that's why he'd invited me to come to Cambridge. I mean, why else would he do that, and also pick up my hotel bill, if he wasn't going to make me an offer?"

"Did he?"

Yedenok drew on the cigar and blew a puff of smoke. "I never saw him."

"How come?"

"I was standing at his door, ready to knock, but I thought I heard someone talking in the suite. I assumed Mel was with someone, or maybe on the phone, so I decided, screw this, I'm not about to give the son of a bitch the satisfaction of beating me. So I got the hell out of there. I was in such a hurry to go into the elevator when it came that I ran smack into somebody getting off. I was surprised as hell."

"Why were you surprised by somebody getting off?"

"Because the person I ran into was a big redheaded kid I'd seen picketing in front of the hotel. They were protesting against smoking. I guess they were some of the people who caused the mélée earlier in the day when Mel was going to autograph books at a cigar store."

"Let me be clear about this," said Lerch. "You went up to the penthouse floor to have a talk with Chandler about settling your lawsuit, but you never went into the suite?"

"Yes. I changed my mind about settling."

"When you were standing at the door, did you notice the smell of something burning?"

Yedenok thought a moment, finished the whiskey, and exclaimed, "I did, as a matter of fact." He looked at the cigar in his hand. "I assumed that it was Mel smoking."

"How well did you know him?"

"Personally?"

"Yes."

"Ours was strictly a business relationship. I wrote articles for his magazine and he bought them and published them."

"I understand he'd banned your stuff from the magazine."

"The bastard did more than that," Yedenok said, wagging a finger toward the bartender. "He got me blacklisted as an unreliable drunkard."

"Not that it's my business," said Lerch as the bartender arrived, "but it seems to me that you might have a problem on that score, Mr. Yedenok."

"You're right, Mr. Detective. It's not your business. Have you any more questions?"

"Not at the moment, but I will require that you stay in Cambridge a while longer."

"If you need me, I'll be sitting right here. Since my lawsuit has probably been rendered moot by this murder, I intend to stay here running up as huge a bar tab as possible, to be paid for by the unlamentably deceased Mel Chandler's accountants."

"I'm not a lawyer," said Nick, "but I'm pretty sure you'll be able to continue your suit against Chandler's estate."

"What's the point in that? I was looking forward to making Chandler eat his words."

Leaving Yedenok and exiting the Plimouth Lounge, Lerch said to Nick, "I find it curious that Devonshire didn't mention to me that he ran into someone when he got off the elevator."

"He was probably so scared after stumbling onto a murder, and then being suspected of committing it, that he forgot about it."

"I'm going to have another talk with him, in case he's also forgotten about seeing other people on that floor. It seems to have been a very busy spot. Devonshire was up there. Salter was in the suite. Now we've learned that Yedenok was lurking around. I wonder who else might have gone looking for Chandler at that time?"

"I'm pretty sure you can eliminate Devonshire as a suspect."

Lerch's eyes narrowed to slits. "How so?"

"Yedenok said that he smelled smoke while he was outside Chandler's door. He then ran into Devonshire as the kid was leaving the elevator."

"That's his story."

"If it's true, Chandler's bed was already on fire," said Nick, "so Rob Devonshire could not have started it."

"But Yedenok could have," said Lerch. "We've got only his word that he changed his mind about going in to see Chandler. He could have killed him and started the fire. But after he bumped into Devonshire, he saw that he might have to explain his presence on that floor, and so he concocted the story about hearing Chandler talking and getting cold feet about seeing him."

"Possibly," said Nick.

"You have to admit, it makes sense."

"Now that you've interviewed everyone connected with Chandler who's staying in this hotel," said Nick, "who's next on your list?"

"The next stop is Beacon Hill," said Lerch, "to pay a call on the grieving son."

"Has Richard been informed that Chandler's death has been confirmed as a murder?"

"Nicky, Nicky, my dear friend," said Lerch, "if you'd landed exactly the same case when you were a murder cop in the Big Apple, would you have immediately told the son who you'd put at the top of your suspect list in his old man's murder?"

Taking the cigar case from his pocket, Nick responded with a sly grin.

WHEN A MAID opened the white door of the house on Beacon Hill, she greeted the three men she found on the stoop with an apprehensive look. "If you're reporters—"

Lerch pulled out a wallet containing his shield. Flashing it, he asserted, "The Cambridge Police Department, homicide squad. My name is Lerch. These two men are my deputies. We're here to see Richard Chandler. Is he in?"

"Yes, but—"

"Tell him we're here."

"Just a moment," she said, closing the door.

A few moments later, Richard Chandler opened it wide. "Come in, gentlemen. We'll talk in the parlor. It's off to the right."

As Nick followed Lerch and Goldstein into a large foyer, Richard greeted him smilingly. "I'm surprised to see you, Nick. But happy to have you here nonetheless."

"Thanks, Richard. I only wish I could say I was happy to be here."

Richard looked at Lerch quizzically. "What is it, Lieutenant?"

"The medical examiner's report is in."

Richard pointed to the parlor doorway. "Please go in."

Entering a large room, the men found Veronica Redding seated beside a lit fireplace.

Looking at her, Lerch said to Richard, "I'd rather we talked alone."

"I want Ronnie here, Lieutenant."

"Very well. The medical examiner's report leaves no doubt your father was murdered."

Veronica gasped and rushed to Richard.

Hugging her, Richard asked, "How was it done?"

"He was poisoned."

"Good Lord. How could that be?"

"I'm not at liberty to tell you that. I can tell you that whoever did it tried to make it look as though he was lying in bed smoking and had a heart attack."

As they were speaking, a woman entered the room and demanded, "What's going on?"

"Mother," Richard exclaimed, "this is Lieutenant Lerch of the police."

"Mrs. Chandler," said Lerch. "I was informed you were in Miami Beach."

"There was a fortuitous change of plans, Lieutenant."

Lerch gave her an incredulous look. *"Fortuitous?"*

"In view of what's happened, had I stayed in Miami, I'd have had to pack up immediately and return to Boston to be with Richard. Are you arresting him?"

"What makes you think I'm here to arrest your son?"

"Didn't I just hear you say that his father was murdered?"

"Yes, but that doesn't explain why you assume I'm going to arrest him."

"As Mel Chandler's only child, he's the logical suspect. I told Richard last night to expect the police to regard him as such. That's why my return from Miami Beach was fortuitous."

"May I ask what promoted this fortuitous sudden change in your plans?"

"When I received an invitation to Mel's book-signing and celebration party at Farley's, my impulse was to get as far away as possible. But on the flight down to Florida, I decided that I wanted to attend after all. That change of heart was thwarted when weather delayed my landing at Logan Airport. Upon my return to this house, Richard told me what had happened to my ex-husband. Richard said that because the police had taken names and addresses of people at the party, he did not believe the theory being proposed that Mel had had a heart attack. That was a very astute deduction on Richard's part. As soon as he shared it with me, I called my attorney."

Lerch jerked with surprised. "What for?"

"When I expect my son to be suspected of patricide," said Anita as she sat in a chair by the fireplace, "I always call my attorney."

"There's no need for sarcasm, lady."

"Unfortunately, my attorney is snowed in at his ski resort in Vermont, so I found myself limited to conferring with him by telephone. I'm sure I needn't tell you what he advised."

"Hardly."

"You'll understand, therefore," she said, reaching for a silver cigarette box on a table by the chair, "that I must insist that you reserve your questioning of my son until such time as my attorney can be present to counsel him and protect his constitutional rights."

Lerch turned abruptly to Richard. "Is this woman speaking for you? Are you refusing to cooperate with my investigation into your *father's murder?*"

"First of all, Lieutenant, I resent you referring to my mother as *this woman*. Second, I don't need a lawyer to tell me that it would be stupid of me to answer your questions when it's obvious you regard me as a suspect."

"When did I say you're a suspect?"

"You mean I'm not? I don't know whether to feel relieved or insulted."

"There's no call for lip from you either, young man. If your lawyer were here and not stuck in the snow in Vermont, he'd tell you that by taking that smart-ass attitude you're tempting me to take you into custody as a material witness. It's up to you, fella. You can cooperate with me now, or you can accompany Detective Goldstein to police headquarters. In handcuffs. And wouldn't that make a nice video clip for the evening newscasts and on the front pages of tomorrow's papers?"

"I understand why you might think of me as your prime suspect in my father's murder, Lieutenant Lerch, but I swear to you that I did not kill him."

Anita slammed down the cigarette box and bolted out of the chair. "Richard, shut up."

Lerch glared at her. "Mrs. Chandler, you either keep your trap shut, or I'll order Detective Goldstein to remove you from the room."

"In my own house?"

"It's either I talk to your son here and you stay out of it, or he goes to headquarters and remains there until your lawyer digs himself out of Vermont and shows up with a writ."

"If you're planning to charge my son with murder, do it now so he can invoke his right to remain silent."

"He's had that right since I walked in the door. But if it's true, as he insists, that he didn't kill Chandler, what's the problem in him talking to me? When he spoke with me last evening at Farley's, he volunteered that if his father had been murdered and I was looking for suspects, he could think of several candidates."

Anita chuckled. "Only several, Richard?"

"Since you now find all this amusing, Mrs. Chandler, I'd like to know where you were at half-past six last evening."

"I was in a taxi. I was fortunate in having secured one to bring me from the airport."

"Can you provide a way for me to verify that? The cab registration number, for instance?"

"Who takes notice of taxi registration numbers?"

"Is there someone who can vouch that you were fortunate in finding a taxi?"

"As a matter of fact, there is. I shared the cab with a charming man who happens to be in the cigar business. He'd come up from Florida because Mel had invited him to the party. It was quite a bizarre coincidence."

"What's the man's name?"

"I never thought to ask. However, he said he was staying at the Palmer House. Someone at the hotel should be able to help you by checking the registry."

"Did he drop you off here, or did you leave the cab at the hotel?"

"He was kind enough to bring me to my door."

"At what time?"

"I didn't look at my watch. He may be able to tell you."

"So you don't know where you were at half past six."

"I know that I was not murdering my former husband. Why on earth should I?"

"I have reason to believe you feel you were cheated in your divorce settlement."

"Whoever caused you to adopt such a belief was correct, except that it's not a feeling that Mel cheated me. I know he did. He continues to do so. But I assure you I did not seek to redress my grievance by killing Mel. That's why I have lawyers. Not to kill him, of course. You know what I mean."

"May I assume that because your son inherits the Chandler fortune, you'll have no need of lawyers to collect what you feel you've been cheated out of?"

"Assume what you wish, Lieutenant. But do not assume because Richard stands to be a major beneficiary of Mel's last will and testament that he resorted to murder to collect it. As he told you, in the category of who had a reason to kill Mel Chandler there are many. I suggest you get a printout of his computer address book. Mel had an amazing genius for turning people against him, both in business and personally. There was a standing joke about him. In it he'd ask Ben Salter, 'Why does everybody take an immediate dislike to me?' Ben would answer, 'It saves time.' "

"At the moment I'm concentrating on people who were invited to the party."

"By starting with my son."

"Actually, I talked to four people before I came over to Beacon Hill."

"It's getting on to lunchtime. My cook has prepared a very nice meal. She makes a magnificent soufflé. I'd invite you to join us, but there's only enough for three."

"There's one more matter on my mind, if I may."

"What is it?"

"It concerns the body."

Richard blurted, "What about it?"

"It's just that none of you has asked about when the coroner will release it. I thought you'd want to know that he has. You may now go ahead and make arrangements for the funeral. But until the direction of my investigation becomes clearer I must require that you not leave Boston, Mr. Chandler."

"Am I a suspect?"

"Let's just say that because of your familiarity with your father's business affairs, I consider you vital to the investigation and a potentially important and helpful witness."

"I'm ready to do whatever you require, Lieutenant. There's no need for me to rush back to New York City. As to arranging the funeral, my father long ago wrote out instructions that he wished to be interred in a memorial vault he had built on the grounds of a small house he owns in Vermont. It contains the remains of his second wife and their son, Donny. At some point, I suppose, there'll be a memorial service for Father in New York."

"I appreciate your cooperation, Mr. Chandler," said Lerch. Leaving the parlor, he glared at Anita. "Enjoy your soufflé."

"Goodbye, Lieutenant."

Pausing in the doorway, he said, "There is one more question, Mr. Chandler. It nearly slipped my mind. It has to do with your phone conversation with your father."

"What phone conversation?"

"I was informed that you had one with him last evening. I was just wondering what the two of you were arguing about."

With a nervous glance at Veronica, Richard replied, "Whoever told you that I had an argument with my father was mistaken. The last time I spoke to him was . . . over a week ago. It was the day before I left New York for the cottage on the Cape."

Lerch smiled. "I see. Apparently I misunderstood."

As the maid closed the white door of the Chandler house behind the departing trio, Nick buttoned his coat to the neck and said, "Very well done, Jack. That was quite a nifty Columbo you pulled in there."

Lerch pulled up the fur collar of his car coat. "I pulled quite a *what?"*

Goldstein put on gloves as he answered, "Nick's referring to the old cop show on TV."

"Ah, yes," said Lerch as they descended snow-cleared steps. "The one starring Peter Falk where the audience knew who the killer was because the show started by showing the murder being committed."

"Every time Lieutenant Columbo was on his way out of a room after he'd questioned the murderer," Goldstein continued, as they walked single-file on a narrow path between heaps of shoveled snow, "he would stop and say, 'There's one thing that's been bothering me.' "

"I was afraid you'd forgotten about the phone call," said Nick as they approached Lerch's vehicle, "but I see now that you were holding off to hit Richard with it when he thought you were done questioning him. It worked. The kid was really rattled."

"Something about young Chandler is not copacetic," said Lerch, stepping over a pile of snow to go around to the driver's side of the vehicle. "What do you think, Nick? Is he our man?"

"Richard is certainly a leading contender."

As the men got into the vehicle, Lerch asked, "What about Mother Dearest?"

"Of all the stories we've heard about who was where at the time of the murder, hers is the easiest to confirm, or not confirm, as the case may be. If it turns out that she was sharing a cab from Logan Airport at six o'clock, there's no way she could be at the Mayflower at half-past."

"Maybe she and Darling Son are in this together."

"Possibly."

Lerch groaned.

"If they *were* in it together, I think Mother Dearest would have given Darling Son an alibi by telling you that when she was dropped off at her house by the taxi, she found Richard there. Since she didn't, it's clear that he wasn't. If there was a conspiracy, they would have coordinated their stories. As it stands, Richard's alibi is Veronica Redding."

"With an inherited fortune at stake," said Goldstein as Lerch started the engine, "he lies and Veronica swears to it."

"This guy Appleton," said Lerch. "He lives where, Sid?"

"Commonwealth Avenue, near Exeter Street."

The plows had done their work. But in clearing Commonwealth Avenue for traffic they had pushed snow aside to trap and even entomb parked cars. This forced Lerch to leave his vehicle blocking one of the lanes of the northbound side of the broad, divided old boulevard. To reach Charles Appleton's address, the men had to climb over a three-foot ridge of plowed snow, wade through half a foot of unshoveled snow on the sidewalk in front of the house, and ascend seven uncleared steps. Finding the door unlocked, they entered a small vestibule.

Examining names on mail boxes, Goldstein read aloud, "Appleton, Charles. Top floor." He pressed an intercom button. It went unanswered again and again.

Lerch asked, "Do you have his phone number on you?"

Goldstein plunged a hand into a pocket and drew out a small notebook. He then took out a cell phone. Appleton's phone also went unanswered.

"Damn," grumbled Lerch. "Stick a note in the mailbox telling Mr. Appleton to phone our office the minute he gets back."

Thirty-two

WHEN LERCH'S VEHICLE turned onto Brattle Street, Nick looked toward his store. On the cleared sidewalk, Professor Woolley was bundled up like an Eskimo as he observed four men in denim jackets and blue jeans defying the cold and installing a new window.

Bounding from the vehicle, Nick exclaimed, "What's all this?"

"Since you weren't around this morning," said Woolley, "I took it upon myself to have your glass replaced."

Lerch and Goldstein appeared on the sidewalk.

"Good day, gentlemen," said Woolley. "How is the investigation into the murder of Melvin Chandler progressing?"

The four men paused and looked hard at Woolley.

"It's nothing to concern you, fellas," he replied with an admonishing gaze.

"Not nearly as well as this window job appears to be going," Lerch replied as the men returned to work. "How did you find somebody willing to come out to replace glass on the day after a snowstorm?"

"A former student of mine owns a glazier company with branches up and down New England. Although he earned a divinity degree, he discerned after a hurricane that a better means of earning a living that would also help God's creatures was to go into the window replacement trade. I daresay that if I had asked him to send a team of young men out to replace a window *during* a snowstorm, they would have raced to my rescue even if it meant employing a team of huskies and a dog sled."

Woolley assessed the progress of the men's work.

"With matters well in hand here, Nick," he said, "I insist that you and these stalwarts of the homicide squad come up to my apartment, where I shall provide soup to warm you and some sandwiches to fortify you while you fill me in on the case."

"Then we can all have a smoke," said Nick, "while Woolley tells us who did it and why."

"Motive," Woolley muttered as they left the glaziers to their work. "Motive is the key."

"It generally is," Lerch replied, "and we've got motives up the wazoo."

"I'm not referring to the motives of suspects, Jack," said Woolley, holding open the door to the stairs to the apartments above Nick's store. "I'm interested in Chandler's motive in asking enemies to his party. It's as if he was inviting his murder."

"That's a very provocative thought, Professor," said Goldstein.

"It's been provoking me since the moment I learned that Chandler was dead. It kept me awake most of the night. That's when I made the soup. Nothing can stimulate mental faculties more than standing at a stove tackling a challenging soup recipe. In this case I elected to make a pot of vegetable. With bologna sandwiches, it's just the thing for talking murder on a cold and snowy day."

When they entered Woolley's apartment, it was suffused with the aroma of his night's work. A round table in a corner of the large living room held plates, utensils, and four large bowls.

As Woolley went into the kitchen, Lerch said, "It looks as though you were expecting to have company for lunch, Professor. The table's already set."

"When I found Nick was not at home this morning," Woolley replied from the kitchen, "I deduced that he'd gone to meet you and Detective Goldstein and that the three of you would in all likelihood show up here at some point, and that you would be hungry."

He emerged from the kitchen carrying a large pot and long-handled ladle.

"The nice thing about soup," he said, setting the pot in the center of the table, "is that it can be served for lunch or dinner. Help yourselves while I fetch sandwiches from the fridge. There was hardly room for them in it. When I heard the weather forecast of a big snow, I stocked up my larder. Tell, me, gentlemen, is there anything more beautiful than a full refrigerator?"

"Yes indeed," said Nick, scooping soup from pot to bowl. "Two full refrigerators."

Woolley returned with a heaping plate of sandwiches. "Thank you, S. H."

Goldstein asked, "S. H?"

"Sherlock Holmes. In one of the stories Holmes rewarded a helpful lad with a shilling. He asked the boy if he could think of anything better than a shilling. The lad replied—"

"Two shillings?" asked Goldstein.

"In the organization of Sherlock Holmes aficionados which calls itself the Baker Street Irregulars," Nick continued, "when someone is inducted into the organization, he's given what's called an investiture in the name of a character, place, or thing in the stories. The symbol of the investiture is a shilling coin. Woolley's investiture is in the name of Wilson Hargreave, who was a detective with the New York police. If an invested member of the BSI is deemed to have done extraordinary service on behalf of keeping alive the memory of the great detective, he is awarded *two* shillings. Woolley received his three years ago."

"What was your extraordinary service, Professor?" asked Goldstein.

"The reason for the two-shilling award is never explained," Woolley replied. "But Nick believes it's because I've managed to work a mention of Sherlock Holmes into all my books."

"He even inserted Holmes into a scholarly treatise on the subject of the Roman Empire."

"Enough of this dillydallying," said Woolley, taking a chair. "I invited you in for soup so you could bring me up to speed on the Chandler murder. Have you interviewed the obvious chief suspect, the son?"

Lerch slurped a spoonful of soup.

"Pardon me, Jack," said Woolley, "but as Charlie Chan once advised one of his children, 'Soup is not a musical instrument.' "

"It's very hot, Professor."

"I know of a case many years ago in England in which a wife who'd reached the end of her rope concerning her husband's decades of soup-slurping silenced him with a hatchet."

Lerch put down his spoon. "Why do you regard Richard as the obvious chief suspect?"

"First, he inherits a fortune. Fathers have been killed by sons for much less. Second, the woman he was with last evening at Farley's is the sort a man might kill for if she asked him to. I presume they have alibied each other."

"They have."

"I have no doubt that their alibi is such that you have no way of verifying it."

"Right again, Professor."

"Have you interviewed the two men on Chandler's self-described enemies list who were staying at the Mayflower?"

"Dave Selden claims he was in his room at the time of the murder."

"And Yedenok?"

"He admits he went to the penthouse floor at Chandler's invitation," said Nick, "but he says he changed his mind about seeing Chandler."

"Did he explain why?"

"He just said that he left without seeing him."

"Yedenok says when he was getting on the elevator," Lerch continued, "he ran into Rob Devonshire getting off. But Devonshire made no mention of meeting anyone. He said only that when he got to Chandler's door, he smelled smoke. When he looked into the bedroom, he saw the fire and discovered that Chandler was dead."

"If Devonshire has told the truth, it doesn't look good for Yedenok," said Woolley. "On the other hand, if Devonshire killed Chandler and concocted the story he told you about finding Chandler dead, it stands to reason he'd omit the part about being seen by a man at the elevator."

"We know from David Selden that Yedenok was on the penthouse floor," said Lerch, "because Selden met Yedenok on the elevator when it stopped on the seventh floor."

"You said that Yedenok told you he heard Chandler talking to someone in the room?"

"He probably did," said Nick, "but what Yedenok could have heard was Chandler talking on the telephone."

"Benjamin Salter told us that Chandler had put in a call to his lawyer," Lerch continued, "and had been waiting for the call to be returned when Salter left him about an hour earlier."

"The interesting thing about Chandler's call to his lawyer in New York," said Nick, "is that according to Benjamin Salter, Chandler made it after he had a shouting match on the phone with Richard."

"That's very interesting, indeed," muttered Woolley. "The question is, from where might Richard have placed the call? He could have been in the hotel, made his way to the suite, continued the argument, and—"

"If you're thinking that Chandler wasn't on the phone and it was Richard who Yedenok heard Chandler talking to," Lerch said, ignoring his soup, "I don't see how it could have been."

Woolley let go of his spoon. "Why not?"

"Because a few seconds after Yedenok got on the elevator, Devonshire was at the door of the suite. He smelled smoke. He went in and found Chandler dead. If Richard had been there, the kid would have seen him."

Woolley reclaimed the spoon. "Richard heard the door opening and ducked into a closet. When Devonshire beat a hasty retreat, Richard emerged and fled the suite."

"Impossible. The maid would have seen him coming out."

"Richard escaped when the maid was in the bathroom, wetting towels."

"Speculation, Professor," said Lerch.

"What can any of us do but speculate?"

"Good point, Professor," said Nick, also disregarding soup and sandwiches. "There is another name on Chandler's enemies list we have yet to interview—Charles Appleton. You knew him and Chandler in their Harvard days."

"I remember them vividly."

"Tell us about him," said Lerch.

"When I spoke to him at Farley's last night," said Woolley, "he appeared to be mystified at having been invited. While we chatted about the old days, he seemed to be in another world. Distracted. Staring off into space. I thought he might have been ill, or on drugs. I hadn't seen him in decades. The youth I remembered carousing with Mel Chandler and another member of their club, Kevin Rattigan, was quite an athletic, robust hale-fellow-well-met. Last evening I found myself appalled. He looked awful. Like death warmed over."

Lerch asked, "Do you know what Appleton does for a living?"

"I believe he's on the faculty of Boston University."

"I guess that's why he wasn't there when we went to his apartment to question him," said Goldstein. "He was probably conducting a class."

"That can't be it," said Woolley. "There was an announcement on the radio that morning classes at B.U. were canceled because of the snow."

Goldstein grinned. "Good old snow days!"

Woolley surveyed the bowls and with a pained expression demanded, "What's the matter, fellas? Your soup's getting cold. You don't like it?"

Nick, Lerch, and Goldstein exchanged looks, lifted spoons, scooped soup from their bowls, and in unison slurped loudly.

Thirty-three

WHILE NICK, LERCH, Goldstein, and Woolley finished soup and sandwiches and left the table to settle into chairs to smoke cigars, Kevin Rattigan worried as he walked down Commonwealth Avenue from Kenmore Square as fast as possible on snowy, icy footing.

When he'd spoken to Charlie Appleton on the phone just after midnight, Charlie had blurted out the shocking news that Mel Chandler had not shown up at the party because he'd dropped dead.

"I thought something was wrong when policemen appeared at Farley's," Charlie explained. "According to them, Mel suffered a fatal heart attack in his hotel."

"I suppose that high lifestyle and smoking that he touted in his magazine finally caught up with him. I never liked the guy when we were at Harvard together, but I'm sorry he's dead. Still, it's a shock, considering that you and I are only a year younger than Mel."

"As shocking as his death is, Kev, you're never going to believe what happened before the cops arrived. I suddenly saw why I was invited to the party. It's now perfectly clear what Mel meant when he wrote about 'auld lang syne' on my invitation."

Hearing Charlie breathing harder as the excitement in his

voice increased, Kevin had pleaded, "Take it easy, Charlie, or you'll have a heart attack yourself."

"I'm feeling fine. My heart's still got years of pumping ahead of it."

"Not if you let yourself get worked up like this."

They had agreed to talk further about the extraordinary events at Mel Chandler's party at Farley's over lunch at noon. Considering the snow and that Kevin lived near Boston College, they'd decided that to assure Kevin plenty of travel time, Charlie would provide a wake-up call at ten o'clock. When Kevin awoke on his own at eleven and calls to Charlie were not answered, he recalled Charlie's worrisome state of excitement during the midnight phone call.

There had been three suspected heart episodes in as many years before Charlie had given in to pressure from worried friends and consulted a cardiologist. The result had been immediate hospitalization for angioplasty.

Four years later, the chest pains had recurred and Charlie had been advised to undergo bypass surgery voluntarily, rather than on an emergency basis.

Instead, he'd put it off again and again while dealing with increasingly frequent angina pain by taking nitroglycerine.

Fearing something suddenly had gone awry during the night, possibly a fatal heart attack, Kevin pondered during the seemingly endless journey into Boston how ironic it would be if fate decreed that two men who had been close friends in college and then inexplicably estranged for more than three decades should be looking forward to reuniting at a party, only to be stricken by heart attacks on the very same night.

Arriving at Charlie's apartment house just past noon, Kevin entered the building's foyer and saw a slip of yellow paper protruding from Charlie's mail box. He plucked it out, unfolded it and read:

Mr. Appleton, please contact Lt. John Lerch, Cambridge Police Dept., as soon as poss. 498-9300.

Taking a key ring from a pocket, Kevin unlocked the box and found junk mail and three bills. After climbing four flights of stairs to the top floor, he found the key to Charles's apartment on the ring, slipped it into the lock, gave three quick knocks on the door, and went in.

"Charlie? It's Kev. Are you okay?"

Unanswered, he went to the bedroom and found the door closed.

This was not unusual if Charlie had been to a gay bar the night before, gotten lucky, and come home with a boy. But last night had been Mel Chandler's affair at Farley's.

He knocked hard on the door several times.

"Charlie? May I come in?"

Unanswered, he opened the door a crack and found the room dark.

"Charlie, I'm coming in."

When he switched on a light, he found Charlie on the bed with eyes open and mouth gaping. Tightly encircling his neck was a black cord.

Backing out of the bedroom, Kevin shut the door gently and rushed to the telephone on Charlie's desk to call the police.

AT JUST PAST two in the afternoon, finding the outbound lane of Commonwealth clogged with cars and vans of the Boston Police Department, Lerch parked his vehicle around the corner, on Exeter Street. The chain of events which had brought him, Goldstein, and Nick to Charles Appleton's address had begun with Kevin Rattigan's report of a murder. This resulted in a response by a pair of radio patrol car officers, followed by the arrival twenty minutes later of two homicide investigators. When the senior detective, Lieutenant Thomas Lindlaw, was presented with the note which Rattigan had found stuck in Appleton's mailbox, Lindlaw used his cellular phone to request the Boston Police Department's communications room to locate and connect him with Lieutenant John Lerch of the Cambridge P.D.

Reached at his office and informed of the apparent murder of Appleton, Lerch placed a call to Nick's apartment.

When Lerch, Goldstein, and Nick reached Charles Appleton's top-floor apartment, they were met by a tall, stocky detective with reddish skin attesting to years of imbibing in cop bars. His sparse white hair was a comb-over. The coat of a rumpled double-breasted brown suit that should never be worn by a man with his build was strained by a big beer belly.

"Hello, Jack," said Lindlaw. He held out a hand. In it was

the note that Goldstein had left in the mailbox. "This case has got your name on it, literally."

"Tommy, meet Detective Goldstein," said Lerch, glancing at the note and handing it back, "and say hello to Nick Chase. Nick's retired from the NYPD and is lending me a hand."

Lindlaw winked at Nick. "You couldn't borrow a better one, Jack."

"You two know each other?"

"Thanks to Nick's daughter working in the crime lab," said Lindlaw, "Nick and I bump into one another at Jean's occasional dinner parties. She'll be showing up here at some point, heading up the crime scene unit." He shoved Goldstein's note to Appleton into a pocket. "So, my friend, what is it you wanted to talk to the late Mr. Appleton about?"

"He's a suspect—was a suspect—in the Melvin Chandler murder."

Lindlaw gave a little whistle. "The TV news last night said that it was a heart attack while he was smoking in bed."

"That's what I wanted them to say. What happened here, Tom?"

"There was no indication of a break-in. The body was found by a friend of Appleton, Kevin Rattigan. He has his own key. He says Appleton has been in poor health lately, so Rattigan took it on himself to check up on him, which is his explanation for having the key. I think they're gay. Until you said you were interested in Appleton as a murder suspect, I was inclined to think he and Rattigan had had a falling out. Rattigan says he came here around noon because Appleton was supposed to call about having lunch. He never did."

"How was he killed?"

"Strangled with a lamp cord. It looks as if he was taken by surprise from behind."

"How long has he been dead?"

"The m.e. says it probably happened between one o'clock and seven this morning. Rattigan says Appleton had been to a party in Cambridge. Maybe he picked up some guy."

"It wasn't that kind of party," said Nick. "I was there myself. So were Jack and Detective Goldstein at one point."

Lindlaw rubbed his jaw. "What does all this have to do with Melvin Chandler?"

"It was Chandler's party," said Lerch, "but he never showed up for it, on account of having been murdered."

Nick said, "Appleton's murder poses some interesting questions, Jack. Did he arrive home and find someone waiting? Did somebody he met at Chandler's party come home with him? Might they have agreed to meet here later? Are these two murders actually related?"

"Nick, you believe in coincidences as much as I do. Which is never."

"If these cases are related," said Detective Lindlaw, shaking his head ruefully, "it will be fun watching the struggle between the DAs of Suffolk and Middlesex counties wrestle to get jurisdiction to try the killer."

"Before the trial," said Lerch, "must come the arrest. And to make an arrest, one must have evidence and witnesses. Tommy, when you're done questioning Rattigan, I'd like to have a chat with him to see what light he might shed on the Chandler murder."

"Appleton's body's been removed. I'm done with Rattigan for the moment. You'll find him in the living room. The place is half library, half museum. Appleton appears to have saved everything he ever laid hands on."

When Lerch, Goldstein, and Nick entered, they found a room with shelves stuffed with books, photo albums, scrapbooks, and souvenir knick-knacks; file cabinets; and walls festooned with theatrical and movie posters. Looking disconsolate, Kevin Rattigan sat slumped in a corner of an over-stuffed chair draped with a slipcover of large yellow leaves. A slightly built, middle-aged man with lank yellowish hair that in his youth probably would have been described by a poet as flaxen, he looked at the three intruders with wide, teary cornflower-blue eyes.

"Who are you? I already spoke to someone."

"I'm Jack Lerch, Cambridge police. We're investigating the murder of Mel Chandler."

Rattigan jumped a little. "Mel was murdered?"

"I understand you spoke to Charlie around midnight."

"He called me when he got home from a party. It was in Cambridge at a restaurant by the name of Farley's."

"We know. We were there."

"You were? Oh, yes, I remember. Charlie told me the police came to the party and broke the news that Mel had died. What a shock! I could hardly believe it. Mel was only a year older than Charlie and me. We went to college together. We belonged to the same club."

Nick interjected, "Charlie was president and you were—"

"Vice-president. How did you know, Mr. Chase?"

"I'm a friend of one of your former teachers, Professor Woolley."

Kevin grinned. "What a small world this is. I haven't seen him in years and supposed he was dead. I was surprised when Charlie told me he spoke with Woolley at the party."

"Did Charlie mention whether they talked about an incident involving Mel Chandler and a theft of money from your college club? It's a mystery that's bothered Woolley for thirty years."

"What's the mystery? The money was embezzled by Mel Chandler. He confessed to it at the time and was punished by being kicked out of school."

"In the years since Woolley retired from teaching, he's become quite a successful mystery writer. He can't stand the idea that there's a mystery in his own life in which the loose ends have not been tied up. A loose end in Chandler's theft of club money is why Mel needed it. He must have been awfully desperate, knowing that if he was caught he'd be booted from Harvard."

"That was a long time ago, Mr. Chase. I'd like nothing more than to set Woolley's mind to rest, but in view of what's happened to Charlie, money that was taken back in 1968 seems of little moment."

"What could be of moment, as you put it, Mr. Rattigan," said Nick urgently, "is that two of the men who were involved in the theft of money thirty years ago have wound up murdered on the same night."

Kevin rose to his feet. "If you think that I had anything to do with this, you're wrong. I couldn't have killed Mel Chandler because I wouldn't have known where to find him even if I'd wanted to. Nor did I have any reason to kill him. I haven't seen him since the day he left Cambridge. And why on earth should I kill Charlie? He was the dearest person in my life."

"Would you agree that it's likely that whoever killed Mel Chandler also killed Charlie? Or do you believe their deaths were a coincidence?"

"I guess either one is possible."

"Set aside coincidence and do your best to think about how it might be that Charlie and Mel's murders could be linked."

"All I know is that right out of the blue Charlie received an invitation from Mel to come to a book-signing and a celebration of the book's publication in Cambridge. Charlie showed me the invitation he'd gotten. It was very fancy, printed in gold. Mel had written on the bottom of it that he hoped Charlie would accept the invitation for 'auld lang syne.' Charlie took that to mean that Mel wanted to lay the past to rest."

"To lay what past to rest? Did Charlie *say* what he took that to mean?"

"According to Professor Woolley," Nick said, "Mel Chandler, Charlie Appleton, and you were quite a trio in Harvard Square back in 1968. Did you wonder why Mel didn't invite *you* to lift a cup o' kindness to auld lang syne?"

"Mel was Charlie's friend. I was involved with Mel because Charlie was. Mel put up with me only because he wanted Charlie and me to sponsor him for membership in our club. He also needed Charlie in other ways."

"In what other ways?"

"Back then, Charlie was the guy everyone went to for things."

"Such as what?"

"Charlie was a smooth operator. He knew how to cut the corners. How to obtain stuff like term papers. Marijuana. He knew all the ins and outs of Boston. Charlie was a fixer."

"What did he fix for Mel Chandler that was worth a thousand dollars?"

"That money did not go to Charlie!"

"Who did it go to? Woolley said Chandler was a gambler. Was the grand needed to pay off a big debt? Or was Chandler on the hook to loan sharks?"

"It's true that Mel gambled, but not in great amounts. It was by gambling that he planned to eventually replace the money he took from the club treasury, a little at a time, before the next audit of the club's accounts. He needed a thousand in a lump sum."

"What did he need it for?"

"The money went to a girl."

Goldstein blurted, "A grand, for a call girl? She must have been quite a number."

With a pained expression, Kevin replied, "She wasn't a prostitute. Mel got her knocked up. He gave the money to Charlie to pass on to her. Charlie knew an abortionist in Charlestown."

"In 1968 a thousand bucks was a lot of dough for an abortion on Park Avenue!"

"The abortionist only wanted a couple of hundred. The rest was for the girl to get the hell out of town and not come back."

"That makes more sense," said Nick. "But what I don't understand is why Charlie went along with Mel's taking the thousand from the club's treasury."

"Charlie had no other choice. Mel said that if he didn't go along, all of Harvard would be told that Charlie was a homosexual. You have to understand that Charlie was a star ice hockey player. He got into Harvard on a scholarship from an alumnus. There was no way Charlie could let it be known that he preferred to have sex with guys."

"He could have denied it."

"Unbeknownst to Charlie and me, Mel had taken Polaroid pictures of us making love."

"Dangerous invention, the Polaroid camera," said Nick, going to Appleton's desk.

"The funny thing is that the whole thing unraveled because there was a surprise audit of the club's books. To my amazement, Mel did the right thing and confessed in such a way that neither Charlie or I came under suspicion."

Goldstein grunted. "The right thing for Chandler to have done was marry the girl he'd knocked up."

"That would have meant real trouble for Mel," said Kevin. "Emily—that was the girl's name. As I recall, her last name was Mason—like the famous Jewish comedian who was always appearing on the Ed Sullivan show and used to be a school teacher. Mel's problem was that she was only sixteen years old."

"There's the Swingin' Sixties for you," said Lerch disgustedly. "A girl is knocked up at sixteen, then given money to get an abortion and clear out of town."

"Did Charlie speculate as to why all of a sudden he got an invitation from Chandler?"

"He was intrigued, of course. That's why he went to the party. When he told me about it, he said he felt as though he'd entered a time warp and been taken back to the 1960s."

"Just for the record," said Lerch, "where were you around half past six last evening?"

"I was at home."

"Where is home?"

"I have an apartment near Boston College. I'm on the history faculty, adjunct."

"Do you live by yourself?"

"Alas, yes." He smiled knowingly. "There is no live-in lover, Lieutenant, or even one to drop in occasionally. Since the outbreak of the AIDS plague, I have been as celibate as a monk. As was Charlie. So you can rule out his murder having been committed by a trick he picked up."

Surveying Appleton's desk, Nick saw the workplace of an academic who appeared to have nothing in common with Melvin Chandler but college memories. Flipping through pages of a scrapbook, he asked Kevin, "Is there anyone you can think of who would want to kill Charlie *and* Mel Chandler?"

After a long moment, Kevin sighed. "They lived in different worlds. The last time Charlie saw Mel was in 1976 in New York City. Except for myself, I can't think of anyone they had in common. Maybe their deaths are just a coincidence."

"Possibly," said Nick as he left the desk and moved quickly toward the door. "Thanks, Mr. Rattigan. You've been very helpful. I'm very sorry about your friend."

Following Nick from the apartment, Lerch exclaimed, "Helpful? I don't see how that guy was of any use at all. In fact, since he's got no alibi for either murder, he could be our killer. You know the first rule of homicide investigation: the one who reports finding the body probably is the culprit."

Nick took out his cigar case. "By that rule the hotel maid who reported Chandler's death should also be a suspect. What did you expect me to say to Rattigan? The man has just lost the love of his life. I couldn't tell him, 'I'm sorry, but you really haven't been much help to us. And by the way, you're a suspect,' which, for the record, I don't consider him to be."

With jaw jutting and fists jammed against his hips, Lerch asked, "Why not?"

"A better question is why should I?"

"C'mon, Nick. It was probably a gay lovers thing."

Going through the ritual of preparation for lighting the cigar, Nick replied, "That might explain Rattigan killing Appleton, which I don't buy, but it doesn't account for Chandler. These murders are related, Jack, and I can't see Rattigan as the one who committed them."

"I'm not so sure of that."

"However, Rattigan probably knows who did, without realizing that he knows."

"That's quite a leap of imagination, Sherlock!"

"Not at all. It seems clear to me that Appleton knew, or thought he knew, who killed Mel Chandler. That's why he had to go. It's too bad Appleton didn't stop and think about what he was doing when he contacted Chandler's killer."

"Excuse me?"

Nick lit the cigar. "I could be wrong about this, but it's the only reason I can see for what happened here. The murder of

Mel Chandler was planned; Appleton's was improvised. The methods suggest that's the way it went. Chandler was poisoned, therefore it was premeditated. Appleton, however, was spur-of-the-moment. Find Charles Appleton's murderer and you find Mel Chandler's. As for me, now that my front window has been replaced, I have a cigar store to re-open for business. May I impose on the Cambridge Police Department's top murder cop to give me a ride to Brattle Street?"

"Sure, I'll drop you off," said Lerch, "but don't think I'm going to let you walk away from this case, my friend. You're stuck with it right to the finish."

WHEN NICK ENTERED the Happy Smoking Ground, a large stack of autographed copies of *Smoke Dreamer* stood as a mute reminder of the extraordinary and tragic events which had occurred since Friday afternoon. Chandler's riotous reception on Brattle Street. His murder that evening in the Kennedy Suite at the Mayflower. The quick thinking of a maid whose wet towels quenched a fire and preserved the evidence of a murder. The snowstorm, preventing suspects from leaving the scene of the crime. Questioning possible suspects. The pathetic story of Charles Appleton, coerced to become an accomplice in a crime and the arrangement of an abortion because he was a closeted gay athlete, then strangled on the very night that his blackmailer was murdered. Kevin Rattigan, discovering Appleton's body amid souvenirs and relics of an apartment as overstuffed as the flowery chair from which Kevin had explained the motive for a theft of money which had nettled Professor Woolley for more than thirty years.

Realizing that Woolley did not know of Appleton's murder, Nick left, locked the store, and went up to Woolley's apartment. Woolley was seated by a window in his usual reading chair with book in hand and pipe in mouth. The table at which a few hours ago he had proudly served soup and sandwiches was uncleared. He looked at Nick reprovingly, plucked the pipe from his mouth, and demanded, "Where the devil have you been? Has there been a break in the Chandler case?"

"I'd call it a *complication.* There's been another murder."

Woolley slammed shut his book and sat up straight. "Who?"

"Charles Appleton was strangled in his apartment early this morning," Nick replied as he sat on a couch. "He was found by his old college buddy Kevin Rattigan."

Woolley placed the book on a table and slouched back into the chair. "Nick, this is a very interesting development!"

"You'll be relieved to know, I'm sure," said Nick, taking a cigar from his pocket case, "that Rattigan has explained why Chandler took that money that got him booted out of school. He needed it to get out of a spot of trouble with an underage girl."

"The cad!"

"The grand was meant for her to have an abortion and to finance her permanent departure from town. But according to Rattigan, she declined to use the services of the abortionist Charlie Appleton had lined up."

"Was the poor girl Catholic?"

"Rattigan said her name was Emily Mason. Is that a Catholic name? Whatever church she belonged to, she took the thousand and apparently was never seen again."

"I told you Melvin Chandler considered himself a ladies' man," Woolley said, as Nick lit the cigar. "But I'll wager that story isn't found on the pages of his memoir. I must say that I'm surprised and disappointed to hear that Charlie Appleton became a willing participant in such a sordid affair. Charlie always struck me as a paragon of virtue. Athlete, scholar, gentleman."

Nick puffed a cloud of smoke. "Charlie was also homosexual."

Woolley sat up. "Charles Appleton, gay? I don't believe it."

"That's why Appleton went along with the abortion plan. Chandler had pictures of him and Rattigan going at it."

"The dirty blackmailer!"

"Be that as it may, what Chandler did back then didn't keep Appleton from accepting his invitation to the party at Farley's. Rattigan said that Chandler wrote on the card that he wanted to get together with Charlie for what Chandler called *auld lang syne*. Obviously Appleton was in the mood to join him in saluting their past. He was at the party."

"The question now," said Woolley, pointing the bit of his pipe toward Nick, "is which of the others at Farley's had a reason to kill *both* Chandler and Appleton." The pipe went back into his mouth. After chewing the end a few moments, he exclaimed, "Wait a minute! Suppose that Charlie was an accomplice in killing Chandler. That would explain why he seemed distracted at the party, as if his mind was miles away. He kept looking toward the entrance as if he expected someone to walk in. He might have known that his accomplice was on his way to Farley's from the Mayflower Hotel after killing Chandler. Then, for some reason, that person decided that he also had to kill Charlie."

Nick studied the esthetically satisfying lengthening cigar ash as he said, "Possibly. All I know is that someone was in Appleton's apartment between one and seven this morning, caught him by surprise, and strangled him. As to why he seemed to be detached from the festivities at Farley's, maybe he was nervous about seeing Chandler after so many years. I know he'd been thinking about the reunion. There was a scrapbook from their Harvard days on his desk full of articles about Charlie's exploits on the hockey rink and at fraternity parties and the like."

"I don't suppose it contains the blackmail pictures Chandler took of Charlie and Kevin."

"When I flipped through the book I saw no dirty pictures, Professor."

"Since Charlie was gay, none of girls, either, I expect."

"There were a few, actually," said Nick, "but they were surrounded by other guys, including the notorious ladies' man named Mel Chandler."

"He certainly was a popular campus figure," said Woolley. "When I saw Appleton at the party, I assumed Chandler was using the occasion to renew all his old college ties. Perhaps that's what Appleton also expected. It's an alternate explanation as to why he kept looking toward the entrance. He may have been searching for familiar faces from the Sixties. But he said that the only person he recognized in the cigar room was me."

A frown creased Nick's brow. "Appleton said that you were the only person at the party that he recognized?"

"That he recognized from the *Sixties.*"

"How curious."

"I don't follow you."

"Kevin Rattigan said that Appleton phoned him after coming home from the party and said that Kevin would never believe who Appleton had seen that night. He told Kevin that at the time he'd felt as if he'd entered a time warp and been taken back thirty years."

"An obvious reference to me."

"He did tell Kevin about talking with you," Nick said. "But the time warp reference was to somebody else."

"If Charlie said it was as though he'd been taken back thirty years," said Woolley, as he used a pipe tool to tamp the ash in his pipe bowl, "that person must be unscathed by age. Perhaps he's like Dorian Gray and has a very old-looking portrait hidden away in an attic."

Nick abruptly laid his cigar in an ashtray. "Of course," he exclaimed. "That explains the scrapbook."

"Beg pardon? What scrapbook?"

"The one I saw on Appleton's desk."

"What of it?"

"I assumed Appleton had been looking through it before he went to the party. But what if he'd gotten it out *after* the party?"

He left the couch and went to Woolley's desk.

Picking up the phone to call Lerch, he smiled at Woolley and asked, "Professor, are you feeling up to a quick trip across the river into Boston's Back Bay?"

"Hot diggety dog," Woolley exclaimed, bounding from his chair. "The game's afoot!"

"The game in question may be a wild-goose chase," Nick

said as Lerch's phone rang. "If it isn't, we'll be unraveling a fantastic plot worthy of one of your thrillers."

In the following hours Woolley observed Nick with the same excitement, fascination, and bemusement he invariably felt in writing a Jake Elwell novel.

At some point Jake could be counted on to grab hold of the story and barrel ahead toward a solution of the case which was not the one envisioned by the author whose name would adorn the cover of the book.

Nick's actions began with a phone call to Peg Baron.

Woolley heard, "I may have another job for you to handle . . . You might have to go out of town . . . I'll let you know as soon as I can. You're a doll . . . Where will you be an hour from now?"

A second call was a request that Jack Lerch contact Tommy Lindlaw to arrange a second visit to Charles Appleton's apartment.

With streets and roads plowed almost back to normal, they arrived on Commonwealth Avenue less than an hour later. A Boston police officer awaited them with a key.

In the tradition of the official police in countless mystery novels since Sherlock Holmes's first appearance in crime literature, Lerch was Scotland Yard's Inspector Lestrade, standing aside, watching and waiting, as Nick entered the cluttered room.

He went directly to Appleton's desk, opened the scrapbook, and leafed through it.

"Two questions, gentlemen," he said. "Why was Appleton looking at this? Did he look at it before or after the party?"

He turned to Lerch.

"May I take this scrapbook with me?"

"Tommy Lindlaw said his people are done here," said Lerch, "so I don't see why not."

"Good," said Nick, tucking it under an arm and striding toward the door.

Following him, Lerch asked, "What's so important about an old scrapbook?"

"Should auld acquaintance be forgot, Jack, and never brought to mind? And days of auld lang syne?"

As the Boston cop locked the apartment door, Lerch muttered, "Auld lang syne! Right!"

"And now, my friend," said Nick, as they went down the stairs. "I'd appreciate it if you'd drive me in your trusty utility vehicle to Symphony Hall."

Lerch shrugged. "Your wish is my command."

When they arrived, Nick said, "You fellas can wait here. I won't be long."

As Nick got out of the vehicle and stepped over a pile of shoveled snow, Lerch said, "I hope you're not here just to buy tickets for a concert."

Less than ten minutes later, Nick was back in the front seat.

Grinning, he looked at Lerch, gave the lieutenant's broad shoulder a friendly squeeze, and declared, "Home, please, Jeeves!"

"I hope that at some not too distant point, Nick," said Lerch, grumpily, "you're going to let Woolley and me in on what all this is about."

"It's a hunch, Jack. It's possible that I've gone way off base, but I don't think so. I hope to know tomorrow. If it turns out I'm right, I'll be asking you to host another party. But it will be one with a much shorter guest list."

PART VII

Smoke Screen for Murder

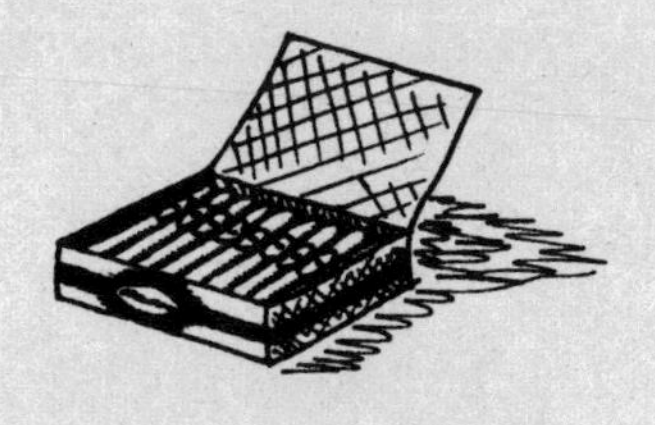

With my cigar, I'm sage and wise—
Without, I'm dull as cloudy skies.
When smoking, all my ideas soar,
When not, they sink upon the floor.
The greatest men have all been smokers,
And so were all the greatest jokers.

ANONYMOUS

Thirty-six

AT FOUR O'CLOCK the following afternoon Nick stood to the left of Lieutenant John Lerch of the Cambridge Police Department in the large parlor of the John F. Kennedy suite. Detective Sid Goldstein and Professor Woolley sat together on a long couch set against a wall decorated with a painted mural. Titled "A Thousand Days of Camelot," it consisted of idealized scenes inspired by Kennedy's short tenure in the White House. Facing it in a semi-circle of chairs were Richard Chandler, his mother, Veronica Redding, Dave Selden, Steve Yedenok, Rob Devonshire, Benjamin Salter, and Madeline Lewis.

"I'm sure you are all thinking that this is the sort of thing that only happens in detective stories and old Charlie Chan movies," said Lerch, "and I admit that it's not the custom in real life for the police to assemble the people who are, uh, involved in a murder case."

Richard Chandler exclaimed, "Quit dancing around the word, Lieutenant. We're here because you regard us as *suspects.*"

"At this point," said Lerch, "I'll turn this meeting over to Nick Chase."

As Lerch joined Goldstein and Woolley on the couch, Nick said, "I'll try not to detain you long. But Richard is right about not dancing around why you've been assembled in a way that seems melodramatic."

"*I'll* say it does," blurted Dave Selden. "Mel Chandler would have loved it!"

"The way for me to begin," said Nick, "is by telling you how Mel was murdered. It was done with a large dose of nitroglycerine in the form of tablets. Dissolved in a glass of cognac and combined with medication Mel was taking for his coronary artery disease, it was a lethal brew. Mel's body was then put onto the bed. A cigar was placed in his hand. The bed was set on fire, apparently in the hope that it would seem that he'd been smoking and suffered a heart attack. If that was the plan, it almost worked. Note that I said *if* that was the plan."

"Noted," said Woolley emphatically.

"I now pose two questions. The first is obvious: who murdered Mel Chandler? Second, why was it necessary for that person to kill again?"

Nick's audience stirred nervously.

"Yes, there's been a second murder," said Nick. "The victim was a man who had been a friend of Mel's in college, Charles Appleton. I'll talk about Charles and his relationship with Mel presently. For now, I ask you to turn your attention to how this complicated drama began. I refer to Mel's book. I'm not a literary critic, but I found *Smoke Dreamer* to be exactly what I expected in an autobiography of a man such as Mel Chandler—self-serving and lacking in candor. But its pages were nonetheless revealing. They show Mel to have been a man who made it very easy for people to dislike him. The book brims with accounts of persons he abused to varying degrees, personally and professionally. A few hours before he was killed, he jokingly told Lieutenant Lerch and me that if he was murdered, we should look for suspects in the book's index. We did not have to do so. It was immediately clear to me that his killer had been a guest at the party at Farley's. That list of names proved considerably shorter than the book's index."

Richard groaned. "We all get your point, Nick. That's why we're here!"

"A suspect," said Nick, "is generally determined by asking if that person had a motive, the opportunity, and the means. When a wealthy man is murdered, it's practically a rule in the investigators' handbook that suspicion falls on the person who inherits."

Like a schoolboy, Richard raised a hand. "That's me."

Nick stood before him. "You'd learned that Mel was planning to give a million dollars to Harvard University. There is evidence in the form of a witness that you and Mel engaged in a rather boisterous argument on the phone on that very topic shortly before Mel was murdered."

"I've already denied that."

"As Mel's son, you were well acquainted with Mel's heart condition and would have known what medications he was taking, and the contraindications."

"Speculation!"

"May I assume," Nick continued with a slight smile, "that now that your father is dead the million-dollar grant to Harvard is not going to happen?"

"You can bet on it."

"I'm not a wagering man," said Nick, leaning down until his face was close to Richard's, "but if I *had* been at the time I heard of Mel's plan to give a million to the college which expelled him, I would have bet against it ever happening."

He came up straight and faced the others.

"The proposed gift to Harvard was nothing but a publicity gimmick to attract attention to his book," he continued. "So if Richard's motive was to keep Mel from doing so, he need not have murdered him."

"For God's sake," exclaimed Richard, "how many times must I repeat that I didn't kill him? I was nowhere near the Mayflower Hotel."

"When Richard was questioned concerning his whereabouts at the time of Mel's death," Nick explained for the benefit of the others, "Miss Redding attested that she and Richard were either in a taxi or trying to find one in Boston. If that's true, there goes Richard's opportunity."

Veronica blurted out, "It certainly is true."

"Setting aside Richard as a suspect for the moment," Nick

said, "who else stood to gain financially from Mel's death? Richard is the only surviving child. Mel's second son, Donny, was killed a few years ago with his mother, the second Mrs. Chandler, in a hit-and-run accident on Cape Cod. Therefore the only other person with a familial tie to Mel is his first wife."

"That's me," said Anita.

Nick addressed her. "It stands to reason that you were familiar with Mel's heart problem and his medications."

"Why should I deny it?"

"In the course of this investigation, I learned that although you and Mel divorced several years ago, you believed Mel had cheated you in the settlement. And that he continued to do so. There's motive. What about opportunity?"

"I had none."

"You stated that you'd gone to Miami Beach, had had a change of mind, and had come back to Boston, arriving around the time of the murder. You said you were in a taxi on the way to my house on Beacon Hill. If your story and Richard's are true, that strikes members of Mel's family off the list of suspects. Who's left? As I said, it's my opinion, and that of Lieutenant Lerch, that the murderer is someone whom Mel had invited to the festivities on Friday. Out of a hundred or so guests at Farley's, only a handful had a personal relationship with him. Three of those guests' invitations bore a handwritten appeal by Mel to attend the party—Dave Selden's, Steve Yedenok's, and Charles Appleton's."

STANDING BEFORE DAVE SELDEN, Nick said, "After many years as the managing editor of *Cigar Smoker* magazine, you were fired in a brutal fashion. Chandler ordered you to clear out or find yourself escorted off the premises by security guards. Correct?"

Selden shifted nervously. "Yes, but so what?"

"That must have been awfully humiliating, Dave."

"I got over it."

"We all know," Nick continued as he moved away from Selden, "that in this day and age it's become common for a fired employee to return to the office to seek revenge in a violent way. Of course, Dave Selden was not the type one would expect to storm into Mel Chandler's office with guns blazing. But he could have easily gotten into Mel's hotel suite on Friday evening with murder in his heart."

Selden leapt to his feet. "No, I couldn't. I was—"

Nick turned abruptly toward him. "You say you were in your room on the seventh floor preparing to go to Farley's."

"I was indeed."

"You offer Steve Yedenok as your alibi."

"It's not an alibi. It's what happened. At the time of the murder I was on my way to the party. Steve was in the elevator when I entered."

"This is true," said Nick to his audience. "Steve verifies

that when the elevator stopped at the seventh floor, Dave got on. That's good for Dave."

He moved toward Yedenok.

"But it's not so good for you, Steve," he continued. "While Dave was waiting for the elevator, he noticed that it began its descent on the penthouse floor. It did not stop till it reached seven. Because your room was on eleven, you had to be on the penthouse floor at the very time Mel was murdered."

"I explained that to you," Steve retorted.

"You said you went there in the hope of talking with Mel and perhaps reaching a settlement of your libel suit. You said that you heard Mel speaking to someone in the suite, so you changed your mind about seeing him at that time."

"That's right," said Yedenok. "I also told you that when I was getting on the elevator to leave, somebody was getting off."

Nick moved from Yedenok to Devonshire. "That person was you, Rob."

"I went up to that floor because I got a call from Mr. Chandler. He said he wanted to talk with me about my concerns with smoking."

Richard blurted, "What nonsense."

"I'll return to the matter of that call. Right now, what's significant about Rob's getting off the elevator just as Yedenok was getting on is that it was a stroke of luck for both of them. That fortuitous timing proves that Rob could not have committed the murder. Steve said he smelled smoke when he was outside Chandler's door. He ran into Rob at the elevator. Rob says he also smelled smoke, and when he looked into the suite's bedroom he saw a small fire. If the bed was burning before Rob arrived on the penthouse floor, Rob could not have murdered Mel."

Richard Chandler interjected, "But Yedenok could have."

"It seems to me that if Steve had committed a murder and set a fire to cover it up," Nick replied, "he would not have chosen to stand around waiting for an elevator. He would have made his getaway by the route Rob took after he discovered the body, the fire stairs."

"That's guesswork," said Richard.

"I believe it's what happened," said Nick. "Futhermore, because the fire was burning at the time Yedenok got on the elevator, and because the fire Rob discovered was small, indicating that it had been started minutes before Rob entered the suite, I don't see how Dave Selden could have started it. If he'd set the fire after he killed Chandler, by the time he got back down to his own floor, the fire would have to have been much bigger than it was when Rob discovered it."

"Since you've apparently eliminated this kid, Selden, and Yedenok as suspects," Richard said, "the only one left of the people who had special invitations is Charles Appleton."

"As I pondered all of this and eliminated Devonshire, Selden and Yedenok, I was indeed left with the possibility that Mel had been murdered by a man he knew when they were students at Harvard. But why would someone whom Mel had not seen in more than thirty years suddenly decide to kill him? What did I know about Charles Appleton? Fortunately, in seeking the answer, I had the benefit of a friendship with a man who'd known Appleton and Mel Chandler when they were students at Harvard."

He turned with a smile and pointed to Woolley.

"Without Professor Woolley's remarkable memory of events some thirty years ago and keen observations of Appleton made during the party at Farley's," Nick said, "this unique double murder might have gone unsolved. Without Professor Woolley, Lieutenant Lerch and I might not have been able to prove that these murders are connected. At first, we found ourselves with two ways of looking at them. Were they a coincidence? This seemed very unlikely. But it was a possibility. The other explanation was that Chandler's murder required Appleton's. In weighing that scenario it seemed reasonable to wonder if Charles Appleton was killed because he was involved in Mel's death."

"I see what you're saying," said Dave Selden. "Whoever killed Mel felt for some reason that he had to eliminate Appleton!"

"But that theory raised a tantalizing question," said Nick. "Why would Charles Appleton, who hadn't seen Mel Chandler in decades, suddenly become enmeshed in a plan to murder him? What could have been his motive? Just as intriguing was that Mel had invited Appleton to the book-launching events here in Cambridge."

As Nick paused, Madeline Lewis ventured, "You know why Mel did that, Nick. He was being nasty, spiteful. He wanted people on his enemies list to see him gloat."

"Possibly," said Nick. "But what if Appleton was actually invited for the purpose which Mel had written on his invitation? What if Mel truly hoped to see Charlie in the spirit of auld lang syne? It was a sentiment in line with Mel's notations on the invitations to Dave and Steve."

He again stood before Selden.

"You thought the invitation meant that Mel wanted to patch things up and bring you back as managing editor."

"Correct."

Nick looked to Yedenok.

"Steve hoped his invitation would lead to settling the lawsuit."

"That's right," said Yedenok, "even though my lawyer was against my seeing Mel."

"But what was there," Nick asked, "between Mel Chandler and Charles Appleton that Mel felt a need to address after so many years? Or should I say '*re*dress'?"

He threw up his hands as if in dismay.

"Unfortunately, the explanation that I hoped to hear could not come from Appleton," he said, "because by the time Lieutenant Lerch and Detective Goldstein and I got to his apartment, he was dead. Murdered. We got the full story of Mel and Charlie's time together at Harvard from Kevin Rattigan. I'll return to that extraordinary episode presently. At the moment, it's important for your understanding of this tangled tale that I deal with Charlie Appleton's unusual behavior at Farley's on Friday evening."

Thirty-eight

"ACCORDING TO PROFESSOR WOOLLEY," Nick continued, "Appleton had appeared distracted and remote at the party. He had a faraway look. He kept staring toward the doorway. Why? What could have been on his mind? Professor Woolley speculated in hindsight that Appleton somehow was involved in Mel's murder and was waiting nervously for his accomplice to arrive at Farley's after having carried out their plan. But I had to ask myself again why, after thirty years, Charles Appleton would conspire to kill Mel Chandler. And with whom?"

The questions hung heavily over the room.

"Later, Kevin Rattigan provided me a different explanation for Charlie's behavior," Nick continued. "He said that on Charlie's return to his apartment after the party, Charlie phoned him. He told Kevin that while at the party he had felt as though he was in a time warp that carried him back to Harvard in the Sixties. Unfortunately, Charlie didn't explain what he meant. He promised to do so when he and Kevin got together for lunch the next day. When he failed to phone Kevin at ten o'clock, and Kevin got no answers to *his* phone calls, Kevin went to Charlie's apartment and found him dead."

Lerch interjected, "He'd been strangled with an electrical cord between the time he spoke to Kevin and seven o'clock that morning."

Nick continued, "When Lieutenant Lerch, Detective Goldstein, and I were asked to come to Charlie's apartment by the Boston police, who were investigating Charlie's murder, I noticed a scrapbook on Charlie's desk. I glanced at it and found that it dated from Charlie's Harvard years. I assumed he'd taken it from its place on a shelf prior to going to Mel's party, just as everyone who's invited to a class reunion digs out the school yearbook."

"This is all very interesting," declared Richard, "but what's Charles Appleton's trip down memory lane got to do with anything?"

"It would have meant nothing," Nick replied, "if Appleton's invitation hadn't contained a reference by Mel Chandler to 'auld lang syne.' Since the man who wrote those words on the invitation and the man who received it had been murdered on the same night, I felt that whatever I could learn of their days of 'auld lang syne' might be helpful. That's where Professor Woolley's memory of them came into the picture. To make a long story short, when Chandler and Appleton were at Harvard in 1968, Charlie helped Mel get out of a scrape by letting Chandler help himself to a thousand dollars from their club treasury. Also involved in that escapade was a close friend of Appleton's, Kevin Rattigan. In questioning him I learned that Chandler had needed the money to finance an abortion for an underage girl Chandler had been romancing. Could this episode from long ago be what Mel referred to when he wrote on Appleton's invitation the words 'auld lang syne'? Did Mel want to find some way to atone for what had happened in 1968? It seemed reasonable to think so. Mel had also invited Selden and Yedenok in a way that suggested Mel wanted to make peace with them. I wondered if in writing his life story, Mel had decided to tidy up some of the less than pretty things he'd done in that life."

Dave Selden barked a laugh. "Mel Chandler, the penitent? I hardly think so. If Mel wanted to ask me back, it wasn't because he felt bad about firing me. The magazine is in trouble."

Nick shrugged. "Who can ever know a man's true motives?"

"Excuse me," said Veronica Redding, "but I thought that's what a detective's job is."

"All a detective can hope to do is try to understand whatever evidence he finds."

"It seems to me," said Richard, "that you haven't found much."

"There is physical evidence that's instructive," Nick answered. "It speaks of the how of this murder: the means and the method. But not the why. If Mel Chandler had been the only one killed, learning the why might not have been necessary. A prosecutor at a trial has no legal obligation to present a motive. Am I right, Lieutenant?"

"You certainly are."

"The real puzzle regarding motive for me," said Nick, "concerns the Appleton murder. Why was he killed? In thinking about it, I was struck by the difference between his murder and Chandler's. Mel's was cunningly planned and cleverly carried out. Appleton's seemed ad-libbed, on the spur of the moment. An urgent *necessity.* What could have happened after Chandler's murder to make Appleton's death necessary? While I was pondering this and the relationship between Charlie and Mel at Harvard, I got to thinking about Woolley's observations at the party."

Woolley blurted out, "Appleton was very distracted. His mind seemed miles away."

Nick continued, "Was he nervous about seeing Mel again? Could it be possible that, as Professor Woolley suspected, he was involved in the murder of Mel Chandler? Had he been an accomplice who had to be eliminated? Possibly."

Dave Selden said, "Obviously, you don't think so."

"Why do you say that, Dave?"

"You're clearly building up to something. Little by little, you're cleverly heightening the tension in this room. As a writer, I find it fascinating. Since you apparently don't believe that Appleton was involved in Mel's murder, why *do* you believe he was killed?"

"It occurred to me that the motive might be found in Kevin's account of Charlie saying that he felt at the party as if a time warp had taken him back to his college days. When he said that to Kevin, he was speaking on the phone on his desk. Lying upon that desk at the scene was the scrapbook that I've mentioned. I told you I assumed Charlie had been looking through it *before* going to Farley's. But in the light of Professor Woolley's feeling that Appleton had seemed distracted, far away, and Charlie telling Kevin that at the party he felt as if he were in a time warp, I asked myself, what if something occurred at the party, what if he had seen something that caused him to get out the scrapbook when he got home?"

Nick began pacing the parlor. When he stopped, he gazed through a picture window at the snowy banks of the Charles River glistening in bright sunlight.

"Was something in the scrapbook," Nick asked, as he turned from the view, "that might explain this amazing series of events which started with Mel Chandler sending party invitations to his enemies list and ended with Chandler and one of the men on that list murdered?"

With an impatient expression Richard Chandler asked, "Well? Was there? Did it?"

Anita Chandler demanded, "For heaven's sake, man, get on with it."

"Yes, if you're going to arrest one of us, then do it," said Yedenok angrily as he looked at his watch. "I, for one, have better things to do than hang around here."

"Bear with me just a while longer," said Nick. "I'm almost finished."

"SOMETHING HAPPENED AT the party at Farley's," Nick continued, "that caused Appleton to feel as though he'd gone back through time to Harvard in 1968. But what? Might he have heard a remark made by someone? Possibly. If so, from whom? The only people at the party who had been at Harvard in 1968 were Appleton and Professor Woolley. If Woolley had said something to send Appleton's thoughts reeling backward in time, I think Charlie would have mentioned it to his former professor."

"He didn't," said Woolley. "There was not a word about the old days."

"Was it music? A song will trigger nostalgia. As I recall, there was no music Friday night in Farley's cigar room."

"You remember correctly," said Woolley.

"What was your impression of Appleton?"

"He seemed distracted."

"On the phone to Kevin Rattigan after the party," Nick went on, "Appleton chose to use the phrase 'time warp.' When he employed that colorful expression, he had open before him on his desk a kind of time machine—the scrapbook I mentioned a few minutes ago. My impression when I saw it on the desk was that he had taken it from a shelf of scrapbooks and photo albums before he went to the party. But Professor Woolley's description of Appleton's odd behavior at the party and Kevin Rattigan's account of Appleton's one o'clock phone call got me wondering about that scrapbook."

Benjamin Salter raised a tentative hand and offered, "He'd just learned that his old college buddy was dead. He got out the scrapbook to reminisce."

"He'd appeared distracted when he was talking to Professor Woolley before anyone at the party knew Chandler was dead. On the theory that something had occurred at the party to prompt him to get out that scrapbook, I returned to his apartment with Lieutenant Lerch and Professor Woolley to see what Appleton was looking for in it."

Richard Chandler interjected, "Apparently you found something, else why would you be regaling us with this fascinating piece of detective work? If you know who killed my father and Charles Appleton, stop dragging it out and tell us. Then Lieutenant Lerch can slap the handcuffs on the killer and the rest of us can go home."

"I'll show you what I found," said Nick.

He plunged his right hand into his right coat pocket and took out a small photograph.

"A date in pencil on the back of this picture notes that it was taken in the summer of 1968 at the amusement park in Revere. It's of three very youthful-looking men and a very pretty girl. Written under the images is, 'Kev, me, Mel, Emily. July '68.' "

"What could possibly be significant," said Richard with a dubious expression, "of an old picture of four college kids at Revere Beach?"

"The picture is actually of only *three* college kids," Nick replied. "The girl, Emily, wasn't old enough to be a co-ed. That Emily considered herself Mel's girlfriend, and that Mel felt the same way, is evident in the picture. They've got their arms around each other's waists. It's easy to understand what Mel saw in her. Emily was a beautiful girl. But not long after this picture was taken, she informed Mel that she was pregnant. And that she was fifteen years old. Mel's response to this double shocker was, as I've said, to embezzle a thousand dollars from his club treasury, with the cooperation of Charles Appleton and Kevin Rattigan. Mel also turned to Charles to give the money to Emily to pay for an abortion in Charlestown and then use the rest of the cash to leave town. Rattigan said Emily took the money but did not keep the appointment with the abortionist Charlie had set up for her. Kevin said Charlie assumed that she'd handled it on her own. Apparently, no one considered the possibility that Emily could have decided to have the baby."

Richard Chandler groaned. "Are you going to tell us that this girl Emily suddenly showed up after all this time and killed my father and Appleton in revenge for the way they'd treated her back in 1968?"

"That would certainly have been a sensational occurrence," said Nick, "but I assure you that Emily was not the person Charles Appleton saw at Farley's."

Richard's eyes went wide open. "What? Have you actually found this woman?"

"I'm sad to report," Nick said, looking around the semicircle of astonished faces, "that Emily died seven years ago. She'd suffered a series of strokes."

Dave Selden slowly shook his head as he asked, "Nick, how the hell do you know that?"

"Discovering Emily was dead was the brilliant work of a friend of mine," said Nick. "I'd asked her—Peg Baron is her name—to look up the birth records for the latter months of 1968 and early 1969. When Peg found what I'd told her to look for, she took it upon herself to check thirty years of marriages and deaths. She found no marriage record for Emily. But she did locate a death certificate dated seven years ago."

"Wait a minute," blurted Dave Selden. "How did you know where to tell your friend Peg to do all this record-checking?"

"Kevin Rattigan told me Emily's name was Mason. He remembered that Emily's last name was the same as that of an ex-teacher who became a comedian and appeared regularly on the Ed Sullivan TV show. With a last name for Emily, I asked Peg to look into birth records of Massachusetts and Rhode Island. But the last name I gave to Peg wasn't Mason. Jackie Mason was on the Sullivan show often. But before

Mason turned to comedy, he'd been a rabbi. The comedian who'd been a teacher and then became a comedian who appeared frequently on the show was Sam Levenson. But to be sure, I told Peg to check birth records under both names. She found one in the files in *Providence.*"

He slipped his left hand into his left pocket and withdrew a paper.

"This is a photocopy of the certificate," he continued. "It's for a very healthy, average-weight, full-term, blue-eyed, brown-haired infant. Although the father is listed on it as Melvin Chandler, Emily chose to give the baby her own last name."

SHOWING MADELINE LEWIS the birth certificate and the picture of Emily and the three young men on their outing to Revere Beach, Nick said, "I assumed Peg would find that Emily had given birth to a girl. Foolish me. I'd forgotten a basic rule of detection: never assume. But I did recall a maxim of Sherlock Holmes. 'When you have eliminated the impossible, whatever remains, however improbable, must be the truth.' "

He turned toward Benjamin Salter.

Holding up the photograph, he continued, "Ben, you look very much like your mother. But there's not a hint of resemblance to Mel Chandler."

"I have no idea what you're getting at, Nick."

"I'm getting at your plot to kill Mel Chandler and get his money and property."

"How could I get anything? Richard is the heir."

"He wouldn't be under the law if he were convicted of Mel's murder. That was the aim of your plan, wasn't it? You planned to kill Mel and set up Richard to take the fall for the murder."

"Oh, Nick, you've been reading too many of Professor Woolley's novels. But just for the fun of it, assume that what you think is true. Where's the evidence to back up your theory?"

Nick waved the birth certificate. "I have this."

"It proves only that I was born and that my mother put down Melvin Chandler as father. It doesn't prove that he *was.*"

"No wonder Appleton was so distracted at the party. He saw you and noted that you look like Emily! That's what sent him hurtling through that time warp. He later confirmed what he thought he had seen by digging out the scrapbook. Looking at the photograph must have been an astonishing moment for him. When he phoned you and said that you two had to meet, he sealed his fate."

"Ah, the plot thickens! We were to meet! When? Where? Why?"

"Very soon, I would think, and wherever Charlie wished. Why? I can only presume that he planned to tell you his terms for keeping quiet."

"For keeping quiet about what?"

"That you are Mel Chandler's illegitimate—no, these days that word is politically incorrect. That you are Mel Chandler's *unacknowledged* son."

"Why should I meet to talk terms with Charles Appleton about keeping quiet about that?"

"Because you'd killed Chandler, you feared Appleton had figured you for the murderer. You couldn't risk Appleton revealing who you are. Charlie's mistake was the one made by so many blackmailers. He thought he had the upper hand."

"Absolutely fascinating, Nick. A riveting story. Please continue."

"This is surmise, but I'm confident it's close to what happened. Appleton phoned you at this hotel. I assume he got your number from the press releases at the party. He probably sounded very excited. He said he had known your mother and was pleased that she hadn't gone through with the abortion. Then he said he was glad that Chandler had finally gotten his comeuppance and that you and he must get together and talk about the matter as soon as possible. You agreed. You knew his address because you'd sent him an invitation to the party at Farley's. You went to his apartment and killed him to silence him. But Appleton hadn't mentioned the photograph in the scrapbook. That was too bad for you."

"All of this is based on your supposition that I murdered Mel. Tell me again, why did I kill him? Oh yes, to claim my inheritance after I had set up Richard to be blamed for murdering his father. Richard's reason for killing Mel, of course, would be to claim *his* inheritance."

"Exactly."

"What a clever boy am I. Or should I say *bastard?"*

"Indeed you are. Half your genes are from Mel Chandler. And half are from a mother who as a girl outsmarted him. You might have become Chandler's rightful heir if you hadn't brought in an accomplice who overacted."

He turned to Madeline Lewis. "You really overdid your part, Maddy."

She looked puzzled. "I'm afraid you've lost me, Nick."

"In talking to Professor Woolley and me, you shouldn't have been in such a rush to point out suspects in a murder that as far as we knew had not happened. You named Steve Yedenok, Dave Selden, and, of course, Richard Chandler. You also tossed in a red herring, no pun intended, by suggesting that Rob Devonshire was a dangerous character. You had to bring Devonshire in because you knew that Ben had set Devonshire up to discover Mel's body."

"What a flight of fancy," exclaimed Salter. "Why would I want Rob Devonshire to find the body? And how could I know that the kid would do what I wanted?"

"If you could arrange for Devonshire to come to the suite at a specified time, you would have more control over the situation. It was you, not Chandler, who invited Devonshire up to the suite. Your plan was to murder Mel and arrange it to make it seem as though he'd died while smoking in bed. You expected that the investigation would show that Mel had been murdered. As I've said, the plan envisioned Richard becoming the prime suspect. With Mel dead on the bed, it was a matter of waiting to set it ablaze and escaping down the fire stairway a few minutes before Rob Devonshire was to come to the suite. Everything went pretty much as planned. Then you had to plant seeds of suspicion regarding

Richard Chandler. That's where Maddy came into the plot to point the finger at Richard while making red herrings of Selden and Yedenok. But the wild card in all this was Charlie Appleton."

"Nick, you flatter me," said Salter. "I am overwhelmed that you're asking everyone in this room to believe that all that was done by me. But you still have not presented one shred of evidence to back up your scenario in which I am a brilliant murderer. Please tell me again, how did I kill Mel?"

"Several nitroglycerine pills were mixed into Mel's cognac. The nitro and alcohol reacted fatally with the medication he was taking for coronary artery disease."

"He could have taken the pills and washed them down with cognac by mistake."

"Nitro pills aren't washed down. They're dissolved under the tongue. You knew what the effect would be on Mel of putting the nitro in his cognac."

Lerch rose to his feet. "Mr. Salter, Miss Lewis, I think the proper place to continue this conversation is my office at police headquarters."

Madeline blurted, "I had nothing to do with this."

Nick smiled and took out his cigar case. "Take my advice, Maddy, and cut yourself a deal with Lieutenant Lerch before Ben pins it all on you."

THAT EVENING, LIEUTENANT Lerch barged into the Happy Smoking Ground and found Nick closing the store and smoking a cigar while Professor Woolley and Peg Baron waited.

Nick plucked the cigar from his mouth. "Jack, you're just in time to join us for a great dinner at Farley's."

"Nick, you son of a gun," Lerch exclaimed, "you had it right almost exactly."

"Who spoke up first?"

"Lewis took your advice. She said Salter started thinking about this when his mother revealed his father's identity on her deathbed."

Woolley asked, "How did he manage to get his job as Chandler's assistant?"

"He started as a copyeditor with one of Chandler's magazines and worked his way up."

"Good lord! What patience! Why didn't he just get rid of Chandler and Richard and then come forward to claim his legacy?"

Nick answered, "The second son intervened. He had to dispose of Donny first."

Peg gasped. "Salter killed the child, too?"

Lerch said, "He hasn't owned up to that yet, but it doesn't matter. I've got his confession to the Chandler and Appleton murders."

Woolley asked, "How did Salter get Madeline Lewis involved?"

"Love and the prospect of lots of money."

Woolley chuckled. "I should have known."

"They've been working on this scheme for two years," said Lerch. "When Chandler wrote his book, that gave Salter the idea of suggesting to Chandler that he hire Lewis as his publicist."

Nick laid his cigar in an ashtray and said, "Jack, this is strictly a hunch, but I think you should find out where Madeline Lewis was when the second Mrs. Chandler and Donny were run down at Hyannisport."

"Holy cow! Do you think Lewis was responsible for that?"

Nick retrieved his cigar. "Possibly."

New York Times Bestselling Author

J.A. JANCE

The J.P. Beaumont Mysteries

"[Beaumont is] . . . a disillusioned, cynical hero in the classic hard-boiled tradition."
Journal-American

UNTIL PROVEN GUILTY	0-380-89638-9/$6.99 US/$9.99 CAN
INJUSTICE FOR ALL	0-380-89641-9/$6.99 US/$9.99 CAN
TRIAL BY FURY	0-380-75138-0/$6.99 US/$9.99 CAN
TAKING THE FIFTH	0-380-75139-9/$6.99 US/$8.99 CAN
IMPROBABLE CAUSE	0-380-75412-6/$6.99 US/$8.99 CAN
A MORE PERFECT UNION	0-380-75413-4/$6.99 US/$8.99 CAN
DISMISSED WITH PREJUDICE	0-380-75547-5/$6.50 US/$8.50 CAN
MINOR IN POSSESSION	0-380-75546-7/$6.99 US/$8.99 CAN
PAYMENT IN KIND	0-380-75836-9/$6.99 US/$8.99 CAN
WITHOUT DUE PROCESS	0-380-75837-7/$6.99 US/$8.99 CAN
FAILURE TO APPEAR	0-380-75839-3/$6.99 US/$9.99 CAN
LYING IN WAIT	0-380-71841-3/$6.99 US/$8.99 CAN
NAME WITHHELD	0-380-71842-1/$6.99 US/$8.99 CAN
BREACH OF DUTY	0-380-71843-X/$6.99 US/$9.99 CAN

Available wherever books are sold or please call 1-800-331-3761 to order.

JAN 1000